AN OPTIMIST'S GUIDE
TO HEARTBREAK

HEARTSONG DUET
BOOK ONE

JENNIFER HARTMANN

For Elizabeth and her brave heart

Beautiful things never last,
and that's why fireflies flash.

Ron Pope

PROLOGUE

With a last name like Hope, one would assume I'd be the equivalent of a walking, talking sunbeam. All buoyant optimism and jaunty cheer. A light in the dark, harnessing a perpetual smile to go with such a name.

Well, one would be right.

I'm all of those things, even on my bad days...even on my worse days.

Especially on my worse days.

So, when the little red real estate icon pops up on my notification bar alerting me of a new house hitting the market, that house calls to me in a way I can't explain.

I need it, I want it, I have to have it.

I choke on my muffin as the familiar honeyed bricks stare back at me, and my skin flushes hot, beet red to match warning flags waving behind my eyes. My belly churns with nerves, my palms sweat, and my mind spins like a rickety old Ferris wheel circling around and around in the sky.

But...a different feeling wins out. Something else, something mightier. It punctures through the uncertainty, through the awful memories, ringing loud over the little voice inside my head screaming that this is bound to go badly.

That Ferris wheel will crumble and fall, turning to rubble at my feet.

I don't care.

I can't seem to care because all I see is a past destined to be rewritten.

A new beginning.

A fighting chance to turn tragedy into magic, catastrophe into hope.

Ultimately, I think that's why I do it.

I think it's because of hope.

Five minutes later, I'm on the phone with my agent.

One day later, an offer is made.

A lifetime later, I beg, I plead, I pray for this not to be the greatest mistake of my life.

Mistake or not, I'm doing it.

I'm finding my way back to them.

Hope wins.

CHAPTER 1

"Lucy! Your dog puked up a dildo!"

I lurch into a sitting position. Alyssa's voice is followed by a clamor of dog nails in desperate need of trimming stampeding across the hardwood floors as the front door claps shut. I blink, her words registering. "*What*?" Scrambling to my feet, I pace down the hallway, finding my best friend flustered in my living room. "A dildo?"

Key Lime Pie and Lemon Meringue, my two Welsh corgis, are busy exploring the new turf while Alyssa visibly shudders and plops down onto the couch. "It wasn't mine."

"Well, it wasn't mine."

"I don't know, Lucy, but it sounded like Kiki was having an exorcism in the backseat. Instead of a demon being expelled, it was a dildo." Alyssa reaches into her oversized purse and pulls out a plastic bag that houses the evidence. Craning her neck and looking away, she holds the bag open while making elaborate gagging noises.

I'm literally horrified as I peer inside. Then my eyebrows dip when I recognize what it really is. "Lys, that's a Banana Bunker."

"Excuse me?" She whips her head toward me, expression pinched with bewilderment. "That sounds obscene. Tell me more."

I laugh. "I use these to keep my bananas from bruising. It's not a sex toy."

"Disappointing."

Key Lime Pie, Kiki for short, hobbles over to me on her stubby legs and collapses at my feet. She's a little overweight thanks to all of Mom's not-subtle, under-the-table snack handouts over the years, where Lemon is more high maintenance when it comes to treat selections. Alyssa transported the dogs over to the new house for me, while I drove the moving truck and carried in the furniture with my Uncle Dan. Alyssa has been essential in helping me transition into my new life.

"So, this is the new place, huh?" Alyssa fluffs her light blond bob and gives the modest space an approving sweep. "It's perfect for you. I hate that you're forty minutes away from me now, but you'll still be playing at the wine bar on Fridays, right?"

I take a seat beside her on the cream-colored sofa and bob my head. "Yep. As long as I can find a job that will work with my schedule."

Part one was moving.

Part two is securing a job that will cover my bills and living expenses.

The house was paid for in cash, thanks to the inheritance money I received from Grandma Mabel, and my car was a gift from my parents four years ago, but I still have taxes, gas, utilities, food, and all the other costs that go along with freedom and independence. While I still have some money left over from the inheritance, I want to find a job that will leave me with a little extra savings each month that I can put away for college one day.

One step at a time.

"Well, I think it's great." Alyssa perks up. "There's a fenced yard for the dogs and enough space to add your inevitable live-in lover. And let's not downplay the privilege of an attached garage."

My stomach pitches.

The garage will be for storage.

I will not be using the garage.

Clearing my throat, I pop up from the couch and fiddle with my hair. "Live-in lover. You're hilarious."

"*Inevitable,*" she parrots.

All I can do is shake my head at her, evading her misfire of a statement. I realize I'm not a troll, and I'm aware enough to admit that.

But, I'm also a tad neurotic.

Quirky, a little strange, and, as some might say, *too* bubbly.

I'm a good person, yes; kind and giving—but men don't necessarily want to jump into bed with blundering women who never stop rambling. It's not sexy.

I'm aware enough to admit that, too.

I live vicariously through Alyssa, and that's enough for me.

After giving my friend the grand tour, we settle down to share a bottle of wine on my scattered furniture with dogs in our laps and laughter on our tongues. It's a nice first night that will only be made better when I can whisk myself away to a familiar bedroom and uncover the sacred memories I know are waiting for me.

I see Alyssa off a few hours later, then race down the narrow hallway to a room that used to be draped in lavender and lace. It's gray now—gray and drab—and I can't wait to transform it into something sweeter, with love and a paintbrush.

Heart skipping, I seat myself cross-legged on the bedroom floor beside the bed.

Her bedroom floor.

Before I can get too comfortable, my phone pings from my back pocket like a little warning bell telling me to keep the past in the past.

It's too late for that, though.

It was far too late the moment I picked up the phone and dialed my agent, telling her I'd found the house of my dreams. Nightmares, some nights, but mostly, a new dream in the making.

She was surprised, yes, but she didn't know just how outlandish my decision really was. I didn't tell her that I grew up right next door in the cornflower blue raised ranch. I failed to mention that this fifteen-hundred square foot property was practically my second home for eight incredible years.

And I never did admit how eager I was to see if Emma's secret hiding place still held a trove of long lost treasures.

Pivoting my attention from the floorboards, I pull out my phone and glance down at the screen.

It's my mother. Shocking.

MOM:

Lucille Anne Hope.

ME:

The full name is less effective in text form, Mom.

MOM:

Just pretend you can hear the ominous inflection in my tone.

ME:

Okay. I'm thoroughly threatened. What's up?

MOM:

I miss you.

I smile, sending her a flurry of hearts and teary-eyed emojis before tossing my phone onto the top of an adjacent box.

At twenty-two years old, I moved out of my parents' house.

After a health scare dashed my dreams of leaving the quiet suburbs of Milwaukee and going off to Berklee to pursue a song-writing major, and my father's subsequent passing kept me from seeking a full-time job due to Mom's crippling grief and loneli-ness, I finally decided to chase a taste of independence. It was hard leaving my mother behind, but I think it was even harder for her. We've always been close, even more so after Dad died. But we both knew it was time for me to spread my wings and fly the nest.

I just never imagined that my nest would be here.

Right back at the beginning.

A sigh leaves me as I lean back on my palms and stare up at the ceiling that used to be home to dozens of glow-in-the-dark stickers and a giant poster of One Direction. It's the same ceiling I'd fall asleep staring at over the course of our eight years of sleep-over adventures. We'd stuff ourselves with Sour Patch Kids—me hoarding all of the green ones, Emma stealing the reds—and write songs that never had the chance to turn into more than hopeful notes on paper.

I drink in a deep breath, the wine only heightening the buzz filtering through my bloodstream, and straighten back into a sitting position. Then I pull apart the shoddy floorboards, nails popping, splinters scattering along with the rest of my reservations.

My whole body trembling, I peer inside.

And one by one, I pluck the items out.

Emma's diary, the face of it doodled with multicolored sharpies and peeling stickers.

Loose sheets of music.

Cal's old clarinet.

Cal, Cal, my Cal.

My eyes mist at the sight of the well-loved instrument, and I graze my fingertips over it, pondering how it became lost in the floorboards, wondering if it still plays. There's a crack through the center of the wood, the fracture patched with a dab of glue, telling me that Emma was in the process of bringing it back to life.

She was always the glue.

She was always *our* glue.

I reach for the diary, letting it shake inside my hands, unable to help the prickle of tears from blurring my vision. It's been a long time since I've heard Emma's voice, but I know it'll speak to me, loud and clear, as I read over these entries. I think I even heard it when the little red real estate icon popped up on my phone, spinning my life in a totally new direction.

Setting the diary aside for the moment, I keep rummaging, landing on a small photograph buried amid the precious relics.

My breath all but stops.

It's a picture of us, of my adventure people, and it's a picture I've never seen before.

Me, Emma, and Cal, our arms tangled around each other, our smiles woven with untouchable joy. The night is dark, the fireflies as bright as the light radiating from our faces. I'm tucked tightly inside of Cal's arm as it wraps around my neck, pulling me right to him, like I was never meant to leave. Emma is on my opposite side, doubled over with laughter.

I recall the moment.

Cal and Emma's father called out, "*Ready?*"

We weren't, but he snapped the photo anyway.

Then he asked us again, and again, and again, until we were a mess of undignified giggles and snorts, halfway falling onto each other.

We were never ready.

We were inherently, forever ready.

I press a finger to the photo, tracing the faces that have only lived inside my memories for nearly a decade.

Where are you, Callahan Bishop? Where did you go?

He may be an entirely different person now. Someone new, someone I'd hardly recognize, but I have to cling to hope that the boy I loved is still out there somewhere.

Hope.

Hope is why I'm here—it's my name, after all; it's in my blood.

But, I suppose the trouble with hope is that it's nothing more than a feeling, and feelings are fleeting. Names are eternal, but feelings don't last forever.

And neither do we.

All I know is that I'm going to use the time I have left to make up for the time lost.

I know, now...I need to find him.

I need to find my old friend.

CHAPTER 2

3/12/2013

"Deceptive Cadence"

A deceptive cadence happens when a chord progression seems to be coming to an end, but doesn't. It's a musical trick. It's a tool that plays with a listener's expectations, and I think that's pretty neat. I've been thinking about how a term like that can apply to real life situations. Everyday stuff. You think you know what's coming, but you never really do. And sometimes, when you think something is coming to an end, it's actually the beginning of something beautiful.

It's kind of like when the next door neighbors moved when I was five. I really liked their cat, so I cried for a whole week thinking it was the end of the world. But then, a pretty cool thing happened. A new family moved into that house.

They didn't have a cat, but they had something even better.

They had Lucy.

Toodles,

Emma

I'm not a stalker. Not technically.

Well, maybe technically—I need to look up the exact definition—but my intentions are far from sinister, and that's what counts.

I hope.

Curiosity swims through me as I pop the car door closed with the heel of my sandal and gaze up at the worn lettering of the auto shop sign.

Cal's Corner.

It's a small shop perched, fittingly, on a corner lot. The road that it sits off of isn't very busy, so the business must rely heavily on word of mouth and a loyal clientele. The prior day, I was on a mission to track down Cal, coming out of the excursion successful. Equipped with nothing but a name and the semi-blurry face of a fifteen-year-old boy, I strolled from house to house like I was a troop leader pandering for Girl Scout cookie orders. Eventually, an older woman recognized him.

"Cal? Cal Bishop?"

I positively beamed through a frantic head nod. "Yes, you know him?"

"Oh, sure," the woman said. "He owns that auto repair shop in town. Used to live down the road before his mama up and moved him away after..." She lowered her head, tinkering with her eyeglasses. "Well, after they went through some family trouble."

I swallowed, my stomach souring. "I know. I used to live next door to him. We lost touch over the years, and I'd love to see how he's been doing."

"He's doing fine, dear. They do wonderful work over at the shop—my husband, Roy, is always running into car problems, and Cal is quick and affordable."

"That's great," I smiled with gratitude, eagerness fusing with nerves. "Thank you for the information."

"Come back over here and let me know how the reunion goes. I'm a lonely old bat in need of some new gossip."

My laughter saw her off, and I've thought of nothing else over the last twenty-four hours.

Only seeing Cal.

Armed with a platter of freshly baked banana bread, my questionable resume, and a nervous smile, I head toward the pewter gray bricks and silvery door that greet me at the front of the building. A little bell chimes when I step inside. I glance up to find a pair of jingle bells tied with red ribbon and plastic holly berries, which is interesting because it's August, but I'm not one to judge. I love Christmas—which also happens to be my birthday.

My eyes case the lobby as the door closes behind me. Aside from the splash of festive flare, its overall aesthetic is cold and uninviting. Two folding chairs are divided by a wood table snagged out of a 1980s garage sale's "free to good home" bin. It's topped with a stack of car magazines that look well-loved. My nose scrunches up because it smells like a marrying of carburetors and sweaty men, but that can be fixed with some air fresheners, or a wax warmer. A reception desk sits abandoned against the far wall, drowning in piles of manilla folders and bookkeeping notes, and I can easily see why this little shop needs help.

Smiling, I set my resume and banana bread platter on one of the chairs, hoping I have the opportunity to breathe new life into my old friend's business.

"Can I help you?"

A deep, gravelly voice has me swiveling around and coming face-to-face with a man with shaggy dark hair. He wipes his hands on a rag as he studies me with cautious curiosity.

With the name "Cal's Corner," I'm anticipating someone who looks like Blippi. So, when the towering beast of a man approaches me, decorated in equal parts oil and ink, I'm convinced it's one of Cal's surly associates. "Hi!" I beam, flashing my whole set of teeth.

Silence.

He just stares at me, unblinking, managing to intimidate everything within a five-mile radius, including the potted orchid sitting on the reception desk. I swear it wilts before my eyes.

Clearing my throat, I start fidgeting with my thumb ring. There's a sizable oil stain a few feet away, and I wonder if it doubles as a black hole I can dive into. "Um, so, my name is Lucy. Lucy Hope. I grew up with Cal, and I was wondering—"

"I know who you are."

My lips shape into an *O*. "You do? Cal's mentioned me?" That's weird. We haven't spoken in over nine years, and I'd like to think that I don't still look like a gangly thirteen-year-old with braces and uneven bangs that were self-minced with a pair of dull scissors. Not knowing what else to do, I hold out my hand and harness my smile. "Well, it's nice to meet you. Is Cal around?"

He glances at my hand like it's holding the disease-infected monkey from *Outbreak*. "Yeah, I'll go get him."

A sigh of relief leaves me when the man turns and trudges away.

I freeze when he comes right back.

Folding two impossibly muscled arms over his chest, he looks down at me with light tawny eyes that spark a tingle of recognition deep inside me. I squint, then inhale sharply as my heart thunders with awareness. "Cal," I breathe out.

There's the slightest crack in his armor when his name leaves my lips, but he recovers quickly. "What are you doing here?"

It appears he's not capable of saying more than five words at once, but even more mindboggling is the fact that I can't even manage one.

I'm in a trance.

Memories burst to life, as if I'm hearing a beloved song that hasn't been played in years. My body hums with nostalgia. I can't help but replay a million moments in my mind, from hide-and-seek in the backyard, to secret forts and friendship pacts, to sleep-overs with Emma that Cal would always try to compromise with silly pranks and antics.

He looks completely different now. The boy I knew emanated softness and warmth, where twenty-five-year-old Cal is standoffish and gruff. If I hadn't already memorized the sound of his laughter, I might be afraid of him.

While always tall, he'd been on the lanky side growing up. Athletic but skinny. He was a star basketball player in his freshman year of high school before—

Before everything changed.

Despite the sleeves of tattoos that adorn bronzed arms, the layer of scruff lining his jaw, and his impressive brawny build, his eyes look the same. Light, light brown, almost copper. Waves of soft dark hair fall over his forehead in a strikingly similar way.

He swipes at his bangs, tossing the rag onto a side table beside him.

The gesture snaps me back to reality. Tinkering with the end of my braid, I suck in a breath. "I'm sorry I didn't recognize you. It's been so long."

His jaw tics. Cal drops his eyes, then pulls them back up, giving me a quick sweep. "You look the same."

I feel like that's not a compliment, but I bob my head anyway. My hair has darkened from honey to light brown over the years—like coffee with extra cream. It's long and thick, often in a messy bun or side braid to keep it contained. My boobs didn't start growing in until I was nearly seventeen, so I have curves now, accentuated by my surplice wrap dress.

But my eyes are still the same smoky blue.

And my heart beats the same.

I realize I never answered his question when he arches one eyebrow and tilts his head, waiting. "Well!" I chirp, overcompensating for the long stretch of awkward silence. "Anyway, I came by to inquire about the front desk position. I was hoping I could apply."

Because I've driven by fifteen times since I moved into your childhood home and saw you were hiring.

My smile stretches, bordering on creepy.

Cal flicks his thumb over his bottom lip as he stares at me, considering my words. Finally, he sighs, looking off to the side. "I'm not hiring."

Not subtly, I peek over at the giant sign that reads: *Now Hiring.* When my eyes pan back to Cal, I squeak out, "Oh. I must have misread."

"Position's been filled."

Gliding my bottom lip between my teeth, I can't help but notice the sad, empty reception desk with the droopy orchid. Piles of receipts and paperwork litter the small cubicle, a sure sign that this place is being run by a bunch of unorganized mechanics.

Which means he doesn't want to hire *me*, specifically.

"I see," I nod, forcing my smile to stay put through the sting of tears. "I'm sorry to have bothered you."

He frowns a little before glancing at the plate of banana bread behind me on the chair. "What's that?"

"Banana bread. It used to be your favorite."

The scowl deepens.

Somehow, I've offended him with banana bread.

I follow his line of sight, gulping. "Homemade. No walnuts. You used to pick out the walnuts when we were kids." My cheeks burn when the silence thickens. I hate long silences, and often find ridiculous things to ramble on about in order to fill the awful void. One time, I started listing off our nation's presidents in a linear timeline because I wasn't sure what else to do.

Cal folds his arms, his biceps flexing. I do my best not to stare, quickly shifting my gaze from his remarkably muscled forearms to the unreadable expression staring down at me.

His face has a roughness to it, but it's not weathered. Long, curving eyelashes and full lips soften the sharp angles of his jaw and jaded look in his eyes. There's a smudge of grease smeared across his cheekbone that I want to erase with the flick of my thumb, but I keep my hands occupied by playing with my hair some more.

The silence has lasted painfully long, so it feels like word vomit is the only way out at this point. "So, yeah," I continue, my voice wobbly. "Enjoy your banana bread. And your day, of course. It was...really nice to see you again, Cal. Maybe we can—"

"Good to see you, Lucy."

His words are pleasant enough, but his tone is distant and his interruption a clear indicator that he wants me to scram.

I nod my head half a dozen times through my dying smile and pivot toward the door. I feel his eyes on my back when I push it open and step outside, but he doesn't say anything else. He doesn't stop me, and I feel like the jingle bells sound far less cheerful on my way out.

Deflating with defeat, I shuffle to my Volkswagen, my sandals slapping in time with my thumping heart. I collapse into the driver's side seat, closing the door and dropping my forehead to the steering wheel.

I'm not sure what I was expecting, but it wasn't that.

It wasn't that cold, brutish version of the sweet boy I grew up with and thought I'd marry one day. They were childlike fantasies, of course, but they held merit at the time. Cal was adorable, kind and fun, never treating me like the annoying neighbor or his little sister's pesky friend.

He was *my* friend, too.

Now he's a complete stranger—and I suppose that's what happens when you lose contact with someone for almost a decade, but I *did* try to find him. His mom uprooted their lives in the wake of what happened, putting their house on the market and moving within months. No goodbye, no contact information. I tried looking Cal up on social media over the years, but have always come up empty. Sometimes I wondered if he was nothing but a ghost. Emma and Cal were just imaginary friends I'd made up to quell the loneliness that came along with growing up as a sick kid.

Smack!

I almost hit the ceiling when a palm slaps against my driver's side window. Pressing a hand to my chest, I turn my head and discover my resume staring back at me, smashed up to the glass. When Cal pulls it away and twirls his finger in the air—signaling for me to roll the window down—I catch my breath and do as he says.

I swear he looks even more fearsome beneath the hazy August

sun, but it could be the fact that the time of day is causing his shadow to stretch out like Goliath.

Also, he's really mad.

"What the hell is this?" Cal barks, waving my resume in front of my face. He plants his opposite hand along his hip, his stare accusing.

"M-my resume," I stammer. "I know my references are a little dodgy, but I promise I—"

"Not that."

I blink, wetting my lips. "Okay, so, Mr. Garrison isn't actually a former boss. He watches Key Lime Pie and Lemon Meringue for me sometimes. My dogs. I usually call them Kiki and Lemon, but they'll respond to—"

"Not the goddamn references, Lucy. The address."

Oh.

Swallowing, my hands immediately start trembling as I fidget in my seat and pull my eyes away from his death glare. "Right. You noticed that."

"Yeah. I noticed that," he says, his voice dipping so low he kind of sounds demonic. "What were you thinking?"

"I wasn't. I mean, not really," I sputter. "I've been looking to buy a house with my inheritance, and everything was wrong. Nothing felt like home. And then your old house went on the market, and I just got this feeling—it called to me, you know? There was this...*pull.* I knew it was the one." My lip quivers pathetically, so I chomp on it. Then I add with a touch of hope, "You looked over my resume?"

The cords in his neck strain as he pinches the bridge of his nose. It feels like he's about to say something, but he lets out a long sigh instead, taking a step backward and refusing to look at me. With a final glance at the resume, Cal grits his teeth, spins around, then stalks away.

I watch the planks of his back ripple beneath a tight sleeveless shirt, his tattoos looking more menacing with each angry stride. When he disappears around the side of the building, I let out a breath and sit there for a while, idle in the parking lot.

It feels like I'm in trouble.

I suppose telling a man I haven't seen in almost ten years that

I bought his old house while simultaneously tracking down his business and applying for a job there, might throw up some red flags.

But, I meant well.

Cal has no idea what it's been like living in that house. The memories. The sentiment radiating from the same taupe plaster walls. Emma's diary entries, detailing a beautiful childhood.

A childhood filled with him.

My Cal.

As I billow my cheeks with air and get ready to pull out of the parking lot, voices float over to me from the side of the building where another well-built man is working on a car.

"Who was that? The Mazda I'm working on?" the man clips from beneath a hood.

Loud rock music fuses with the conversation. I watch as Cal reaches for an abandoned pack of cigarettes on a shelf, falters briefly, then tosses it back down and plucks a piece of gum out of his pocket instead. "Just someone applying for the front desk position."

"You hire her? She was hot."

"She was unqualified."

The associate pops his head up with some kind of wrench in hand. "To answer phones and swipe credit cards? Shit, Cal, this isn't the fuckin' Ritz Carlton. Hire the hottie."

Cal tosses back the gum. "I thought you wanted me to bring in Edna for an interview."

"Edna doesn't look like that. Forget I mentioned it."

"Tell her she has an eleven o'clock interview tomorrow."

"You're a dipshit."

Flipping the man off, Cal stomps off through the garage, leaving the mechanic shaking his head and returning to work.

My fingers are curled around the steering wheel, my knuckles white.

Unqualified.

Maybe I am, but he hadn't even glanced at my resume before sending me away like I was a complete stranger. Like we didn't have history together, sprinkled with memories of spending endless summers counting stars and selling lemonade and banana bread slices at the edge of his driveway. Like we didn't share a powerful common thread—*his sister*.

I tell myself it's fine as I drive the five minute trek back home and enter the house, ambushed by happy tongues and wagging canine butts.

I tell myself it's okay while making a honey and cheddar sandwich for lunch and refilling the dogs' water bowls.

I tell myself it doesn't matter when I shuffle between the unpacked boxes in Emma's old bedroom and collapse to the floor, pulling up the loose plank of wood and reaching for her diary.

But the lie doesn't stick.

As I flip through the crinkled pages of her journal and her words come to life, I can't help the tears that burst through like a broken-down dam.

Quietly weeping, I fall backward with the diary pressed against my heart, and I wonder why she left me.

I wonder why they both left me.

CHAPTER 3

5/18/2013
"Heart and Soul"

You know that amateur piano song every single person on the planet knows how to play? It's one of the easiest songs to ever exist, but it's called "Heart and Soul"—which just so happens to be the two most complex and extraordinary things to ever exist.

Isn't that weird?

Anyway, Lucy is coming over after dinner for a sleepover, and I can't wait to talk about our summer plans. I want to start a band. Me and Cal on piano, Lucy on guitar, and all of us can sing.

I wonder if they'll let me name the band Deceptive Cadence?

Or...maybe Heart and Soul.

After all, Lucy is my heart, and Cal is my soul.

Toodles,

Emma

Peachy sunset pours in through the floor-to-ceiling window, matching the feeling soaring through me as I belt out the last few notes to my rendition of *Losing My Religion* by REM with nothing but a tambourine. I'm so lost in the music, I don't notice anything else.

I'm addicted to the feeling.

Singing, performing, creating. I've never truly been in love before, but it's the only thing I can think to compare it to. There's a certain kind of magic in sharing something soul-deep with someone else. It's almost like you're making an imprint on *their* soul.

I grin wide through the final note, shaking my tambourine until the jangling fades into applause. The crowd goes wild, and I finally snap back to the wine bar. People holler and cheer. A motorcycle revs to life right outside the window. Nash claps from behind the bar as he pours a glass of my usual post-performance Riesling, while Alyssa whistles from a high-top table like one of those enthusiastic dance moms. I flash her my teeth before standing from the stool.

Familiar faces shine back at me when I pluck my guitar off the stage and lift it in the air, taking a final bow. "Thank you all for coming out tonight," I say into the microphone. My voice is steady as I address the audience. As awkward as I come across on a regular day, I'm a different person on stage—calm, collected. Music has always given me confidence. "As always, I'm blessed to be here. I'm Imogen, and I'll be back next week with more mediocre covers and subpar originals for you. Goodnight, everyone."

Imogen is my stage name. I chose it as a nod to Emma and

her favorite pianist, Imogen Cooper. Still grinning, I bend over, and Alyssa hollers, "*Ass*-stounding!"

I would flip her the bird if I was capable, but my finger has never cooperated. Instead, I shake my head as laughter falls out of me, collecting my tips and packing up. It takes me a solid twenty minutes due to a flurry of patrons strolling up to thank me for the show, applauding me on a job well done, and sneaking me a few extra tips, but I take my time engaging with every single one of them. Appreciation and pride fill me from toes to top, and a smile hasn't left my face all evening.

Bliss Wine Bar is packed. It's Friday night, and I play live music here every week at seven, bringing in a bigger crowd each time. It's both a part-time gig and a therapeutic outlet.

For me, music is medicine. It's healing.

It reminds me of her.

My two long braids fall over both shoulders as I tug the skirt of my sundress down, finally securing my Hummingbird guitar into its case. When I skip over to the table for two, where my best friend since freshman year of high school sits, a glass of wine is already waiting for me on a bar napkin with familiar scribbling etched onto it.

Alyssa waggles her eyebrows as I approach. "He's obviously dedicated, and has great handwriting," she observes, fingering the stem of her own glass. "All we need to know at this point is his Enneagram, love language, Zodiac sign, and credit score."

My eyes roll up through a laugh. I've never met anyone quite like Alyssa Akins. She was the popular, pom pom-waving homecoming queen, while I was the quiet music enthusiast who spent her spare time volunteering and doing charity work—but despite our difference in high school social status, we clicked. And I think it's because, deep down, we were the same. Soul sisters. While she was effortlessly outgoing and adored by everyone, she never acted like she was above them.

I discovered that the day I got into a minor car accident near the school one afternoon, and Alyssa happened to be driving by to cheerleading tryouts. She spotted me shivering on the curb, scared out of my mind, and pulled over, staying with me until my parents showed up, missing half of tryouts.

She didn't care, though. Giving me comfort during a crisis was more important.

We've been inseparable ever since.

I spare Nash a quick glance, receiving a wink in reply. Blushing, I return my attention to Alyssa who looks to be frantically punching his name into her Google search bar. "He's sweet," I say.

"Ouch. The kiss of death."

"He's not really my type."

Her eyes narrow. "I'm beginning to think your *type* only consists of the four-legged, flea-prone variety."

As she says this, I peer down at the little note written on my napkin in blue ink that just happens to read: *"I have a dog."* It's accompanied by a questionable drawing of a canine that looks more like a lemur.

Okay, so he knows me pretty well.

I bite down on my bottom lip to prevent the smile from stretching. Every week, Nash leaves me notes on bar napkins, identifying all of his best qualities and character traits, hoping I'll go out with him. While his dedication is admirable, my reason for rebuffing his advances is nothing personal.

It's necessary.

"Maybe I just prefer to live vicariously through you, Lys," I shrug, sipping my wine.

She grimaces. "I don't know why. The last guy I was serious about ended up being married. To two separate women." Eyes popping, she reaches for her phone again. "Nash...Meltzer... wives..." she murmurs as she types.

"He's not married," I shake my head. "He has honest eyes."

"Ted Bundy had honest eyes."

I wrinkle my nose. "Valid point. Keep me posted."

Leaving Alyssa to play Nancy Drew, I pull my own cell phone out of my satchel and skim through the notifications, intermittently chatting with a handful of show regulars and returning the smiles and waves sent my way.

As I'm saying goodbye to an acquaintance, a text comes through.

UNKNOWN NUMBER:

Tomorrow. 9 AM.

I narrow my eyes at the screen, the talk of Ted Bundy still fresh in my mind.

ME:

Who is this?

How did you get my number?

UNKNOWN NUMBER:

I got it the same way I know that your address is 919 S. Maple Ave.

My gut twists with dread.

I'm toast.

He's one-thousand percent a murderer, and my time of death is tomorrow at nine a.m. I mentally prepare for the occasion, wondering if I have time to write up a will. Attorney offices are probably closed by now.

My hand starts to tremble as I type back a response.

ME:

Just don't hurt my dogs.

A few minutes tick by before he responds.

UNKNOWN NUMBER:

What the hell are you talking about?

Puckering my lips, I blink down at the screen, realizing I probably jumped to conclusions. A real killer would never send me a warning text.

I try to backpedal.

ME:

Never mind.

What are YOU talking about?

UNKNOWN NUMBER:

An interview, Lucy. Jesus.

The dread morphs into a fluttery tickle. Kind of like a dead butterfly that's been resuscitated.

> ME:
>
> Cal?

I'm inputting his name into my contacts when he sends a reply.

> CAL:
>
> Don't be late.

Alyssa peers over at my furiously typing thumbs, her interest piqued. "Who's that?" She gasps. "A guy? Is he the reason you've been rejecting Nash?"

"I'm not rejecting Nash. There's nothing to reject," I tell her, still typing as zombie butterflies zip around my belly. "He hasn't officially asked me out."

I click send.

> ME:
>
> Thank you!
>
> Sorry about that!
>
> I'll see you tomorrow!
>
> :)

"Way too many exclamation points!" Alyssa yells in my face. I lurch back, blinking.

"See?" she says, her long, sunny bob tickling her shoulders.

"Crap. I do sound excessively caffeinated. How do I unsend?" The text shows "read" almost instantly, so I massage my temples with my fingertips, hoping I didn't completely botch this already. "He saw the exclamation points," I grimace.

"Well, maybe he'll think they're charming. Maybe he—"

I'm already attempting damage control, shooting off another message.

ME:

Sorry, I was just excited.

I really appreciate the opportunity.

Frowning, I stare at the phone screen. "Now it looks like I'm upset. Exclamation points show enthusiasm."

Panicking, I keep going.

ME:

Have a great night! :) :)

"Oh my God, Lucy. You're making it worse."

Alyssa whips the phone out of my hand, holding it hostage before I can act anymore unhinged.

I reach for the wine glass and start to chug, bouncing my feet restlessly on the rung of the stool. Swallowing three giant gulps, I suck in a deep breath. "Sorry. He's my potential boss, and this particular position means a lot to me. I didn't think I had a chance, but then he texted me about an interview out of the blue."

"Ooh." She purses her lips, eyeing me curiously. "What's the job?"

"Answering phones at an auto repair shop."

"That sounds terrible."

"Well, I used to know him," I explain. "He's the owner."

"So, he's hot."

I fluster, chewing on the inside of my cheek. "I didn't say that."

"Heavily implied," she breezes. "Nobody desperately wants to work at an auto shop and deal with enraged customers who thought they were bringing their car in for an oil change, only to be slapped with a two-thousand dollar bill. Obviously, he's hot, and you want to bump fuzzies."

The sun has dipped lower in the sky, so only a hazy low light seeps in through the glass, but it might as well be a scorching fire-ball. "No."

"What's he look like?"

"Like he was this-close to getting a role on *Sons of Anarchy*," I say, pinching my thumb and index finger together. "Tall and muscley, lots of tattoos. Scruffy and edgy. Steady scowl."

Her eyes bulge. "You just described my future husband. Name?" She reaches for her phone, already in research-mode.

"Cal Bishop. He owns Cal's Corner, the auto shop a few miles from my new house. I grew up with him when I was a kid, and—"

"Holy shit, Lucy."

A phone screen is shoved in my face as I inch back, trying to see what she's showing me. When the article comes into view, I read the headline: ***Local Man Buys Back Auto Shop Originally Owned By Late Father.***

My heart swells with both pride and melancholy as a smile pulls on my mouth. I knew Cal and Emma's father worked with cars, but failed to piece together that he first owned the mechanic shop. Sentiment prickles my eyes before a frown settles in, and I say, "Wait, how did you find that? I've typed his name into Google a hundred times."

"Typed in 'Cal's Corner' and scrolled down a bit," Alyssa says, then shakes the phone as if that will help me see the image better. "But forget the article. Look at the picture. Your new boss. He was your next door neighbor you lost touch with, right?"

"That's him," I confirm, pushing her arm away. "'New boss' is presumptuous considering I don't know how to phone properly. Did he reply?" I wring my hands together in my lap, then reach for the wine glass, which I realize is regrettably empty.

Alyssa glances at my cell phone that she set down on her side of the table. Shaking her head, she delivers the blow. "Nothing. He read them, but didn't respond."

"God, I ruined it."

"He doesn't look like a texter to me," she notes, still ogling the photograph of Cal. Her muted berry lips pucker with appreciation. "Silent, broody. Probably owns a motorcycle. Definitely a beast in the bedroom."

My skin flushes, and I reflexively start fanning myself with the bar menu. "He probably has a girlfriend. Or a dozen."

"Very likely. I'll happily jump in line."

When I finally snatch my phone back—while confirming that

Cal had, indeed, not returned my messages—Nash saunters up to our table with two fresh glasses of white wine. Dark green eyes catch the streaks of fleeting daylight, twinkling in my direction.

"Thank you," I tell him, accepting the refill and gifting him with a shy smile.

He winks. "You bet."

Nash is good-looking. Boyishly cute with prominent dimples and thick curls of caramel blond hair that resemble honeycomb.

Those dimples are out in full force at the moment, acting as little weapons aimed right at me.

"I like your drawing." I gesture with my pinky finger at the lemur-dog drawn onto the bar napkin. "Very cute."

"Yeah? That's Buttons. I'll relay the compliment."

"Great." Both of our smiles broaden at the same time, and I duck my head.

Nash raps his knuckles against the table, taking a step back. "Let me know if you ladies need anything else," he says, his focus skipping over to Alyssa, then returning to me. Our eyes hold for another beat before he pivots away and heads back to the bar.

Alyssa sighs, reaching for the new glass of wine. "You should sleep with him."

My cheeks burn as I twirl my finger around one of my braids. "He's probably a player. I saw him flirting with another girl a few minutes ago."

"Okay, but he isn't leaving her cute little napkin notes. I say go for it."

I shrug a maybe, even though I know I'm not going to "go for it."

I've seen what relationships can do. Napkin notes turn into dates, dates turn into kissing, and then sex, and then *love*, and then...

And then there's Jessica.

I can't ever be Jessica.

"Anyway," I tell Alyssa, hopping down from the stool and swigging back a quick sip of wine before sliding the rest over to her. "I need to get going. Interview tomorrow."

"Ahh, good luck, babe." She hugs me tightly, her bubblegum-scented body mist tickling my nose. "Let me know how it goes."

"I will. See you next week." I throw my guitar case over my shoulder and send her a wave, making eye contact with Nash before I traipse toward the front door.

His dimple-infused wink sees me off, right as my phone pings from my dress pocket. I fish it out, glancing down at the screen.

Cal's name lights up the face.

CAL:

You too

Those two words have me smiling the whole way home, reminiscing about a little girl I desperately miss.

Deceptive Cadence: When you think something is coming to an end, it's actually the beginning of something beautiful.

CHAPTER 4

I'm late.

There is nothing that gives me more anxiety than running late. I even put on my resume: *PROMPT AND PUNCTUAL*. I capitalized it for emphasis.

Now, I'm a liar. A *late* liar.

Granted, I didn't predict a power outage last night. We didn't even have bad weather—it was one of those freak things that nobody really plans for.

Except for me. Normally, I *do* plan for freak things. I leave an hour early to drive five minutes away in case there's a stalled train, or never-ending construction, or a meteor shower, or someone's unfortunate dice roll during a game of *Jumanji*. But when I plugged my cell phone in to charge last night at a feeble three-percent, I did not predict that someone would drive their car into a utility pole and cause the entire street to lose power.

So, my phone died, my alarm died with it, and so did my best hope at landing the receptionist position at Cal's Corner.

The jingle bells chime when I race through the main door, alerting everyone within earshot of my tardiness.

"You're early."

Cal steps out of an office situated behind the front desk, wearing a plain white tee and black denim. His espresso-brown hair looks even darker, damp from what I assume was a recent shower. It's tousled and messy, drying in an assortment of different directions that he somehow manages to make look attractive. There's a silver chain around his neck, tucked into the collar of his shirt, but I can't make out the shape of the pendant.

Wait.

When his words register, they catch me off guard, and my eyes instinctively skate over to the dust-sheathed wall clock. The time shows ten-past-nine.

"I said nine-thirty," he continues.

The interview was most definitely for nine a.m. sharp—a girl doesn't forget her imaginary time of death. But I accept the tiny miracle and choose that moment to believe in a higher power. "Right. That's me. I really love being early."

Wow. I said it like it's at the top of my list of interests: I love a finely aged wine. Sloppy dog kisses. A tangerine sunset.

Being early!

I scratch at my collarbone and start to fidget, picking at my fingernails.

"Come in." Cal nods his head toward the office and disappears inside.

Smoothing down the wrinkles in my dress, I follow behind him, watching as he makes his way to a desk littered with invoices and folders. The office is dim and musty, void of any character or personal touches. No pictures, no knick-knacks. Just a shoddy old desk, two chairs, and a filing cabinet in the corner of the room decorated with cobwebs belonging to a spider family from the nineties. I itch to pull open the blinds and bathe the space in natural sunlight, but I remain where I stand, waiting for direction.

Cal waves his hand at an empty chair and sits down in his own, releasing a long sigh that borders on irritation as he glances up and catches my eyes. "Sorry about the other day. I lied when I said the position was filled," he admits, leaning back and folding his tatted arms. "I thought we'd start with an interview and see if our chemistry is conducive to a comfortable working environment."

I dwell on the word *chemistry* and my teeth start clacking. "Okay. Great," I manage. Pacing forward, I sit down in the chair he's gesturing at and almost miss the seat. Blush settles into my cheekbones as I regain my composure and clear my throat. "I really appreciate the interview, Cal. I know I don't have much experience with cars or mechanics—well, any, really—but I'm a hard worker and extremely reliable."

I inwardly cringe. I basically confessed that I have zero knowledge in the field I'm applying for, but hey, at least I'll show up to do a job I'll suck at.

Cal holds my gaze for another second before looking away and reaching for a pen. "Do you have good phone etiquette? Can you handle customers?"

"Yes. I'm great with people."

"Assuming you don't think they're trying to maim your dogs."

He says it so straight-faced, it takes me a moment to realize he's kidding—*I think*. Cracking a smile, I laugh lightly. "Sorry about that. I really am good with people, and I'm a fast learner. I'm sure I'll figure out your processing system and software in no time."

Jotting down some notes, he nods. "Good. I don't have time to micromanage."

"Okay. That won't be a problem."

"It says here you're available any time, except for Friday and Saturday nights, and preferably no Sundays?" he inquires, not looking up.

"Yes...if that's okay. I can move things around if necessary, but I'm a performer. I play live music every Friday night, and on the occasional Saturday night. And on Sundays I volunteer at a local animal shelter called *Forever Young*."

His eyes lift. "Should be fine. We close at six p.m. during the week and are closed on Sundays."

"Oh, that's perfect," I smile. "I can definitely work with that schedule."

Cal flicks the end of his pen against a yellow pad of paper, still studying me. His eyes narrow as he asks, "You play music?"

I'm not sure if he's showing interest in my life, or if this applies to the job position somehow, but I latch onto the question like it's my oxygen mask dropping on a plummeting aircraft.

"I do. A little of everything, but I primarily sing and play guitar. I actually wanted to go to college for songwriting. Unfortunately, my health..." I trail off, nibbling my lip, not sure how much personal information I should offer. "Well, I was in the hospital for a while. I'm fine now, so you don't have to worry about the job. And then my dad passed away, so it was just hard to focus on—"

"Your dad passed?" Cal's eyebrows pull together, his expression painted with a tinge of concern. "Sorry. I didn't know."

Touched, I smile despite the subject matter. "Thanks. He had cancer. It was really hard on me and my mom."

We stare at each other for a few charged beats. Memories dance between us, and I wonder if he's thinking about family bonfires in the backyard in late September when the leaves would float from maple tree branches, looking so burdenless, so carefree, matching the feeling in the air that we thought would last forever.

Cal blinks. Shadows steal the flickering of light in his eyes, and he throws the mask back on, returning to the stranger who replaced my old friend. "Well," he says, clearing his throat and rising from the chair. "I think this will work. You can start tomorrow."

I stand as well, my heart galloping beneath my lavender halter dress. "Really?"

He pulls a piece of gum out of his pocket, peeling back the wrapper and popping it into his mouth. His gaze falls over me, the muscles in his jaw twitching when he slides his eyes back up to my face. Throat bobbing, he gives me a curt, "Yeah."

"Wow, okay...that means so much to me. I really—"

"Under one condition," he interrupts.

Chewing on my bottom lip, I fold my hands in front of me and twirl my thumbs. "Of course. Anything."

His stare is hard, stance rigid. Copper irises fuse with steel as he says, "We don't talk about her."

A sharp breath leaves me.

Emma's face skips across my mind, from her freckled nose to her ribbons of brunette hair that were often pulled up into a ponytail with her favorite scrunchie. I see her waving to me as she races from my backyard to hers. I hear her shouting, *"Toodles!"*

when she reaches the patio door, a gummy smile shining back at me before she slips inside.

I don't want to not talk about her. I don't want to pretend she's not real.

But Cal is staring at me from behind his desk with a dark expression that tells me I don't have a choice. His "condition" is not up for negotiation. His eyes are blazing, daring me to counter him.

Nodding my head slowly, I do what I do best. I smile. "I understand."

"Good."

That's all he says before storming out of the office, leaving me in a cloud of sandalwood and spice, a trace of something minty, and remnants of a girl he longs to forget.

Before I step out, something catches my attention on the desk. I tilt my head, recognizing the platter of banana bread.

And then my grin brightens because all that he left of the bread were the two end pieces—just like he would do when we were kids.

CHAPTER 5

I realized I was never told a start time, so I'm waiting in front of the shop at seven a.m. the next morning in a summery lemon skater dress with a basket of homemade apple cinnamon muffins, and a smile that swells when I spot Cal careening into the parking lot forty minutes later.

Alyssa was right. He has a motorcycle.

The guttural rumbling of the engine and the aroma of faint gasoline fumes have me flinching back while I watch him zip into a space and draw to a halt. As he pulls off his helmet, traces of early morning sunlight bathe him in a delicate glow, contrasting his hardened exterior and sour expression.

Cal ruffles his mop of hair and hops off the motorcycle, reaching for a stainless steel thermos mounted onto the bike's seat tube. When he spots me standing by the door waving at him, my messy top-bun almost as big as my grin, he does a double-take, then stops in his tracks. The look on his face tells me he either forgot that he hired me, or he's regretting that he hired me.

"Good morning!" I greet brightly, still waving. I'm not sure why I'm still waving, but my arm probably thinks that if it waves long enough, he'll feel compelled to wave back.

He doesn't, but he does give me a terse nod, which I convince my arm is almost the same thing. It lowers to my side.

"Morning," he says in a gruff, pre-coffee voice—which is

possibly his all-the-time voice. "You're early again." Digging into his pockets with his free hand, he pulls out a key as he strides toward me, averting his eyes.

Our arms touch when he brushes past. He smells freshly showered, like spice and earthy musk, and a funny feeling skates down my back as I squeeze the handle of the muffin basket. "I forgot to ask for my start time, so I showed up at seven," I admit through a laugh.

Cal falters, sending me a frown over his wide shoulder. "You've been sitting out here for almost an hour?"

"Yep. I was practicing my customer service voice and stress-eating through two muffins."

Glancing at the muffins, he pushes through the main door. "Half expected to see a trail of woodland animals following you around, waiting for a sing-along."

Okay, so he *does* know how to make jokes.

I bite my lip, trying to hide the smile as I follow him into the main lobby, the chime of the jingle bells welcoming me. "Is that a compliment?"

"Don't know yet." He flips on a light. "You can throw your purse and girly stuff in the break room."

I try to follow the direction his finger is pointing, but it's non-specific, so I figure I'll find my way there eventually.

Taking a sip from his thermos, Cal eyes the muffins again. "You bake a lot?"

"I do," I nod. "And I wanted to make a good first impression. You know...with the guys."

He falters mid-sip, his eyes sweeping over me in a slow pull before settling on my face. "You don't need muffins for that, but doesn't hurt."

My skin heats, my insides filling with warmth. I'm fairly positive that was a compliment.

And, shock of the century, I have no idea what to say.

Frowning a little, he swipes a hand up and down the back of his head and musses his hair. Then he makes a sound that resembles a grumble, or maybe a sigh, and marches past me to his office. I stand there awkwardly, not knowing if I should follow him or not, trying to think of something to say that's relevant and normal. Panicking, I blurt, "So, you work with cars, huh?"

I say it as if maybe he doesn't.

A stretch of silence passes before Cal storms back out of the office with a baseball cap on his head. "Yeah, Lucy, I work with cars." Moving behind the reception desk, he powers up the computer. "The guys will be in soon, and I can introduce you. We have three other mechanics here. Ike, Dante, and Kenny. Good guys, but let me know if they give you any trouble."

"Trouble?" I gulp.

He lifts his eyes for a moment before typing something on the keyboard. "If they make a pass at you, or make you uncomfortable. The last receptionist we had here was Kenny's grandmother."

"Oh." My smile strains. "I can hold my own."

"All right." Cal starts typing again. "Are you going to come watch what I'm doing?"

"Oh!" I nearly drop the muffin basket as I shuffle across the room and pop it on a chair along with my purse, then sprint over to where Cal is nearly taking up the entire desk with his bulky frame. "Right. I'm all eyes. And ears. And any other parts you need from me." I wiggle my fingers, but then my cheeks flame when a less-innocent implication settles in. "For work," I add, gesturing toward the computer.

One dark eyebrow arches to his hairline. "Are you always this hyper in the mornings?"

"Sorry, I'm nervous."

"Why?"

"New job jitters. But it's fine. I'm listening." Wishing my hair was down to hide the pink stain on my cheeks, I move in closer and lean over the desk to watch the cursor dance across the screen. A software program shines back at me with a monkey logo, detailing different categories such as workflow, inventory, customer invoices, and technician reports.

Cal goes over everything quickly.

He's one of *those*.

I've hardly grasped one thing before he's showing me how to use the credit card reader, then talking about the petty cash box and listing off client appointments for the day. Luckily, I've been jotting down notes on a pad of paper, hoping I'll have time to reread everything and fully absorb the tasks and system before the shop opens in an hour.

"Make sense?" His palms are splayed on the desk as he bends forward, his corded arms lined with veins and ink.

I look back down at my notes, biting my lip as I internally panic. "Absolutely."

"You sure? I can go over it again."

We glance at each other at the same time, and our eyes catch, his coppery irises glimmering against the dim lighting. I want to ask him a thousand questions that have nothing to do with the job.

How are you?

No, wait...who are you?

Do you laugh the same? Hug the same? Do you still eat your cereal with chocolate milk?

A little crease forms between his brows as he scans my face, and I wonder if he has questions, too. I want him to ask me something. Anything. I want to confess that I never stopped thinking about him, even after all these years. I never stopped thinking about *her.*

"I looked for you," I mutter softly, unable to hold back the heart-rending truth twisting my heart into knots. Cal's frown deepens into something darker, his jaw hardening as he stares at me. I watch emotion dapple the eyes he's trying to keep stone-cold, but my words are like warm sunlight beating down on a block of ice. "I tried to find you. Facebook...social media."

He finally pulls his gaze from mine, bowing his head. "I don't have any of that shit."

"I noticed," I nod. "It was hard not knowing what happened to you. What happened to—"

"I didn't hire you for this." When he snaps his head back up, the frost returns, a silver storm clouding his eyes. "I don't want to do this with you, Lucy."

"You act like the past doesn't mean anything."

"Because it's the past. People fucking change. They move on. I'm not that kid anymore, and if this is going to work—" he flicks a tattooed finger between us, "—you need to get it out of your head that you can break me down with endless smiles, sunshine, and banana bread."

I recoil as he straightens from the desk and looms over me by a solid foot. My eyes mist, locking on the center of his charcoal gray hooded tank, too afraid to lift them and meet the volatile expression I know he's wearing. "Okay," I say, my tone pathetically meek. It shakes a little, causing Cal to let out a tapered sigh.

When I finally find the courage to trail my gaze skyward, he's scrubbing a palm down his face, scratching at the coarse stubble along his chin.

"Fuck," he mutters. "Sorry."

"It's fine. I shouldn't pry."

"I'm being an asshole." With his hand still cupped around his jaw, he turns his attention to the dying orchid sitting at the corner of the work station. The pink and fuchsia flowers are dull, the petals wilted. He closes his eyes, breathing out through his nose. "I just want to keep this strictly business. Tell me you understand."

I nod quickly. "I understand."

"I don't mean to be such a dick," he continues, panning back to me.

I'm already staring at him with a lump in my throat that feels like a chunk of my heart that came loose. I swallow it down, forcing a smile to spread. "You're not."

"I am. I just don't know what to do when you look at me like that."

"Like what?" I murmur.

He peers down at his feet, then back up, a flash of pain crossing his face. "Like you're looking at her."

I don't have time to work through the emotion that seizes me, or the stabbing feeling that punctures my chest like a hot blade, because the main door swings open, revealing a man in a white hoodie with olive skin and sable hair.

He raises his coffee cup in greeting. "Yo."

When he notices me standing beside Cal, hardly visible behind the corner of the desk, he does a second take, stalling his feet. I send him a smile, shaking off the tense moment. "Good morning."

"Are you the new girl?"

I bob my chin, instinctively fiddling with my giant top-knot. "Lucy. Today's my first day."

Cal clears his throat, scuffing a worn sneaker along the linoleum floor and pushing away from the desk. "She's our new receptionist," he intervenes. "Lucy, this is Dante, one of the mechanics."

"It's great to meet you."

Dante takes a sip from his cup, eyeing me with appreciation. "Likewise. It'll be nice having a lady around here keeping us degenerates in line." Grinning, he looks over at the chair that holds the muffin basket. "You make those?"

"I did," I say, gliding around the desk, yellow skirt flaring. "Apple cinnamon."

"Shit. Nice find, boss."

Cal makes a humming sound as he flips his ball cap around and traipses over to the water cooler in the back corner of the room. He fills a paper cup, then returns to the desk to pour it around the base of the potted orchid. Not looking at me, but clearly speaking to me, he says, "Come find me if you have any questions. The guys know their way around the system, but I prefer to be the one in charge of training you."

"Okay. Sure," I reply.

Cal tosses the empty cup into the trash and saunters away, heading back into his office and leaving me with pages of messy notes and an ultra-frazzled mind.

Dante shuffles past me. "A few words of advice," he says, stopping at the desk as he takes a swig of his coffee.

"What's that?"

"One," he quips, holding up an index finger. "Don't try to talk to him before his coffee. Two, don't try to talk to him about his family or personal life before *or* after his coffee. And three…" He flicks three fingers at me, then pauses. "Actually, just keep referring to one and two."

I purse my lips to the side, debating if I should reach for the notepad and jot these things down. Ultimately, though, all of his points seem to boil down to one point: *Avoid Cal.*

"Oh, another thing," he says, tapping four fingers on the desk and waggling his eyebrows. "Don't take anything personally."

With a tight smile, I gulp.

Dante sends me off with a wink, whistling as he disappears behind me. "You got this. Welcome to the team, sweetheart."

His final words race through my mind as I jump into action and try to get organized.

Don't take anything personally.

It's only day one, and I'm already faced with the impossible.

The day flies by in a blur of customers, card reader errors, new faces, and crippling anxiety. Thankfully, the mechanics have all been welcoming toward me, which has been a bright spot in an otherwise stressful introduction to the life of an auto shop receptionist.

Ike is in his early thirties, donning a shaved head, troves of leather, and a collection of tattoos that make Cal look like an ink amateur. He's not as tall as Cal, but he's just as built, his harsh exterior only softened by the fact that he always has a lollipop dangling from his mouth.

Kenny is the oldest, in his late forties. His face is dappled in freckles and sunspots, his hair and goatee a striking shade of amber; almost red in direct sunlight. The giant bear hug he gave me when we met, combined with a distinctive laugh, has me feeling like I've known him for years.

And then there's Dante, who is closer to Cal's age—mid-twenties. He's been friendly and accommodating, quick to help when Cal is preoccupied. I'm pretty sure he's the flirt of the bunch, judging by the mischievous gleam in his eyes and crooked grin he wears whenever he's talking to me.

As for the clients, they've been patient with me, overall, as I work my way through the unfamiliar program prompts, computer glitches, and general lack of knowledge in the field I'm working in, but my luck runs out around four p.m. when the crotchety Roy Allanson strolls in.

He lifts his cane, pointing it at me like I personally tampered with his vehicle. "You," he barks, squinting his beady eyes in my direction.

"Me?"

"Yeah, you. Get the owner."

I stand there like a deer in headlights, even though the request was crystal clear. My body often locks up when I'm being yelled at or chastised.

"Are ya deaf, girl?" he continues, hobbling closer. "You don't even look old enough to be working here. Get the owner before I go back there myself."

My cheeks blaze beet red as I nod my head and rush over to the door that separates the lobby from the service area. "Of course. One moment, please." The greasy garage fumes act as a welcome reprieve from the shame that's suffocating me. I look around one of the bays for Cal, who I find half-hidden beneath a red sedan. "Hey, Cal?"

He doesn't hear me over AC/DC.

Clearing my throat, my voice cracks as I repeat, "Cal."

Finally, he rolls out from underneath the vehicle, tools in hand. "What's up?"

"There's a man here. He's really mean, and he wants to speak with you."

He blinks. "Allanson? Tell him I'll be out in a minute."

The order is simple, yet it sounds equivalent to how a doctor might feel having to tell a family that their loved one didn't make it. Masking the uneasiness trickling through me, I pull my lips between my teeth with a head bob and swivel back around to deliver the news.

The man is bent forward over the reception desk when I return, still grumbling profanities under his breath. I lead in with a weird chuckle-sigh noise, clapping my hands together. "He'll be out in a minute!" I announce cheerfully.

Mr. Allanson slants his eyes at me, roving his gaze up and down my figure with disapproval. He's wearing a *Regal Beagle* t-shirt tucked into a pair of khakis that are drooping off his hips. "They'll hire anyone these days, eh?" he snips, still giving me a onceover.

I swallow, not letting his words get to me.

This guy is just angry and transferring his aggression onto the only person he can right now.

It's fine.

Cheeks still hot, I shift my attention to the desk and make my way behind it, forcing an amiable smile. I fiddle with a stack of paperwork, pretending to be busy as I feel the man boring holes into my proclaimed inadequacy. "Cal should be right out," I squeak.

"Yeah, yeah."

Fortunately, Cal materializes from the service area a moment later, ruffling his hair with a big hand that's stained with some sort of engine residue. When he sees me smiling maniacally, he shifts his sights to the irate customer and takes over. "Good to see you, Roy."

"I'm sure you are," he gripes back. "Tryin' to bleed me dry with that last bill, and the damn thing still doesn't work."

"You tried to replace the air filter yourself and left the plastic on. That's problematic."

The man grumbles. "Your prices are problematic, son."

"Our prices are competitive and in line with industry standards. We do good work."

I try to remain invisible, but my bright yellow dress is like a smoldering spotlight, pulling Roy's attention back to me.

"And this little thing hardly looks a day out of high school." He pops a thumb over his shoulder at me. "How can I expect accuracy when I'm not confident she knows her math?"

Cal's face is unflinching, his stance immovable. "I assure you, she's competent."

"She better be, Bishop, because I don't want to find any surprises—"

Thinking fast, I blurt, "I love surprises. It's funny that you never suspect them."

Everyone goes silent.

Save for the crickets skittering around my brain.

Both Cal and Roy turn to look at me. Cal does a face-palm, silently begging me to stop talking, while Roy narrows his eyes and studies me curiously.

Then he barks out a laugh. "*Three's Company*," he blares with awe, slapping a hand on top of the desk. "You know your sitcoms, girl."

Out of my peripheral vision, I see Cal's posture unclench, his expression shifting from irritation to cautious curiosity as his gaze skips between us. I keep my focus trained on Mr. Allanson, leaning forward on my arms and nodding at his t-shirt. "It's one of my favorites. I feel like today's generation has no appreciation for the classics, you know?"

"You got that right." His laughter rattles his chest as he flashes me a set of yellowing teeth. Then he turns to Cal, his fiery temperament dowsed. "How did ya score this one, Bishop? She's a keeper."

Cal folds one arm across his chest, the other elevated as he scratches at his jaw and glances at me, his surprise evident. He's still looking at me while he replies to Roy. "Lucky find," he says.

"I'd say so."

Relaxing with relief, I keep going. "I brought in some home-made muffins for the clients today," I add, reaching for the basket with two muffins remaining. "Here, take one."

Roy's smile hasn't wavered as he plucks a still-moist muffin from the bottom and nods his thanks. His mood has brightened considerably, allowing Cal to go over his mechanical issues with far less tension, ultimately setting up a payment plan as a one-time courtesy.

I'm feeling proud of myself as I wave Mr. Allanson out twenty minutes later, letting the jingle bells ring through me like I'm cashing out a big win on a penny slot machine.

After Roy leaves, Cal turns to me before heading back into the bays, and an eyebrow lifts with scrutiny. "*Three's Company*?"

"His t-shirt was a nod to the show," I shrug, smoothing out my skirt. "My grandfather and I used to watch all those old sitcoms when I was growing up—*Happy Days, Growing Pains, Family Ties*. I thought maybe I could help."

He just stands there for a moment, silent, studying me. His

eyes slant as he nods his head, faltering briefly, before pushing through the big gray door and finishing up his work.

The last two hours roll by without incident, void of any more customers, and I use the time to make a list of things I can do to add some charm and an inviting ambience to the shop.

I'm creating vision boards in my mind when Cal sneaks up behind me.

"Lucy."

"What?" I spin around, buoyantly. "Hi!"

Cal moves in beside me, tipping his chin to the computer screen with a glower. "Show me the sales summary for the day."

A quiz.

I know how to access the sales summary, but Cal is standing so close to me, radiating authority and command, and smelling like an oddly intriguing cocktail of motor oil and earthy woods, that my fingers zip around the keyboard erratically. I click the mouse a dozen times when the screen freezes up, only causing it to freeze longer.

My knee starts to bob when I feel the fabric of Cal's sleeveless hoodie brush up against my shoulder when he leans in closer.

"You're getting hyper again," he notes. "How much coffee have you had?"

I glance up at him with only my eyes. "None. I don't drink coffee."

"What?" His brows bend with bafflement. "Are you human?"

He asks it so seriously, as if there's a chance I could have been hijacked by an alien replica. I wring my hands together to keep them from trembling. "I'm just nervous, okay?"

"Still? Why?"

I muster a quick, "You."

"Me?"

"Yes, you. You're intimidating. Borderline petrifying," I admit, my eyes skipping over to the orchid plant. "See? Even your flowers are cowering."

It's supposed to be a joke, but something bleak sours his expression. A heaviness washes over him as he looks down at his feet, a muscle in his jaw ticking.

I guess he takes his decorative foliage very seriously.

"I can never keep the damn things alive," he mumbles. Scrubbing a hand down his face, he pivots toward me with a sigh. "I'm not trying to scare you. This is just the way I am."

"Perpetually grumpy?"

He levels me with a hard stare. "Difficult."

"Well, you don't need to be difficult around me. I'm easy." My eyes round when I register the suggestive innuendo, and I try to backpedal, even though backpedaling often digs me into a deeper, more awkward hole. "Easy to work with. You know, to interact with. I don't mean I'm *easy*...like a floozy. I just meant—"

"Got it," he clips, then points at the computer. "Sales summary."

"Right." Filling my cheeks with air, I manage to access the report he's looking for and send it to the printer. "There you go."

"Thanks."

When my gaze pans to the wall clock, I see that it's already five-past-six, signaling the end of my shift.

Cal must notice at the same time. "You're free to go," he says flatly, turning to walk away with the printout in his hands. Before he moves out of sight, he wavers for a moment, and then my name falls from his lips. "Lucy."

I freeze. "Yeah?"

Facing away from me, the muscles in his back twitch as he curls, then uncurls, his fingers. "Good job today. The way you diffused the situation with Allanson..." He pivots then, looking at me as he lifts an arm to palm the nape of his neck, causing his bicep to bulge. "I was impressed."

Pride and elation trickle through me, and I suck in a breath, a smile lifting. "Thank you."

He sends me a curt nod before stalking away, heading toward the back room.

Despite the pitfalls and first-day hurdles, the genuine smile stays put as I fetch my purse and punch out, waving goodbye to Dante, Kenny, and Ike, who are gathering their own belongings.

Cal doesn't exactly smile, or even say goodbye, but his eyes catch mine before I slip out of the break room.

There's a softness staring back at me—something tender,

filling me with shimmery warmth. The moment doesn't last long, as he quickly dips his head and turns around, his shoulders square and rigid, but that look follows me home.

So do his words.

"Good job today."

It wasn't a great first day, but somehow, it feels like it was.

Chapter 6

1/3/2013

"Heart Broken"

Lucy is sick today. She gets sick a lot, but she doesn't like to talk about it, and just tells us she was born with breathing problems.

She never wants to worry anybody. But when you care about someone, you worry about them, no matter what. That's just the way it is.

One time, we went swimming in a pool with extra cold water and Lucy had trouble breathing. She had to go to the hospital in an ambulance. When she came back, she had a heart monitor.

It doesn't seem fair that Lucy needs a heart monitor. She has a perfect heart.

The best heart.

A heart like Lucy's should never be broken.

Toodles,

Emma

O nly one week on the job, and I had to call in.

I woke up this morning with severe shortness of breath, feeling overly winded, so I decided to check in with my physician. After a chest x-ray revealed nothing too concerning, I was prescribed beta blockers and told to take it easy for the next few days. Being that it's Saturday, I'm grateful for the extra recovery day tomorrow so I can get back to work on Monday.

Cal didn't say much when I called him at seven a.m.

"Yeah?" came the husky, sleep-ridden voice.

"Cal? Hi! Um, sorry to bother you, but I need to head to the doctor today. It's nothing serious, and I'm sorry it's interfering with my work schedule, because I know I said it wouldn't, so I apologize that I need to—"

"You okay?"

A heavy pause hummed between us, and I couldn't tell if he was concerned or annoyed. I swallowed. "I'm okay."

"See you Monday," he murmured, then hung up.

Since I'm unable to handle abrupt lapses in communication, I immediately started word vomiting via text, in desperate need of closure.

ME:

Hi again!

I hope you're not mad.

I feel horrible.

I'll come in early on Monday and deep-clean the waiting area and bathrooms, and bring some knick-knacks to spruce the place up.

Have a great weekend!

:)

He didn't respond.

Nearly twelve hours later, he still hasn't responded, nor opened the message. The only conclusion I've drawn is that he hates me, and I'll be jobless come next week.

"It's okay, though, really," I mutter, partially to myself as Key Lime Pie drags me forward down the sidewalk, her attention on another dog a few blocks away. "I'll find something else. Honestly, this will be good for me. I haven't had a lot of experience in the working world, so it's important to start growing a thicker skin."

"You're being dramatic, Lucy, just like me. It's a genetic condition, and I'm sorry for passing it down to you." Mom shakes her head as she shuffles beside me with Lemon Meringue's leash wrapped around her palm.

My mother is right.

I inherited a touch of her dramatics and anxiety, and a pinch of Dad's devil-may-care optimism, molding me into the erratic person I am today.

The thing about me is I'll often jump to the worst possible conclusion while simultaneously convincing myself that it's totally fine if the make-believe disaster somehow comes to pass. It's like I'm trying to get all my ducks in a row before chaos unleashes, so I'm prepared to march through the fire with a megawatt smile and bright-eyed ducks.

"Speaking of conditions," she adds, reaching over and snatching Kiki's leash. "You shouldn't be over-exerting. I've got her."

"I'm feeling better. She's not even pulling me."

"God forbid you collapse right here on the sidewalk, and I have to resuscitate you while trying to wrangle two corgis and dial 9-1-1, just as this inevitable thunderstorm hits us. Better to be safe."

Dramatic.

I forgo arguing and tip my chin toward the leaden gray sky.

Smoky clouds glide over mature treetops, hindering the final remnants of daylight as a crack of thunder rumbles in the distance.

It reminds me of a similar sky on a late-August afternoon, more than a decade ago. A friend from school was having a pool party. She'd invited me, but after a recent scare at the community pool that triggered an episode and landed me in the hospital, Mom wouldn't let me go.

I stared out the window all day, feeling sullen, imagining all the fun my friends were having.

Then, right around dinner time, the doorbell rang.

"Come on, let's go," Emma proclaimed, decked out in her bathing suit, rain boots, and a dinosaur inflatable around her waist. "The weather is perfect!"

Actually, it was pouring.

Rain bucketed down, drenching my smiling friend who stood on my uncovered front stoop. Droplets fused with freckles as rivulets of water trickled down her cheeks and nose.

"Go where?" I wondered, bewildered. "It's raining."

"Right? It's great, isn't it?" She looked up at the sky, her smile only broadening. When she faced me again, licking water from her lips, she said, "I know you weren't able to go to that pool party, so I figured we could make our own."

My heart leaped with joy.

Five minutes later, we were stomping through puddles and mud in the backyard, soaking wet, laughing until our bellies ached. Cal joined us with his water gun moments later, chasing us around the grass until we all collapsed into the lake that started forming near the tree line.

Swallowing, my eyes burn with sentiment as the memories roll through me, and I swear I hear her distinct laughter echoing along with a hiss of wind.

"How is he, Lucy?"

My mother's voice pulls me from the moment. I shake away the lingering emotion, turning to face her as we coast down the sidewalk. "Cal? He's..." Searching for the perfect adjective—gruff, quiet, dismissive, darkly attractive, closed-off, tattooed, anti-social—my brain finally latches onto one: "Different."

I study her expression as it wilts. Strawberry blond hair, now shaded with silver and white, stops at her shoulders, tucked behind two bejeweled ears. My mother, Farrah Hope, wears a pair of earrings shaped like golden angel wings that haven't left her lobes since the day my father passed.

Her eyes pan over to me, glittering light blue. "It kills me that Dana never kept in touch. Everything was so sudden."

My throat stings as I drop my head, fixating on the sidewalk cracks as we skip from one square to the next. "He's changed. A lot. I've only spent a week with him, but he hasn't opened up at all. He hasn't talked about his mother, and he refuses to talk about Emma."

"Refuses?"

"Adamantly. It was his one stipulation if he were to hire me."

"Good heavens," she whispers into the warm gust that blows through. "I always wondered what had happened to him. He was such a bright boy. Handsome and kind." Chuckling to herself, she tugs at Kiki's leash before my dog veers off toward the family of geese crossing the road. "You know, I'd convinced myself that the two of you would become a couple one day...once you grew up some more."

Oh boy. I clear my throat, giving my ponytail a tug. "You were just imagining things, I'm sure."

"Well, he was always protective of you. It was sweet."

"Yeah, like a sister. He was protective of Emma, too."

She shrugs a little, glancing up at the clouds as a few rain-drops leak out. "It was different during that last year. I saw the way your eyes would light up around him, and the way your cheeks would turn all red when he'd call you that nickname." Mom pulls her lip between her teeth, chewing thoughtfully. "What was it again?"

On cue, my cheeks turn all red.

Sunshine.

I feign memory loss and pick up my pace, walking slightly ahead of her. "I can't remember. Too long ago." Then I change the subject. "I bet the zucchini bread is done. Let's head back."

As we turn the corner onto Maple Avenue, my driveway comes into view—along with a motorcycle parked right in front of it. I blanch when my eyes land on the hulking figure leaning against the bike, his arms and ankles both crossed.

"Who's that?" Mom mutters from behind me, almost ramming into me when I come to a dead stop on the sidewalk. The dog leashes tangle around my legs as my mother makes an "oof" sound and tries to gracefully unravel them.

She fails.

Kiki breaks free and dashes toward my friend-turned-boss, her stubby little legs moving so fast, it looks like the stormfront is carrying her through the air like an autumn leaf.

Cal straightens from the bike, watching as the dog charges at him. He's probably watching in horror, but his expression doesn't move from its usual impassive state, so he just stands there waiting for thirty pounds of sable and white to ambush him.

Mom finally gets control of the other leash, stepping around me with Lemon secured. "Are you dating someone, Lucy?" she wonders while Lemon barks her frustration that her sibling managed a thrilling escape and left her in the dust.

Shaking off my surprise, I mutter, "No...that's Cal."

I catch the widening of her eyes as she stares at me for a quick beat, then marches over to where Cal is bent over, trying to pet Kiki as she flits around him. My dog is shameless as she paws at his legs, hopping up and down like a bunny starved for attention.

"Callahan," my mother greets.

Her voice has a breathy sort of wonder to it, having not seen him since the summer of 2013. She always called him by his full name—Callahan. And Emma was always Emmalee.

"Just Cal," he says, standing upright as his eyes flick over to me for a moment, then swing back to my mother. "Good to see you, Mrs. Hope."

"Goodness, how you've grown. I never would have recognized you. How is Dana?"

"She's fine."

Mom doesn't notice the telltale flexing of his biceps or the twitch of tension in his jaw—but I do. Jumping between them, I lean down to seize Kiki's leash and hand it back to my mother with an overenthusiastic smile. "The zucchini bread! Do you think it's burning?" I usher her toward the house while mouthing, *"We'll talk more later."*

She shoots me a weird look paired with an eyebrow wiggle, like we're both in on some sort of juicy secret, then sends Cal a wave with her elbow since both hands are occupied with two corgis trying to wrestle and play-fight around her ankles.

Chaos.

Cheeks heating, I turn to Cal once my mother has successfully disappeared into the house. I wring my hands together, taking a careful step forward as a few more raindrops escape the smog. My hairline starts to frizz thanks to the humidity, so I smooth it back, fiddling with my long ponytail while Cal stares down at me, mute and stoic. "What are you doing here?" I ask him.

His eyes are unreadable, a melding of gold and stone, and the drizzle feels icy against my skin when my blood pumps hotter.

It's then I realize that he just caught me gallivanting around the neighborhood with my dogs and my mother, a picture of health, after I called into work this morning and left him shorthanded.

He probably came over to fire me in person.

"I promise, I really did have to go to the doctor," I add, newly panicked. "My doctor put me on some medication, and my mom stopped by because she was worried, and the dogs needed to—"

"It's fine," he cuts me off. Cal pulls a baseball cap off his head and ruffles his hair—mystical hair that seems to be immune to humidity—before returning it to a forward-facing position. "You didn't sound like you had a cold, and I know you've had some asthma problems, so I figured I'd stop by and make sure everything was good."

My heart warms.

Cal and Emma never knew the truth about my medical issues while we were growing up—I always just told them I had asthma because it was easier that way. More understandable. More palatable, I suppose. After a traumatizing moment as a young child that had me feeling like I was abnormal, I made my parents promise not to say anything in fear of my friends not wanting to spend time with me anymore. The worst thing would have been that they looked at me differently, or treated me like fragile glass, or excluded me because they thought I was too sick.

I couldn't bear it.

Finally, I say through a smile, "You were...checking on me?"

He frowns as if the notion is completely off the mark, but it doesn't offset the brief flash of candidness in his eyes that glints within the gold. "It's not a big deal," he says, looking down at his feet. Then his eyes shift over to the little ranch house sitting before us, the bricks still made of honey, the shutters still white. The giant maple tree stands tall and proud in the backyard, sprouting over the roof, and three thriving rose bushes continue to line the front of the house, just like they used to.

"It looks the same," he murmurs, the words tinged with something softer. "I haven't driven past it in years. Haven't been able to."

Cal stares at the house with haunted, glazed-over eyes, and I can't help my tears from welling.

I want to invite him inside.

I want to show him Emma's diary.

I want to laugh with him, cry with him, reminisce with him.

Inhaling an uneven breath, Cal glances back at me as a sharp breeze blows through. It carries with it the scent of his skin. Something crisp and smoky; bourbon and oak, and a touch of spice.

It carries memories, too. The taste of rainwater on my tongue as the three of us splashed around the flooded backyard. The static of untouchable innocence carved into laughter.

And then, with our eyes still locked, lightning flashes in streaks of pale yellow, and the sky untethers the rain.

It starts pouring.

Hard, fast, relentless.

Cal tips his head skyward, adjusting his cap and scrubbing a hand over his face. "Fuck," he whispers, hardly audible over the storm.

I can't tell if he's cursing the rain, or the memories it brings with it like an uninvited guest. Part of me wants to laugh, part of me wants to sob. All I end up doing is staring at him with my lips parted and trembling, chest heaving, and heart galloping so fast I should probably be concerned.

His throat bobs when he finds me again, his gaze trailing briefly over my soaked blouse with a flickering of heat. When our eyes meet, he mutters in a low voice, "I'll see you Monday."

I manage a pathetic nod as he moves backward toward his bike, t-shirt molding into the planks of his abs and chest and suctioning to his skin. "Okay. See you."

Pivoting around, he hops on the bike.

The rain dies down as the engine revs to life, like it was just a blip, like it was only meant for us. I remain standing idly in the grass, shivering as he drives away.

Cal acted like he didn't care, like his visit didn't mean anything, but I saw the thinly veiled worry reflecting in his eyes.

I swear I saw it.

And I know it had to mean something.

Emma's words sweep through my mind as I watch the tail-lights of Cal's motorcycle evaporate into the fog and mist.

When you care about someone, you worry about them, no matter what.

That's just the way it is.

CHAPTER 7

"What the hell is this?"

I fly around, my hair whipping me in the face when Cal appears from out of nowhere. I'm assuming he came through the front door, but even the jingle bells failed to pull me out of my artistic trance. "Good morning," I beam, a pink dry erase marker tucked inside my hand. When his question registers, tone matching the disgruntled look on his face, I frown. "What is what?"

"The doodles, Lucy."

I glance down at the multicolored board sprawled across the reception desk that's decorated in hearts, stars, and smiley faces. "It's your new welcome board. It has your specials and rates. It's like a menu, but for cars."

"It looks like I'm signing up for circle time at the Montessori school."

Deflating like a popped balloon, I try to defend why I showed up at six o'clock on Monday morning in hopes of sprucing up the shop and its lackluster first impression. "Well, you're Cal's Corner. It's a cute name, so I thought you needed some cute marketing."

"No."

It appears our rain-infused encounter on Saturday did little to breach his cast-iron walls.

"I think the customers will appreciate it," I continue, shaking off his bad attitude. "This place is like a gloomy mancave with sterile walls and weird smells. I added a little table with a wax warmer."

Cal stands in front of me in a pecan-colored beanie, white muscle shirt, and faded blue jeans. Tufts of velvety dark hair sprout from underneath the hat, acting as a boyish contrast to his skull and rose neck tattoo and overgrown stubble. The furrowed brow adds his own unique flare to an otherwise basic ensemble.

He takes a long sip from his thermos, glancing at the glowing warmer perched beside the water cooler. "Is that why it smells like a strip club in here?"

"It's black raspberry and dark vanilla bean," I provide.

"Why is it shaped like a merry-go-round?"

Chewing on my lip, I float around the side of the desk to join him in the center of the lobby. "It reminded me of that time we went to the carnival. You, me, and Em—"

His eyes flash with warning.

"—immense amounts of fun." I cough into my fist. "If it's too weird, I can get a different one. They have floral prints. Fun patterns. Some are shaped like owls."

He already looks irritated with me, and the sun has only been up for an hour. Muttering something incoherent under his breath, Cal steps toward the desk and sets his thermos down, leaning over to fetch a file folder.

I counter his silence with more chatter. "I'm sorry again about Saturday. I didn't mean—"

"Stop apologizing. It's not a big deal."

"I just don't want you to think I'm unprofessional."

"I don't." Flipping through the loose papers, he tosses the folder back down and gives me his full attention. "I wouldn't say no to some wardrobe adjustments, though."

I blink. "What? Me?"

"Yeah. Here." Cal moves behind the desk, rummages through a cardboard box in one of the cabinets, then tosses a t-shirt at me. "Wear this."

"Why? I didn't know there was a dress code." Fisting the

grubby shirt etched with a band logo, I give it a quick whiff. Then I gag. "It smells like feet."

"It's Kenny's."

"Does Kenny use it to clean his feet?"

"Not anymore." He gives me a deadpan look, waiting for me to put it on.

"You're serious."

"Yes, I'm serious. My guys are a bunch of horny teenagers, apparently, and I don't want them staring at you like you're a piece of meat."

My face flames with the fire of a trillion suns. I instinctively glance down at my chest, noting the small amount of cleavage peeking out through my citrus orange tank top, my longtime scar on display. "Oh. Well, I have a cardigan I can wear."

"That works."

Swallowing, I force my eyes up until they meet with his. A flicker of vulnerability skates across his expression, akin to two days ago when we stood in my front yard. He clenches his jaw, the veins in his neck dilating.

"I, um...I know you always saw me as a little sister, Cal, but I'm all grown up now." I stretch a smile, partly charmed by his protectiveness, while still mildly mortified. "I appreciate you looking out for me, though."

Eyes dipping to the floor, he looks like he's about to say something, possibly counter my sentiment, but then the jingle bells chime, and Ike stalks through the door with Dante trailing him.

Cal uses the distraction to make a break for it. He takes the t-shirt from my hands, mutters a gruff "good morning" to the guys, then storms away toward his office.

"Banana bread is on your—"

The door slams shut.

"—desk," I finish with a sigh. Preserving my dwindling smile, I turn to the two mechanics who appear unaffected by Cal's sour mood. "Hey," I wave, swiping my hands along my jeans as I watch them exchange a look.

"Smells good in here," Ike notes, eyeing the room. "Did you infect the place with your essential oils, doll?"

"No," I laugh lightly, popping a thumb over my shoulder.

"Just a wax melt. I thought it would heighten the morale around here a bit, but alas..."

Off my implication, they both glance at Cal's closed door.

"Told you not to take it personally," Dante says. "Though, he does seem extra pissy lately. You're probably a physical reminder of the fact that he hasn't gotten laid in a thousand years."

Ike adds through his lollipop, "Not to mention, it smells like a sex parlor in here, now. Probably ain't helping."

I spontaneously break out into hives. Heat dapples my chest and collarbone as I lift a hand to hide the pink splotches that I know are blooming. Then I laugh again, only this time it sounds unstable. "I'm sure he's, uh, doing just fine. You know...in that department."

Dante swoops past me with a wink. "Not really."

Ike does the same, and both men simultaneously look down at my cleavage before disappearing into the service area.

I purse my lips together.

Then, when they're out of sight, I race to the coat hanger to fetch my cardigan.

It's a little past noon, and we don't have any more appointments on the schedule for the day, so boredom and lack of new tasks have me wandering around the garage, trying to find a way to make myself useful. Spotting Cal with his head underneath a hood, I sprint over to him, my heels clicking across the cement floor. "Hey!"

He hasn't turned the music on, so my voice echoes abrasively.

"What?" Cal doesn't bother looking up, continuing to fiddle with the vehicle as he chews his gum.

"I hung the new sign, swept and mopped, and washed all the glass and windows. Oh, and I also cleaned the bathroom."

A grunt is his only response.

"I really appreciate you giving me a key so I could come in early today. I'm a morning person, usually up by five a.m. I hate sitting around and feeling useless, you know? Plus, I wanted to make up for my absence on Saturday."

Silence is his new response.

Am I shocked by this?

No. But it doesn't stop my disobedient tongue from blathering away. Apparently, I'm incapable of being in a room with someone without forcing conversation, even if that someone probably hates me and is currently holding a steel ratchet.

"What are you working on?" I continue, peeking over his shoulder in an attempt to figure out what he's doing. My knuckles tap against my thigh as I clear my throat.

More silence.

It's fine. It's honestly fine.

Tools clank against engine parts, the only sound penetrating the skin-crawling silence.

I keep going.

Why? Because I have a disease, that's why.

"Maybe you can teach me how to—"

"Dammit, Lucy." Cal straightens, letting out a sigh of exasperation.

Which is pretty much the only sigh he makes.

"Sorry, I'm not trying to bug you."

Two toned arms fold across his chest, the ratchet dangling from one of his hands as he assesses me with a healthy mix of confusion and exhaustion. "How are you like this without coffee?"

"Like what?"

"Like a kitten that just O.D.'d on catnip."

Scratching at my shoulder, I just shrug, unsure of how to respond. He's staring at me like he views me as a toddler who needs to be entertained at all times.

"You can come bug me, sweetheart," Dante's voice sounds from behind us.

I don't miss the way Cal's expression darkens, his eyes slanting as he shifts his focus from me to Dante, then back to me. "You know, I actually needed to run some errands. Dante can hold down the fort while we're gone."

"Both of us?" I squeak out.

"Eh, fuck you, man," Dante chuckles amicably, shaking his head as Cal sets down his tool and stomps past me.

I race after him. "Okay, sure. That sounds fun. You don't need me manning the front desk?"

"Should be good. We're done with appointments for the day. If anything comes up, the guys can handle it."

His long legs carry him what feels like miles ahead of me, forcing me into a permanent state of jogging. I make a quick pitstop at the desk before rushing after Cal and into the parking lot.

Grumbling, he comes to a halt and spins around. "Forgot my coffee. Be right back."

"This coffee?" I proudly display the thermos I retrieved, shimmying it in the air with a smile.

He glances at it. His lips twitch with something that could become a smile if he happened to be anyone else on the planet, and then he moves in to take it from my outstretched hand. "Thanks."

"Any time, boss." When I curve toward my car, pleased, Cal walks up to his motorcycle instead and reaches for the helmet. I slow my pace as the scene processes. "Oh, are we driving separately?" I wonder from a few feet away.

"No."

That's all he says.

Blinking a handful of times, I watch as he just stands there, holding the helmet in my direction, as if I'm supposed to take it and wear it.

On my head.

Because he wants me to ride on his motorcycle.

"Cal, no," I contest, my blood pressure snowballing. Glancing down at my ripped skinny jeans, I curse myself for not wearing a dress. I always wear dresses. If I'd worn a dress, I'd have a viable excuse for not getting on the bike, other than, *"That looks terrifying."* My heart thumps with fear as I glide over to him. "I'm fine driving."

"Why?"

"I've never been on a motorcycle before."

"First time for everything." He shrugs, his eyebrows lifting like he's wondering what I'm waiting for.

I'm waiting for the terror to pass so my legs can become functional limbs again. "What about your helmet?"

"I'm good. We're not going far."

I nod wildly.

Okay. This is super fine. Even if we crash, it'll probably be minor, and I'll have a helmet. And Cal has such an impressive muscle ratio that he basically has built-in protective armor.

I've convinced myself that I won't be dying today, so I continue to nod as I close the gap between us and take the helmet from his hands. "Sure, okay. This will be great. Really great," I ramble, plopping the helmet over my head and scrambling for the fastener.

"I got it," Cal intervenes.

He steps into my bubble smelling like clean, woody bath soap and a trace of mint, his body heat a warm juxtaposition to his frosty demeanor. All my breath gets caught in my throat when calloused fingers graze my jaw to secure the chin strap, his eyes briefly tangling with mine before he clasps it into place, pops the visor down, and steps away.

The helmet feels giant, and my equilibrium wobbles. "I'm pretty sure I look like Toadstool from *Mario*," I decide.

Cal gives me a onceover, staring at my painted toenails poking out through my heels, raking over my legs sheathed in tattered denim, lingering on the tangerine tank top, and landing at the helmet. "You look good," he murmurs. Turning around, he moves toward the motorcycle.

Casual indifference rolls off of him as he situates himself on the bike, and I almost miss the compliment.

"Hop on," he continues as he straddles the seat. "Sit close to me so you can mirror my body language. When I turn, you turn with me. Try not to wiggle too much or shift abruptly. Wrap your arms around my waist and hold on. Don't be afraid to hang on tight—you won't hurt me."

I try to take mental notes, but it feels like he's listing off Einstein's Written Demands, and all I hear is "wiggle." "Got it. Great." Sliding my bottom lip between my teeth, I stroll forward and lift my leg, mounting the back of the seat with little grace. I latch onto Cal before I topple instantly, inching closer to him and digging my knees into his hips. "Is this okay?"

My fingers are loosely curled around the fabric of his shirt, so he snatches both of my wrists and forces my arms around his torso until I'm pressed into him, my breasts smashed against the planks of his back and my palms locking at his abdomen.

I choke on a breath, feeling tingly all over.

Giving me a look over his shoulder, he says, "Hang onto me."

Electricity zips through me at Cal's proximity and the prospect of the ride. I squeeze him as tight as I can as he kicks the bike into gear and drives us out of the parking lot. The moment we gain speed, a feeling of exhilaration washes over me, replacing the fear. I'm almost certain we're going one hundred miles per hour, but the speed limit says twenty-five, so I try to relax and focus on the adrenaline spiraling through me.

Street signs zoom past.

Other vehicles are nothing but a blur.

The late summer breeze causes goosebumps to scatter across my skin.

My thighs clench around him, my right hand latched onto my left wrist as I cling. I want to laugh, or sing, or cry, my lungs burning to release *something*.

I feel free.

But Cal was right—we didn't go far, and we turn into an auto parts store hardly five minutes later, shuffling off the bike and heading inside.

The visit is uneventful. Cal talks to a greasy-haired guy at the front desk about special-ordering a specific part for a Land Rover, while I meander the aisles that host shelves filled with timing belts, engine mounts, driveshafts, and spark plugs.

I'm engrossed in a variety of steering wheel covers when Cal eventually ushers me out the door. "That's it? You're done?" I wonder, scrunching up my nose, curious as to why he wanted me to tag along on such a brief errand.

"I was thinking we could grab lunch next door."

I blink, blindly following him.

A trickling of nerves work their way through me, considering most days, Cal acts like he'd rather dive face-first into a sticker bush that caught on fire than be within ten feet of me.

Any time spent together that goes beyond printing out his sales report at the end of the day, or fetching him his misplaced coffee thermos, feels like an all-expenses-paid trip to Disney World.

I downplay my excitement with a casual, "Sounds great."

We make our way across the craggy sidewalk of the outdoor strip mall and wind into a burger joint a few stores down. Cal pulls what looks like a grid of chewing gum out of his pocket, plucking one out of the foil and popping it into his mouth. That fruity-mint scent wafts over to me, mingling with something oaky, creating an elixir that is purely Cal.

"You two can sit anywhere you'd like," a hostess calls out when we amble into the restaurant.

We slide into a booth, sitting across from each other, and Cal hands me a menu. "You good with burgers?" he asks, his eyes dipped to the lunch selections.

I scramble to find something not made of beef and land on a black bean burger. "Yep, all set. I'm a vegetarian, but restaurants are much better about that these days. I can usually find something of the non-meat variety."

His eyebrows arc. "Really? Do you eat dairy?"

"Yes, because cheese."

Nodding, he adds, "You used to eat meat."

It's such a simple statement. A trivial observation. But it's also the very first time Cal has offered up the tiniest glimpse into our shared past. I can't keep the smile from cresting as I lean forward on my arms and nibble my lip. "Your mom loved to make us liverwurst sandwiches for lunch during the summertime," I reflect, taking note of his micro expressions as he shifts his attention out the window. "We would carry them down to the riverwalk and sit on the dock. I ate them because I felt guilty for throwing away something she made special for us, but you and Emma would always—"

"Feed them to the ducks."

My eyes cloud over, not expecting him to acknowledge the story. Not expecting him to acknowledge *anything* to do with her. I bob my head, carefully weaving my words together, scared of pushing him away and breaking our tether. "Yes. And then we'd head back to my house and secretly raid the pantry while my mom was watching her exercise videos in the den."

The midday glow reflects in his eyes as he stares out through the pane of glass. They glisten with a thousand buried memories. Memories entombed in dirt and soot that I long to dig up and shine new light on. Memories I'm desperate to resurrect.

A waitress saunters over to us then, pulling Cal back into the shadows with a cheery *hello*. I see the shift, the disconnect, as he clears his throat and straightens, blinking away the simmering nostalgia.

Our tether morphs into a noose, and I choke, slinking back into the booth.

"What can I get for you two?" the waitress chirps, flicking her pen against a notepad.

She glances at me, then turns to Cal and gives him sex-eyes, undoubtedly picturing him naked.

Cal orders a cheeseburger and fries, while I list off my veggie burger with cheddar and extra mustard, and a side of fruit. When she struts away with a hair flip and a flirty sashay of her hips, Dante's earlier implication regarding Cal's celibacy burns through my brain. Cal appears unstirred by the lingering balm of the woman's lavender and chamomile perfume, his eyes hardly sparing her a friendly glance—which is interesting because she was pretty, and her boobs were porn star-level.

Since the mood has already shifted, I decide to veer off in a completely different direction. "So, do you date a lot?"

He looks at me curiously, as if not expecting the question. Folding his hands together, Cal inches forward a bit, his brawny build practically taking up the whole booth.

And when his eyes hold with mine, the gold outshining the smoky brown, it feels like his proximity takes up my whole chest.

Finally, he replies, "Not frequently."

"Do you sleep around?" I blurt out next.

No!

Why, Lucy? What is wrong with you?

"Less frequently," he says, the crease between his eyes deepening. "Why are you asking? Is this the Lucy way of telling me you're interested?"

Heat travels from my neck to my ears, then back down my chest, leaving a trail of random pink blotches in its wake, until it looks like I had a seizure while applying sunscreen. My mouth goes dry as I try to muster something intelligible. "I – I was just curious," I stammer. "I don't know much about you anymore. You look like the type of guy who, um—"

"Who, what? Has a harem?"

I'm still flushing profusely, which should be a clear indicator that I need to change the subject, but for some reason, I keep going. And I think that reason is because Cal is talking. He's actively participating in conversation with me, and I find the notion mildly addicting. "I'm just saying, you look like you do okay for yourself."

He runs his tongue along his top teeth as he studies me, trying to read between the lines. That's when I realize I basically admitted, in a roundabout way, that I found him physically attractive.

I imagine myself melting away and dissolving into the floor cracks.

"So, you are interested?" His eyes narrow like he's genuinely wondering where I'm going with this line of conversation.

The melting thing didn't work, so I'm stuck answering the question with beet red cheeks and beads of sweat threatening to inhabit my skin. "No! I mean, no. Definitely not."

"Definitely not," he parrots flatly.

"Not that you're not...you know, *interesting*. You are. You're sort of dark and mysterious, and you have the tattoos, the motorcycle, the muscles..."

"The personality," he provides.

It takes a minute to register the fact that he's joking, poking fun at himself, because he says it with such breezy nonchalance. I burst out laughing, bowing my head until my hair falls all around me, bouncing atop the table. When I glance back up at him, he's not smiling, but his head is cocked in a charming sort of way, and his eyes are as close to twinkling as I've ever seen them. "And the sense of humor," I add with a grin, taming my hair.

Cal folds his arms as he leans back. "I'll relay all these compliments to my hoard of concubines."

More laughter falls out of me.

The pink in my cheeks is now tinged with mirth when the waitress drops off our food a few moments later.

"I don't see you laugh much," Cal notes after taking a bite of his burger and wiping his hands on a napkin. "You usually look like you're in a permanent state of distress around me."

I watch as he sifts through the little paper pocket of french fries, collecting all the crispy ones and pushing the smooshy ones —the *best* ones—to the side.

My expression must shift from joy to distress because he follows up his statement with five words that have my stomach flip-flopping.

"I like watching you laugh."

He doesn't elaborate, returning his attention to his lunch.

My brain revs into overdrive in an attempt to pick apart that declaration, my wheels spinning as I nibble my burger and munch on the chunks of honeydew melon.

I think about it as Cal insists on paying the bill, completely ignoring the waitress' phone number scribbled onto the receipt, crumbling it into a little ball that finds its way to the garbage can.

I think about it when we mount his bike, and his hand reaches behind him to grip my thigh as a means of tugging me closer, so I'm safely secured.

I think about it when a colony of butterflies flit around inside my belly at the gesture.

I think about it when my arms clasp around his waist and hold him tight, while wishing I could remove the helmet and press my cheek to the warmth of his back.

Ultimately, I'm still thinking about it when night falls and a dream pulls me into a make-believe world where we are young again; free and burdenless.

Emma is still with us.

And we never stop laughing.

CHAPTER 8

8/21/2012
"Brotherly Love"

Today, Lucy and I went to the park to watch Cal play basketball. One of his friends, Alex, was being a creep and started whistling at us while we ate roast beef sandwiches on the sidelines. He waggled his tongue and said, "If you run out of meat, I have some of my own you can put in your mouth." Then he grabbed his junk.
High school boys shouldn't be saying that stuff to junior high girls—yuck!
But that's not all.
Cal lost his mind over it! He shoved Alex down and said he'd kill him if he ever talked to us that way again. Alex didn't like that, so he got up and tackled Cal. My brother went down hard and

hit his head on the cement...then he just laid there, not moving.

Lucy screamed. She threw her sandwich and ran faster than I've ever seen her run, dropping to her knees beside Cal and leaning over him. I followed behind her, yelling his name and telling Alex to race home and get our parents. When Cal finally opened his eyes, he looked right at Lucy with the funniest look on his face. He kept blinking and staring at her, like she wasn't even real. Like he was in a weird trance or something.

I didn't hear what he said after that because Alex started hollering behind me.

But when we all walked home together, they both had that same funny look on their faces...

Toodles,

Emma

My eyes have to be playing tricks on me.

Blinking through the diffused lighting of the wine bar, I try not to let my voice waver as I sing through the lyrics of *Edge of Seventeen* by Stevie Nicks with my acoustic guitar. Nerves rattle my chest for the first time since I started doing live performances, causing my knees to knock together as I bob my feet along the rung of the stool.

He's here.

Cal is here, watching me play from the edge of the bar.

Candlelight steeps him in flickering shadow, while the under bar lighting casts an amethyst glow across the stoic expression he's wearing.

He's staring right at me, sipping on a glass of dark liquid. Probably whisky or bourbon. His big build and muscular thighs practically take up two stools, and there's an ardent look in his eyes that sends a shot of firewater to my veins, almost as if I guzzled down my own glass of one hundred-proof liquor.

Focus, Lucy!

I close my eyes and duck my head in an attempt to center myself, but the lyrics jumble in my brain, and I repeat a verse.

Focus, focus, focus.

Hoping nobody noticed, I allow the slip-up to give me fuel as I zone out, straighten my spine, and belt out the rest of the song with my whole soul. When the reverb of the guitar strings fade into applause, I fill my lungs with a plentiful breath and pop my eyes back open.

A smile lifts.

I nailed the ending.

Unable to keep my eyes from skating over to Cal, I brighten my smile and bite my lip, watching as he spins his drink between long fingers, takes a slow pull, then averts his gaze.

I sigh with renewed confidence and grip the microphone in my hand, addressing the audience as the cheers begin to dwindle. "Thank you all so much for coming out tonight. I can't tell you how much performing for you every week means to me. It fills my heart and brings the biggest smile to my face." Someone whistles from the crowd, and I spare Cal another tiny glance, but he's not looking at me anymore. "I'm Imogen, and I'll be back again next Friday to serenade you. And if all goes well, hopefully you'll be smiling, too. Goodnight."

More claps and hollers ring out, soon replaced by idle chatter and a bluesy music station, and I inch my way off the stool, smoothing down my mini tiered dress. It's rust-colored with a floral pattern, the sleeves long and ruffled to match the cooler weather that rolled in with September.

I put a little extra effort into my hair tonight, leaving it down and curled, the light brown ribbons hanging loosely over my shoulders that peek out from the dress.

As I pack up my guitar, my cell phone buzzes from my purse strewn across an adjacent stool.

It's Alyssa.

ALYSSA:

GIRL! I got stuck in a horrendous meeting with Wilshire and I'm running late. Don't people realize that the phrase 'Any questions?' means THE MEETING IS OVER? Nope. People just assume it's time to ask questions. Idiots. Anyway, I'll be there soon to smoosh and love on you. ♡

Grinning wide, I text back a quick response.

ME:

Don't worry! I just finished, but there's still wine to be had.

Cal showed up, so I'm going to go talk to him.

ALYSSA:

eyeball emojis

ME:

I know. Shock of the century.

ALYSSA:

Holy shit.

Okay.

Shit.

ME:

Oh look, my problematic speech patterns are rubbing off on you.

ALYSSA:

Shit.

ME:

LOL.

See you soon!

I slip my phone into my dress pocket, lock up my guitar case, and step off the small stage. Patrons send me smiles and waves as I breeze past and make a beeline toward Cal. He's hunched over the bar with a big palm wrapped around his half-empty glass, his body language equivalent to a neon sign flashing, "*No Vacancies.*"

The kind of sign you take one look at, then keep driving.

But I realize it's no coincidence that he's sitting at my signature wine bar at the precise time I perform every Friday night, so he must be here to show his support.

Right?

Cal shifts a bit on the stool, eyes panning over to me when he senses me marching over to him with my hair swinging back and forth, a wide-eyed stare, and troves of nervous energy. While his attire is consistent with his usual clothing ensembles—a plain white t-shirt, dark denim, black boots—his hair is sans a cap or beanie, mussed with some sort of styling gel. Bed head with effort.

And, *oh*—he smells sensational.

I step into a heady cloud of manly scents, consisting of his usual woodsy soap or deodorant, and mingling with a new cologne designed to lure women into spontaneously removing all of their clothing.

Women who aren't me, of course, but Alyssa is a definite goner.

Straightening more on the stool, Cal brings the glass to his lips, scanning me in a slow sweep from head to toe when I approach. His eyes rest on my chest scar for a heavy beat, the one I lied to him about, telling him it was from an accident when I was just a toddler.

When our eyes lock, and his body heat travels over to me, my stomach clenches with an unfamiliar feeling. It triggers my heart to gallop and my skin to flush.

Inhaling an unsteady breath, I realize I'm being ridiculous.

This is Cal.

My boss. My friend.

I tell myself to be cool.

Dear Lucy,

Please act sane and rational.

And please, for the love of God, say something normal.

Flashing him a dazzling smile, I blurt, "Wow, hey. I saw it and almost blew you."

And then all color drains from my face.

Cal chokes on his bourbon, which might be the strongest reaction I've gotten out of him since the day I walked into his auto shop. Clearing his throat, he doesn't look at me as he mutters, "Nice to see you, too, Lucy."

Stars twinkle behind my eyes like I was clobbered in the back of the head with a frying pan, and it takes every ounce of strength to remain in an upright position. "That's...completely, totally, and not at all what I meant to say," I croak out, placing both palms against my cheeks to hide the scarlet splotches. "Blew *it*. I saw you and almost blew it. Up there on stage—when I was singing. Meaning, I was surprised to see you and stumbled over the words. That's all. God, I'm so sorry."

Nash, clearly eavesdropping on the conversation and now privy to my eternal shame, chuckles as he swipes a rag down the bar top.

"Nice," he says.

I catch his amused glance and slide my hands down my face because I need to use one of them for balance. Latching onto a chairback, I beg my legs to stop quivering. "Riesling, please," I squeak.

He grins as he moves down the bar, pointing at the space beside Cal.

There, a full glass of wine already sits.

My blush blooms tenfold when I spot the familiar scribbling on the napkin underneath it. "Thank you." I fumble with the stool, the legs screeching along the floor, mimicking my dignity. When I maneuver around it to climb up, my knees graze the rough denim of Cal's thigh, and that tingly feeling races through me again.

I'm a mess.

He glances at the contact but doesn't move away. "You were good," Cal says, watching as I manage to situate myself in the seat beside him.

The compliment warms my already feverish blood. "Oh, thanks. I feel like a different person when I'm performing." My humiliation finally ebbs as I finger the wine glass and lean down to take a sip, eyes skipping over to him. "It's like this rush of adrenaline. Something freeing."

Long, dark lashes nearly touch his eyebrows as he stares down into his glass, the ice cubes tinkling. "That last song is hard to sing."

He's right—it is. It took me months of daily practice to perfect my acoustic version of it. "I love Stevie. I'm kind of an old soul," I confess, realizing our shoulders are a hair's breadth away from kissing. "So, um...what made you stop by? I didn't think you knew where I played."

"You mentioned it."

That's all he says, but I'm almost certain I never told him.

Cal shifts his attention to the little napkin I'm attempting to cover up with my forearm, his own tattooed arm inching to the right and brushing against me. "You sleeping with the bartender?"

My eyes round at the bold question and abrupt subject change.

I suppose it's not any worse than my shameless fishing about his sexual conquests on Monday, so I shake my head a little and chug down a few swallows of wine. "No. He just leaves me a note after every set. It's sweet."

Peeking at tonight's message, I silently read it:

"I pissed off three customers tonight because I was so distracted by the way your lips move when you sing."

Oh.

There's a tightness in my chest that crawls up my windpipe. Nash's notes have always been cute and harmless, but this one is much more suggestive, leaving little room to wonder what his intentions are. Clearing the boulder from my throat, I flip the napkin over and chuckle lightly, "So sweet. Anyway..." I swivel toward Cal, observing the dubious arc of one espresso-brown eyebrow and the tic in his cheek. "What are you doing here? You don't strike me as a social butterfly."

"What makes you think that?"

Violet bar lights illuminate his deadpan expression, and I bite my lip to hold back the smile. "Nice try. You've dodged my question twice now."

Blinking away from me, he takes a sip of his drink. "Have I?"

I huff.

"What's with the stage name?" he pivots.

Sighing, I resign myself to the fact that he's not going to share his deep, dark thoughts with me tonight—or likely, any thoughts at all. I'm determined to get them out of him one day. "Emma," I admit softly, watching as he pauses with the glass halfway to his mouth.

Cal's eyes flash with something tortured before he takes a sip, then sets the glass down with more force than I anticipated. Those two syllables always seem to bring out the worst in him, and I long for the days when they brought out the best.

"Her favorite pianist was Imogen Cooper," I continue. "She wanted to be just like her one day. I thought it would be a nice tribute—"

"I got it, Lucy," he practically snarls, stroking his five o-clock shadow and looking everywhere but at me. "You don't have to keep fucking talking about it."

His temper is tangible; I can taste it.

It's caustic and bitter, so I take a giant swig of my wine, needing the chaser.

I know better than to say anything else, and instead, cower in my seat like a scolded child, untucking the hair from behind my ears as a means to curtain the reddening of my cheeks. I twirl my glass, staring at my nails painted in a nutty taupe, while I wait for the cloud of contempt to evaporate.

And then there's a large palm pressing gently to the small of my back.

When I realize it's Cal, actively touching me in a way that feels apologetic—*intimate*, almost—my brain short circuits, my heart skipping a beat or six. It's an innocent gesture. Casual, friendly. He probably didn't give it a second thought when he lifted a hand etched in ink, grazed his fingertips up along the bow of my hip, then splayed that hand over the narrow arch of my lower back.

But, it does something to me.

Heat blossoms *everywhere*—in my face, my chest, my ears, my throat. His touch is a shot of warmth to my womb. I'm so taken aback by the feeling that I go completely still, freezing in place, my fingers curling around the stem of the wine glass until my knuckles turn opaque.

Leaning into me, he dips his lips an inch from my ear. "Sorry."

The word is scratchy like sandpaper, sending a whispering of tingles down my spine. As he says it, his palm slides off me in slow motion, just missing a brush with my backside.

One touch.

One touch and one word, yet it feels like my insides have detonated and I'm choking on the residual smoke.

What is going on?

I finally brave a glance at him, partly horrified for having such an intense reaction to something so insignificant, and praying he didn't notice.

But looking at him is a mistake because he's still so close, *too* close, and his eyes are drinking in the reaction I desperately hoped he'd missed. "It's okay," I breathe out, slicking my tongue along my newly dry lips. Cal drops his gaze to my mouth, lingering there as I finish, "I understand. I won't talk about her again."

The veins in his neck strain as he draws back up. "I just need to get over it."

"That's not true. Some things aren't meant for us to get over."

His eyes slant, unconvinced.

"I just mean...not everything that makes us hurt needs to be forgotten or banished. It hurts because it *mattered*. And things that mattered once, will always matter," I tell him. I'm not sure if I'm making any sense, but he's not cussing me out or stalking away, so I take that as a win. Resituating myself on the stool, I twist toward him until my knees are skimming his leg, just barely. "We need to find a way to carry those things with us in a positive way—instead of letting them bring us down, they should move us forward. Inspire us. Help us grow."

Maybe it's the buzz of the bourbon. Maybe it's the mood music, a lullaby to his inner demons.

Whatever it is, Cal opens up.

He gives me a crumb, and I inhale it like a gourmet feast.

"I think about her every goddamn day," he confesses, low and haunted. His finger taps along the side of the glass as he stares down into the melting ice cubes. "She's my personal black cloud. Follows me around, so any trace of joy is rained out." Lifting his eyes, he skims his gaze across my face, brows bending in that typical Cal scowl. "And now you're here."

The statement punctures me like a hot poker.

It's not hard to read between the lines: *I'm making it worse.*

"I never meant to upset your life, Cal. I just..." Nibbling my cheek, I shift away. "I missed you."

He makes a grouchy "*hmmph*" sound, scoffing at the very notion. "You missed a boy you used to know. You missed a fairytale life before it was stripped away by the villain."

"We can start over," I try, knowing I'm pushing my luck but wanting nothing more than to keep him talking. "We can be friends again."

"Friends," he mutters through another scoff. "No. You live in a little bubble with your head in the clouds, and I'm still...*there.*"

There.

I know where "there" is because, some days, I live there, too.

Folding a section of hair behind my ear, I reach for my wine glass and take a slow sip, peeking at him over the rim. I gulp it down and say, "Then...why did you come out tonight?"

His frown deepens as my implication registers.

Surely, he came to see me. He came because he misses all the same things I miss, but he's too guarded and closed off to admit it.

There's no other alternative. It couldn't have been a coincidence.

Realizing he can only admit it or avoid it at this point, Cal withdraws, swallowing back the final sip of liquor. A long, tapered sigh tells me he's done talking as he sets the glass down and rises from the stool. He tosses a twenty-dollar bill atop the bar counter as he stands, and before he turns to leave, he swipes up the napkin that holds Nash's note and crumples it in his fist.

Then he turns to me.

He turns to me ever so slightly, the musk of his cologne fusing with the spell of his next words.

"You sing like a fucking angel."

A sharp exhale bursts from my lips, the wind knocked out of me.

My knees wobble, my heart in a tailspin, but he doesn't stick around to steady me. He storms away, leaving me painfully rattled. "Th-thank you for coming out tonight," I stammer as he retreats, wringing my hands together so they stop shaking. "It means a lot."

The clamoring of bar noise drowns out my wimpish voice, but he still looks back at me. Just a quick cast over his shoulder, paired with a slow blink. No smile, no nod.

Nothing but a falter.

And then he's gone, tossing the wadded-up napkin into the trash before he walks out the door.

He's gone, but I still feel him everywhere. Those words are crawling all over my skin, heating me like a midday sun.

Not five minutes later, Alyssa rushes through the entrance and bolts toward me, apologies and exaggerated stories about her marketing meeting drifting to my ears.

I hardly hear it.

Just like I hardly hear Nash when he refills my wine glass and inquires about the elusive stranger who came to watch me perform.

I'm pretty sure I provide some sort of answer, but I don't even hear my own response.

All I hear are the words of a young boy, sprawled out on the pavement, staring up at me with a look of awe and wonder in his eyes as the sun sets my hair ablaze like a halo.

"Are you...an angel?"

CHAPTER 9

The weeks whizz by, and it's almost as if nothing ever happened.

I mean...nothing actually *did* happen.

Nothing that would warrant Cal to make a one-eighty personality shift and suddenly start treating me like his new best friend, anyway. It was only a little hand-to-back touch that sent my pulse into hyperdrive, paired with a compliment I've repeated over and over in my nonsensical brain for the last fourteen days.

This is a *me* thing. This is me grasping at straws when the straws are the cheaply-designed paper straws that instantly dissolve the moment they touch liquid.

I have nothing to hold onto.

I'm so desperate for Cal to warm up to me—to see me as the girl he knew, the friend he grew up with—that I'm reading into every scrap of decency he shows me.

And he *is* decent; I'm sure of it. There's a good man hiding behind the grouchy, untouchable mask. People wear masks when they don't want to be seen. But, the thing is, I've already seen him. I know his true heart as much as I know my own, and it kills me that he's worked so hard to bury it.

I'm spritzing glass cleaner along the main lobby window on a Friday afternoon when I hear the break room door creak open, then slam shut.

"Did you get rid of our food in the fridge?"

Glancing over my shoulder, Cal looms behind me with his hands on his hips. An olive green beanie sits partially halfway up his head, revealing scowl lines that are probably reserved especially for me. He crosses his arms over a heather gray sleeveless tee, waiting for me to provoke his anger further.

He didn't come to my show last week. I doubt he'll appear tonight, or at any future performances, either. Honestly, I'll probably never know why he stopped by that night and told me in a husky, haunting voice that he thought I sang like a bleeping angel.

And that's fine. I just need to forget that it ever happened.

I smile brightly as I swipe a rag over the cleaner and watch Cal's eye twitch in time with the squeaky sounds. "Correction: it used to be food. It turned into a biohazard zone three months ago."

"I'm serious."

"Me, too. I felt like I should have been wearing one of those spacesuits from *E.T.*"

He makes a humming noise. "Cute."

I can't help but stretch the smile I'm certain he doesn't appreciate. "I scrubbed the whole thing out and saved what I could. Three out of ten of your peach yogurts survived the purge. The rest of them expired before I was born."

He's not amused. Then again, Cal never looks amused, so I shouldn't take it personally. The man hasn't cracked a single smile in my presence since I walked through the front door for the first time over a month ago.

Sighing at my failure to get even a semblance of a grin out of him, I swivel back to face the window, my hair bouncing between my shoulder blades.

I don't even hear him approach.

When Cal finally speaks, he's standing right behind me, his heat emanating through the fabric of my mustard yellow sweater dress.

The low baritone of his voice follows. "Thanks."

I hate that a shiver races down my spine at his proximity.

At the gravel in his pitch.

At the luring, bewitching energy he emits, even though he's completely unapproachable.

It doesn't make sense.

Cal is a paradox that has my mind reeling, my wits unraveling, and my heart all topsy-turvy, and it's confusing the crap out of me.

I squeeze the rag in my hand and turn around slowly, schooling my face to maintain the easy smile. "Happy to help. You just needed a woman's touch."

He cocks his head to the side, eyes narrowing. There's a heavy pause that crackles between us before he murmurs, "Is that right?"

I swear I hear a touch of flirtation in his tone.

I swear.

"Around here," I add with a cough, wondering why I can't ever talk like a normal human being. "With the cleaning and organizing—"

"Got it."

My belly feels queasy as my brain regurgitates every embarrassing, accidental sexual innuendo I've uttered in his presence throughout the last six weeks.

It's been a lot.

I'm about to change the subject when Cal does a double-take at the reception desk, and the temperate mood suddenly evaporates. His irritation amplifies. "Where the hell is the orchid?"

I blink. "What?"

"The orchid, Lucy. The fucking flower that's been sitting on the desk since I hired you."

I blink again, hesitating. My gaze skips to the newly reorganized desk, then back to Cal. He doesn't look irritated anymore —he looks fuming. Muscles are rippling through the thin layer of cotton molded to his chest and torso, and his eyes are pinned on me, hot and accusing. "Oh, I...threw it away. It was dead."

"It wasn't dead."

I'm not sure what's going on, but the plant was definitely dead. It was so dead, its decay was contaminating the wood grains underneath it. "I – I'm sorry. I can get you a new one. I'll run to the store right now if you want."

He pinches the bridge of his nose, inhaling a steadying breath, before dropping his hand to cup his jaw. Eyes trained on the desk, he shakes his head back and forth like he can't process the fact that the decrepit orchid remains have finally been removed from the lobby. "I watered the damn thing every day. They keep dying on me."

I study him for a moment. His eyes soften as they stare across the room, the brewing storm like a silver-fade from dark to light. Something has his muscles unclenching, his tension dissipating.

This isn't about a flower.

There's something else going on, but I'm too scared to dig.

Then his declaration registers, and I frown thoughtfully. "You can't water them every day, Cal. Orchids only need to be watered once a week. I grew up with a houseful because my mom loves collecting them." I watch Cal glance down at his dirty, scuffed boots, his biceps flexing with wavelets of new tension, before I add gently, "You've been killing them."

His head snaps up.

Gold-spun irises funnel with a new firestorm. My instincts tell me to step back, move away, but I lift a hand, instead, placing my palm against his rigid forearm. I feel the muscles twitch and tense when I trace my thumb along the sleeve of his tattoo.

Skulls and skeletons. Relics and bones.

Death.

All I want to do is breathe new life into him, so I take a small step forward and give his arm a squeeze. For once in my life, I say nothing. I just stand there, holding his arm, and tip my chin up until we're eye-to-eye. A smile crests on my mouth to match the warmth of my touch.

Electricity kindles.

Heat blooms beneath my fingertips.

I suck in a breath and wait for him to say something —*anything*—hoping he'll accept the tiny invitation to unshroud his darkness, to share his demons with me.

Briefly, I think he's going to. His eyes glaze over with a hint of vulnerability, lips parting with all the things I long to hear.

But then he shakes me off of him, sluicing me with the sting of rejection.

I stumble back.

Ripping his arm away, Cal scratches at the spot where my hand just was, as if he's trying to carve out my touch. He takes a long stride backward, gaze shimmering with intensity, stance withdrawn. And his next words slither through me like a plume of black smoke.

"Don't," he grits out, head swinging back and forth as he continues to retreat. "Don't touch things that don't belong to you."

The implication settles in like a weighty brick, and my vision blurs, a whooshing sound humming in my ears. He's not talking about the food in the fridge. He's not talking about the orchid.

He's talking about himself.

He could have shoved his fist through my chest and yanked out a rib, and I would have felt less sucker-punched.

Ouch.

I catch the flash of guilt that skates across his face before I spin around toward the window, spritzing more cleaner onto the glass.

My rag swishes up and down, side to side.

Squeak, squeak, squeak.

Maybe I was wrong. Maybe the boy I adored is long-gone, lost to the fallout of a broken road.

I still hear him standing behind me, sighing his trademark sigh, but I refuse to turn around. I can't let him see how much that hurt.

Smiling right now would be too hard.

So, I keep wiping the glass, keep distracting myself, keep trying to forget what *was*, so I can adapt to what *is*.

I can do this.

I can forget about everything he used to mean to me.

Eventually, Cal's footsteps stomp away, shuffling in time to the rag gliding across the window.

Squeak, squeak, squeak.

Stomp, stomp, stomp.

The service door slams shut, and my tears fall.

10/22/2013

"Yellow Orchids"

There's a million reasons why I love going to Lucy's house— stuffing our faces with Sour Patch Kids and watching the old Goosebumps episodes on Netflix. Writing songs in her bedroom while she practices on her guitar. Sneaking her mom's historical romance novels and giggling until we cry.

And one of them is because her mom collects orchids.

They're such a pretty flower. Kind of elegant, like how I feel when I'm performing at my piano recitals in a fancy dress and Mom's bright pink lipstick. I'm not sure why Mrs. Hope chose orchids as her favorite flower out of all the flowers in the world, but I'm glad she did. They're beautiful.

I decided to look up the meaning of the flower on Dad's computer, and I think my favorite is the yellow orchid. It represents friendship and new beginnings. Cheer, happiness, and joy.

It reminds me of Lucy.

Mostly, it reminds me of us.

Toodles,

Emma

Cal doesn't know it yet, but I filled his office with fresh orchids two hours ago. Kenny heard the ricochet of Cal's volatile mood, likely tipped off by the door-slam and subsequent hostility radiating off of him like the roar of an impending hurricane. Being the nice guy that Kenny is, he sauntered up to the lobby amid my quiet breakdown and told me to take an early lunch and give myself a breather.

Wrought with embarrassment, I offered up my thanks and booked it out of the auto shop, debating if I should head home and have a cryfest with my dogs, or call Alyssa and beg for advice.

It's never good advice, but it always leaves me with a smile.

Somehow, neither option panned out, and I found myself cruising into the parking lot of the local Woodman's. I knew it was both foolish *and* futile, but those things had never stopped me in the past—so, I purchased every single orchid on display in the floral department and filled my car to the brim.

Then, I managed to sneak into Cal's office with armfuls of flowers, setting up the room like a colorful, floral garden.

There are dozens of them.

Pink, yellow, fuchsia, and white.

The little potted plants are scattered around the space, lining his desk, and perched beneath the lone window along with a note that says, "*Water us every Friday, please!*"

I have to believe that even if he never warms up to *me*, the gesture will start to melt his freezer-burned heart.

Just a little.

I'm settled behind the desk a while later, scrolling through the low inventory report, when the service door swings open. My heart jack-knifes in anticipation of seeing Cal for the first time since our charged confrontation, but it's just Dante unwrapping one of Ike's blue raspberry Dum Dums as he moves toward me with a half-smile.

He must notice my brush with panic and realize I was

expecting Cal because there's a weird look on his face as he approaches.

Pity.

He pities me and my pitifulness.

Clearing my throat, I dive back into inventory and pretend like I'm not a mess.

He just huffs a laugh. "The boss getting under your skin?"

"No," I lie quickly. Too quickly.

"You're terrible at taking advice, sweetheart."

Tucking my hair behind my ear, I feel my cheeks heat. "I can't just avoid him, Dante," I say, clicking my fingers across the keyboard as if I'm diligently working, but I'm actually only typing my name over and over again.

"I said to avoid talking to him about personal shit, and not to get offended when he acts like an asshole."

Shrugging my shoulders, I look away, defeated. "It's nothing," I clip. "We used to be friends, so I just thought—" I trail off, blowing out a breath. "Like I said, it's nothing."

"Well," he says, readjusting his coveralls. "I don't think he wants to be your friend anymore."

"I've noticed. Thanks."

"Not what I meant."

I falter mid-keyboard click, my gaze skating back to him, eyebrows pinching together. "What do you mean?"

Dante rolls his neck, letting out a sigh when he meets my confused stare. "There's only two reasons a man threatens anyone who makes a move on a woman," he says, looking at me pointedly. "Either that woman is related to him, or she's a woman he has a personal interest in."

My heart teeters.

I ignore the little tickle in my throat when he says *personal interest* and shake my head. "Or," I counter, "maybe he just wants his employees to be treated with respect."

"On the job? Sure. I'd buy it. But his orders were clear to stay away from you on *and* off the clock."

Wait...*what?*

The tickle morphs into a beehive, and my cheeks flame pink. "Okay," I say, the word drawn out because I need extra time to process his meaning. Then I gulp. "He made it...clear?"

"Crystal."

It feels like my equilibrium is going on the fritz. "I – I mean, it's possible you heard him out of context. He probably sees me as a sister, which falls into the first category."

That makes sense.

There, I solved it.

Dante scrubs a hand up and down his face, trying to hide the You're Really Not Smart expression it's wearing. "He doesn't see you as a sister, sweetheart. Promise."

My teetering heart nearly collapses in on itself when the service door swings open again with double the force, producing a brassed-off Cal.

Dante shoots me a look, stepping closer and whispering, "Watch."

I zig-zag my attention between Cal storming at us, and Dante, who is closing in on my personal bubble. He wraps an arm around my shoulders, causing me to freeze in place. I glance up at him with big, questioning eyes, spotting Cal trudge to a stop out of my peripheral vision.

"What do you say?" Dante asks, eyebrows waggling conspiratorially. "Tomorrow night?"

"What? Oh, sure," I swallow. "Okay."

"Why are you fucking touching her?" Cal snaps from a few feet away.

We both turn to see him glaring daggers at Dante, arms folding over his puffed-out chest. One of his skull tattoos looks like it's sneering when a muscle flexes near his shoulder.

Unwrapping his arm from me, Dante moves away and stuffs both hands into his cargo pants. "Hey, boss. Just having a chat."

"You were touching her. Why?"

I cut in, smoothing out my hair. "It's fine, Cal. We were making plans."

"Plans to do what?"

He looks livid. Sweat gleams off his bronzed skin beneath the overhead light, and his hair is in disarray from work, heightening the chaotic look in his eyes.

"Gonna catch a movie," Dante says, looking nonplussed. "Netflix and chill, maybe."

"The fuck you are."

Oh my God.

My eyes widen to blue saucers.

That Jason Bateman meme spirals through my brain, and I start combing my fingers through my hair—hair that suddenly feels like a heavy wool coat dead set on suffocating me.

Cal's glances at me, confirming that my attempt to become invisible has failed. Forcing an ultra-strained smile, I turn back toward the computer screen and start backspacing the line of "Lucys" before he spots them.

"I need her here tomorrow night. I'm keeping her late," Cal says, sauntering closer until he's only two feet away from us.

Dante intercedes, sending me a knowing wink. "No worries. Maybe next week."

"She's busy then, too." He stares at him, unblinking. "Get back to work."

Chuckling lightly, totally unfazed, Dante gives Cal a punch on the shoulder and tips his head to me in goodbye. "Heard, boss."

I watch Dante slap a beanie on his head and make his way into the garage.

"Print me that inventory report," Cal says when the door closes, sidling up beside me at the desk until our hips bump together. He doesn't step away.

Swallowing hard, I gather my hair in both hands and fidget with it until it's hanging over my shoulder in a loose twist. "Sure, but what was that?"

"What was what?"

"Cal." It's all I say because I know he's not an idiot.

He leans forward on his palms, knuckles looking transparent due to the amount of pressure and tension rippling down the expanse of his arms. Splayed fingers curl into his hands until he's making two fists atop the desk. Then he looks to the left, meeting my eyes. "Because you're sweet, and he's trouble."

His response has my belly fluttering. I try not to obsess over the fact that he called me sweet and shift my focus on the other angle. "Oh...well, I thought he was your friend."

"He's also trouble."

I nibble my lip. "And you don't think I can handle trouble?"

"Just print me the report, Lucy. I need to get back to work."

I inch away from him and scroll through the program to locate what he's looking for. Confusion races through me because I don't know what to think about Dante's assessment of Cal having a "personal interest" in me—it sure as heck doesn't seem that way. But, he also fell right into Dante's little trap and put a blatant stop to any Netflix-and-chilling.

My mind lands on the only explanation: *Sister.*

He sees me as a sister due to our history together and my friendship with Emma.

That's the only scenario that makes an ounce of sense. If Cal was interested any other way, he wouldn't be radiating irritation and loathing so potent, my skin feels singed.

"Here you go," I say, reaching down to fetch the papers from the printer.

He swipes them from my hand, muttering something gruffly under his breath that is either a "thank you" or an "eff you," then turns away.

It looks like he's about to head to the garage but falters briefly, pivoting toward his office instead, likely to put the report on his desk.

I lock up. Cal is about to walk into an enchanted orchid garden, and I have no idea how he's going to react. He's in an awful mood, so my ploy to lift his spirits may ultimately backfire and cause an eruption, like a flame to liquor.

The end result: I'm a flambé.

Holding my breath, I watch him disappear into his office with his head down as he skims the report. My heart is pounding, making me dizzy. I start braiding my hair to quiet my shaky hands, my leg bobbing up and down in time with my heartbeats.

A few moments tick by.

One, two, three, four—

And then, Cal steps back out.

He just stands there, facing me outside the door, totally unreadable. Tense and silent. Something in him deflates a little, and he leans his shoulder against the doorjamb, shoving one hand into his blue jeans. He swallows as he stares at me. Still silent, still blank.

I stare back, my eyes huge and searching. I'm terrified, choking on my own air, desperate to know what he's thinking.

I get my answer when he inhales a quick breath, and then his lips turn up with a smile.

A smile.

A smile.

I'm embarrassed when unexpected tears spring to my eyes to the point where his smile blurs, and I have to blink them away to make sure I didn't imagine it all. But I didn't, and he's still smiling, shaking his head with a measure of disbelief.

A tiny sound falls from my lips. A laugh, a sigh, a burst of impossible relief. I smile back at him, bigger, brighter, flashing all my teeth through misty eyes and a pathetically happy heart.

Cal glances down at the floor, the smile lingering, before turning around and heading back into his office.

When I was seven years old, my parents bought me a shiny new bicycle without the training wheels. Cerulean blue, my favorite color at the time. It had a little bell and pastel pink streamers floating off the handlebars, and I cried when I saw it waiting for me in the garage on my birthday, sitting among a pool of confetti sprinkled at the wheels. My parents didn't have a lot of money at the time and told me they couldn't afford to get me a new bike, so I never expected it.

It was such a surprise. An incredible, thoughtful gift.

I didn't think anything would ever replicate the feeling of joy that raced through me when I saw that blue bicycle, knowing Mom and Dad must have sacrificed a lot to have been able to afford it. Even as a small child, I knew that.

As I stand here with tears tickling my cheekbones, I know that life's truest treasures live inside the unexpected moments. The little curveballs that sweep us off our feet and steal our breath.

I told my parents the bike was the best gift I ever received, and nothing could ever top it.

I meant it at the time.

But then...

Cal smiled at me.

CHAPTER 10

I 'm covered in cats when I get a text from Cal a week later on a Sunday afternoon.

CAL:

Meet me at the shop in an hour.

Blinking down at my phone screen, I shoot him a reply.

ME:

I'm volunteering at the moment. :)

I send him a selfie of me and Mr. Perkins, a black and white domestic shorthair, for good measure.

A few minutes skip by before Cal says:

CAL:

Please

The "please" gets me, just like he knew it would. Whatever it is, it must be important. Sending back a response riddled with exclamation points, I stroke Mr. Perkins' fur as he croons in my lap with contentment. One of the other volunteers, Gemma, sits beside me in the cat room, leaning back on her palms as her auburn hair glows with red streaks beneath the eclectic Ikea light fixture.

"Looks like I need to head out early today," I tell her, glancing at her profile.

Gemma is beautiful; a little older than me, pushing thirty, and engaged to a guy named Knox. I was invited to her December wedding, and I'm looking forward to the winter event that will ring in the holiday season—my *favorite* season.

She looks over at me with shimmery green eyes, laughing lightly when a cat named Lima Bean clasps her wrist between two paws. "Emergency?"

"I'm not sure yet. It's my boss, but we're closed on Sundays. He asked me to meet him at the shop in an hour."

Knowing a little bit about my working relationship with Cal, she, of course, gives me an eyebrow wiggle. This is why Gemma and Alyssa get along so well.

"Could be something simple. Could be scandalous."

"It's not scandalous."

"Show me a picture before I decide," she grins.

I balk at her. Then I relent, scrolling through my cell phone in search of the Google photo Alyssa texted to me with a million melting and drooling emojis.

Sighing, I show her the screen.

Her eyes pop. "Scandal is imminent."

"No, it's not." I can't help but snort, shaking my head through the smile as my cheeks flush crimson. "It's not like that. Cal is...uninterested," I settle on. "In everything."

"Everything?"

"Everything except for his job and..." I scrunch up my nose. "Orchids, apparently."

She shrugs. "So, he's a hard worker who will always bring you flowers. Sounds like a winner to me."

We share a laugh as I unravel myself from the half-asleep cat and rise to my feet, brushing the tuxedo fur off the front of my leggings. I volunteer here almost every Sunday, cuddling cats, walking dogs, refilling food and water bowls, and deep-cleaning kennels. The animal shelter is called *Forever Young*—it's a sanctuary for senior dogs and cats; a place where they can live out their geriatric years and not have to worry about sitting on death row at animal control or a high-kill shelter.

The cause spoke to me.

I've always been a sucker for the things deemed less desirable. The overlooked. Growing up as a child with medical issues, I was never Miss Popularity. I was either teased or ignored through most of grade school, often absent from classes due to surgeries and procedures, and sometimes forced to carry around a heart monitor. I was always picked last for gym class activities, and that was on the days I was even able to participate. Most of the time, I'd become too breathless and have to sit it out. My classmates complained that I was getting special treatment—they had to run laps, while I sat on the sidelines. But, little did they know, I'd have done anything to run laps with them.

It took years for me to feel like my condition wasn't an actual "disability"—it was just a part of me. A different part. A unique part. Sometimes that part hindered activities or plans, but it never hindered how hard my heart loved. And that's what it's all about, after all. Loving other people, loving our blessings, loving ourselves.

Honestly, the more my peers claimed I was less of a person, or lacking in some way, the more love I wanted to give. The more I appreciated everything good around me.

That's why I choose to spend my time with the senior pets who get passed over for the young, energetic puppies and kittens. It doesn't seem fair that these sweet souls are disregarded because their age makes them "less than" in the eyes of many.

Old age is not a disability; it's a gift.

And I've finally embraced the fact that I am, too.

Waving goodbye to Gemma, I promise to fill her in on the Cal updates before leaving the room and breezing down the main hallway toward the front of the building. Vera is perched at her desk, munching on one of the oatmeal cookies I made for the staff of volunteers. She is the incredible founder of this nonprofit sanctuary, having built it from the ground up with generous donations and her own personal savings.

Vera pokes her head up from a magazine when I sweep by, running a hand over her short, cropped hair. "Leaving already, honey?"

"I am, unfortunately. I got called into work today."

"Oh, I understand. You work so hard. See you next week?"

She smiles warmly, the apples of her cheeks rosy and round, reminding me of pink azaleas. I nod, traipsing toward the main entrance and sending her a wave. "Absolutely. Give Snickerdoodle a belly rub for me since I missed her today. I hope her vet appointment goes well."

Swallowing her bite of cookie, Vera waves back. "I'll shoot you a text later with an update—it's a miracle that donation came in so we could front her surgery cost," she smiles. "Make sure you relax at some point, hon."

"One of these days!" I call back over my shoulder before stepping out into the parking lot.

It's the last week of September—officially fall—and there's something in the breeze today that makes me feel nostalgic. It's funny how that happens sometimes. There's no exact recollection that springs to mind, no precise moment, but it feels like I'm lost to a memory I can't quite pinpoint.

It's sort of like déjà vu, but instead of feeling rattled, I feel warm.

My soul feels warm.

Today it's the tickle of an autumn breeze that lightens my steps and fosters my smile as I make the thirty-minute drive to the shop with the window cracked. As I curve into the parking lot, I note that Cal's bike is already sitting alone and idle in one of the empty spaces.

The fuzzy feeling is still burrowed deep inside my chest when I hop out of the car and make my way inside, the jingle bells complementing my mood. "Cal?" I look around for him, peeking inside his office, then checking the break room. He's nowhere to be found, so I push through the service door and glance into the bays. "Cal?"

Finally, his muffled voice trails over to me from what looks to be the storage room. "In here," he says. The door is half open, a singular bulb that dangles from a string providing lackluster illumination to the familiar shadow I see moving back and forth.

Realizing I look like a scrub, I swipe more cat hair off my black leggings and readjust my oversized sweater that falls mid-palms. My hair is a day past due for a wash, pulled up into a giant bun and riddled with dry shampoo, and my face is sans makeup, save for a shoddy mascara application and my berry lip balm.

I'm pretty sure I smell like a kennel, so I panic on my trek over to him and douse myself in the bottle of grapefruit-scented hand sanitizer I purchased for the guys that they have noticeably ignored.

"Lucy," he bellows, poking his head out. "Over here."

"Coming," I tell him, slathering the sanitizer all over my neck, collarbone, and arms while I break into a jog. "Sorry. I'm not exactly prepared."

Cal scratches at his overgrown stubble, squinting at me when I approach. "Prepared for what?"

To see you.

"Work."

"You look good to me." He says it casually, easily, his eyes raking over me in a gradual pull, landing on my cap toe ballet flats, then drawing back up. Blinking, he adds, "You smell like a medical exam room. And Vitamin C."

I give him a strained laugh and tug on my topknot. "So, what did you need?"

Hesitating, he makes a humming noise before swiveling around toward a wall of shelving units stocked with mechanical parts. The storage room is small, so I instantly feel swallowed up by his body heat and earthy man smells as he ushers me farther inside.

"I'm working on a friend's car today. She was in a bind, and I was already here, so I offered to take a look at it. Problem is, I was here combing through inventory so I can get an order in tomorrow. Don't really want to be here all night, and was hoping you could take over. I'll pay you double time."

All I hear is "she."

Scraping my bottom lip between my teeth, I bob my head, perusing the stockpile. I should be asking what the hell an ignition magneto is, but the question that blurts out of me is, "Whose car?"

"What?" Cal's shoulder blades stretch the thin material of his tank as he reaches up to an upper shelf and starts rummaging.

"The car," I clarify, trying to look nonchalant by swinging my arms back and forth as I skim the middle shelf. "The one you're working on today."

He falters, his hand mid-reach for a dusty box. Forgoing the item, he spins around to face me, his eyes glinting with curiosity beneath the tungsten lightbulb. There's a shadow of a smirk on his face. "Why?"

Crap—he's on to me.

"Just wondering," I shrug.

"I told you, she's a friend."

"Okay." I start whistling because whistling makes a person seem disinterested. Totally cool and composed. Not at all fishing.

Cal swipes his thumb and index finger over the corners of his mouth, almost like he's trying to eradicate any trace of a smile. "She's one of my mistresses. From the harem that I have."

It takes a beat for me to realize that he's teasing.

Cal hardly lets his guard down and jokes with me—or anyone for that matter—but on the rare occasion he does, it always shoots a giddy pitter-patter to my heart.

My lips press together to hold in the laugh as I attempt to maintain my composure. "Cool."

"Her name's Jolene."

"Pretty name."

"She is pretty. My favorite out of all my lovers." He crosses his arms, head tilting to the side. "I have dozens."

"Congratulations," I breeze, coughing to cover the giggles while I aimlessly graze my fingers over the boxes of batteries. When I glance up at him through long lashes with only my eyes, I relish in the half-smile that managed to break free. Just one corner of his mouth is tipped up as he gazes down at me with a flickering of humor in his eyes.

I wish I could bottle this moment; package it up and store it inside me, unwrapping it when I need the reminder that my Cal is still in there.

Our eyes continue to hold until the smile fades from his lips, and the levity in his eyes evolves into something else. Something that causes my skin to flush hot. It's the same feeling that possessed me a few weeks ago at the wine bar when Cal pressed his palm to the small of my back, smelling like sin, and whispered a single word against the shell of my ear that had thunder rolling in my chest and lightning climbing my throat.

I'm forced to change the subject before the fire in my cheeks turns this storage room into an incinerator. Darting my eyes away, I break the tether and draw my attention back to the array of mechanical parts. "So, inventory. Exciting. Do I have to—"

I'm interrupted by the sound of a cheery female voice echoing through the bays.

"Cal? I come bearing gifts."

Cal blinks away whatever was brewing inside his light brown eyes and releases a long sigh, sweeping past me. "Sorry. One sec."

Following, I stall right outside the doorway and spot a woman wandering around the garage with a paper bag and a drink carrier that holds two coffees.

"Americano with a splash of heavy cream, and a dozen donut holes," she proclaims, spotting Cal moving toward her.

I glance at the slew of items in her hands, biting my lip at the notion that she seems to know exactly how he likes his coffee.

Then my eyes pan up to her face.

And for some reason, my insides curdle like spoiled milk.

She *is* pretty.

The mystery woman cranes her head around Cal's big frame, noticing me hovering near the doorway tinkering with the edging of my long sleeves. "Oh! I didn't realize you had company, Cal. I would have grabbed another coffee."

Cal stops in front of her before sparing me a glance over his shoulder. He massages the back of his neck with his palm as he makes the introduction. "That's Lucy, my new receptionist. She's doing inventory for me today," he says, meeting my wide-eyed gaze from a few feet away. "Lucy, this is Jolene. My ex."

Jolene.

The friend.

The friend who is actually an ex.

Okay. Well, that's fine. She seems nice.

"Hi," I greet, lifting my hand in a little wave as I saunter forward. "I don't drink coffee, but I appreciate the sentiment."

She eyes me with a smile, bobbing her head up and down as long, curly black hair falls over both shoulders like an obsidian waterfall. Two big green eyes resembling that of a Disney princess skate back to Cal, countering the troves of dark leather that make her look more like the villain. She's covered in tattoos—arms, neck, and the hint of toned belly that peeks out from below her crop top. Her body is athletic and fit, so it's clear she loves working out more than eating muffins all day like me, and her boobs are...impressive. Really impressive.

She's gorgeous.

And I have no idea why that has my chest caving in.

"You don't drink coffee? That's intriguing. You'll have to teach me your ways because I could probably pay off my house in a year with all the money I'd save by giving up Dunkin." Flashing me her teeth, she pops one of the coffee cups from the container and hands it to Cal, the little heat vapors swirling from the mouth hole. "Cal mentioned he finally hired someone. How are you liking it here?"

I smile back, inching closer. She seems friendly and approachable, so I shoo away the ridiculous waves of anxiety spilling into my psyche. "It's been wonderful so far. I'm learning a lot."

Jolene shoots Cal a wink, thrusting the bag of donut holes at him and reaching for her own coffee. She swivels toward a metal desk and hops up, swinging her stiletto-tipped feet back and forth. "Nice find, Cal. Where can I get one of those?"

He glances at me and scratches his cheek. "We were neighbors back in the day. She's been great."

"Great? She's fucking gorgeous," Jolene says before taking a swig of her drink. She winces like it scalded her. "I'm jealous of your eye candy. My receptionist looks like we purchased him off Wish dot com and he got lost in the mail."

Laughter bursts out of me. "Um, thanks," I tell her, pushing my baby hairs off my forehead. "That's really sweet of you to say." Still laughing, I add, "About me. Not the other guy."

Grinning, she pops her eyebrows up and down. "I own a tattoo parlor. If Boss Man, here, ever gives you too much shit, come see me. Actually, come see me, anyway. I'll give you half off your first design and I'll try not to hit on you."

Blush settles into my cheeks again.

"All right, let's get this inventory taken care of," Cal interjects, his stance turning to stone. Arms crossed, he settles his sights on me with a scowl. "Grab the folder off the desk and meet me in the storage room. I'll walk you through it."

"Okay," I mutter.

When he stomps off, Jolene mouths, "*Come see me*," before I duck my head with a smirk and rush off to fetch the folder and a pen. I trot back over and join Cal a few seconds later, geared up and ready to learn my way around gauges and meters.

He's shuffling items around when I enter, his back to me, and his big, muscular body perched atop a midsized ladder that is miraculously supporting his weight.

I seize a shameful moment to eyeball him, taking supreme interest in the way his butt looks in his jeans. The faded black denim is form-fitting today, less baggy than usual, and his shirt is riding up his back a little, showing off a trace of bronzed skin. When he moves, I can't help but—

"When you're done looking at my ass, I'll give you the rundown."

Oh God.

I almost pass away.

Spinning around to look *anywhere* else, I hear him climb back down the ladder until he swipes the folder out of my white-knuckled grip.

"Relax. I'm messing with you."

"I'm fine. It's fine." *Everything is fine.* I clear my throat and attempt eye contact. "Okay. Show me what to do."

He goes over everything quickly, as per usual, and I retain absolutely nothing, still catatonic from embarrassment. But, it's inventory, which is self-explanatory, and I'm pretty sure all I need to do is count.

I can do that.

I think.

Cal points at the ladder and has me climb up, listing off random items on the top shelf. I nod absently, surveying the parts, and then I feel his hand on my lower back.

I try to stay focused, but it's difficult.

Electricity sparks from his touch, lighting me up from the inside out.

"You okay? Just want to make sure you're steady." His hand lowers a fraction when I inch up, grazing my backside. He leaves it there for a potent second before pulling away. "You won't fall?"

"I – I'm good."

"Good."

Knees wobbly, I take a deep breath and head back down the ladder, ready to finish up this inventory lesson that feels far more complicated when Cal is leaning into me. He holds up the report, grazing his tattooed middle finger down one of the columns while our shoulders brush together.

That's when I frown, my eyes scanning over the list in column two. "What's a clitometer?"

I swear he snorts.

Running a hand over his face, forehead to chin, he looks at me as he takes a step back. "A what?"

"A clitometer," I repeat, confused.

"A *clit*ometer doesn't exist. A *clin*ometer is a tilt sensor. It's used for measuring."

"Oh." Cringing at the slip-up, I backpedal. Backpedaling has basically become my whole personality at this point. "Well, part of the N is smudged on the report. It looks like a T. Like *clit*— and oh my *God*, did I really just say that word to you?"

That tiny smirk reappears as he tosses back a piece of gum and scrubs a hand down his face again. And again. After a beat, he flicks his eyes toward the wall of shelves, then back to me, saying, "It's cute that I make you nervous."

Filling my cheeks with air, I hold it in for a second before blowing it out. "There's nothing cute about saying 'clit' to your boss. Multiple times, now."

The smirk stretches.

I tuck my chin to my chest and bite my lip. I feel like I need to change the subject at this point, so I pivot back to his mysterious ex-girlfriend he's never mentioned before. Curiosity trickles through me as I begin, "So, speaking of cute—"

"No, I'm not sleeping with Jolene," he cuts me off.

Creepily clairvoyant.

His gaze swings over to me, the smirk disappearing. "We haven't been together for a long time. We're just friends."

"Oh, well, it's fine if you are."

"Thanks, but I'm not."

Convinced he's lying, I keep going. "She's really nice. And beautiful. And I would never judge you or pry if you—"

"I haven't had sex in two years, Lucy."

I gasp before my mouth snaps shut.

Cal tosses the papers on a shelf and turns toward me, his eyes flaring. Wild and magnetic. Burning into me like violent embers. He takes a single step forward until he's only inches away and sweeps his gaze across my face.

And then he says in a low, steady voice, "God help the woman who breaks that streak."

Swallowing, he levels me with a pointed stare before walking out of the storage room.

He walks away as I reach for a shelf to steady my balance.

He walks away, leaving me shaken and breathless.

He walks away, while I just stand there, dumbfounded, with a throbbing ache between my legs.

I've been at it for an hour, sorting through a gazillion air filters and spark plugs, grateful for the reprieve. Cal's words have been rocketing through my brain the whole time, gripping me in a chokehold, but I've managed to stay focused and organized.

Honestly, the more I've thought about it, the more I realize he was probably just making a generalized statement.

Just because he was staring right at me with his whisky eyes, intoxicating my bloodstream, doesn't mean he was actually *referring* to me.

That would be absurd.

I laugh tersely at the thought.

He hasn't come in to check on me at all, and when I peered out through the crack in the door a little while ago, I found him leaning against one of the stone-gray walls, deep in conversation with Jolene as loud rock music blared from an overhead speaker.

My heart did a weird lub-dub thing at the image, pinging with telltale anxiety again, but I shut that down fast. It's not a big deal, and I'm not jealous.

I'm really not.

I've never had a reason to be jealous before, and I certainly don't have one now. Besides, Jolene is great. She's laid-back and likable. Fun. It's no wonder they dated at one time—she looks exactly like the type of girl Cal would go for. Sexy, adventurous, edgy. She probably has a motorcycle. I bet they used to ride their motorcycles together and had long talks under the moon about black picket fences and little biker babies.

It's fine.

I'm fine.

Well...I'm fine until I'm *not* fine.

In an instant, I'm blindsided.

I lean too heavily on one side of the ladder and lose my balance. The whole thing tips to the left, toppling from underneath me, and I go down, flailing as I try to find something to grab onto as I'm falling.

Unfortunately, I grab onto a nail jutting out from one of the shoddy shelves.

Since I'm in the midst of plummeting, the nail doesn't just puncture my hand—it slices it open. It tears through the underside of my palm while I make my seemingly slow-motion descent to the concrete floor.

The pain doesn't register right away, trumped by shock and adrenaline, as the air whooshes out of me for a split second. Oddly enough, the shooting pain in my tailbone strikes first.

I wince.

I suck in a sharp breath through clenched teeth.

And then...*it hits me.*

Searing, blinding, awful pain.

Propping myself up with my uninjured hand, I brave a glance at the damage and instantly start freaking out. Panic grips me like a noose.

Blood.

Blood everywhere.

It's gushing and oozing and dripping down my arm, soiling my sweater and leaving little puddles on the floor.

I scream. "Cal!"

He doesn't hear me over Sevendust, so I scramble to my feet, holding my hand as far away from me as possible, like it's clutching a rabid raccoon.

Oh my God, oh my God.

I race out the door, frazzled and stumbling, using all my willpower to keep the tears from pouring out of me. "C-Cal," I yell again, tipping my chin up until I zero in on him at the far end of the garage.

He straightens when he sees me, momentarily frozen.

Our eyes lock.

I hold my hand up higher, as if he can't see the gallons of bright red blood trickling down my arm to my elbow, leaving a trail of carnage behind me. "I'm bleeding," I croak out, feeling like I'm about to have a panic attack.

Cal seems to snap back to reality and tosses his coffee cup to the ground, the remaining contents spilling everywhere. Jolene stares in horror, a hand cupping her mouth.

"Jesus Christ," Cal says in a strained breath, beelining toward me.

He reaches me in a blink, only three giant strides, and I think he's going to grab my hand to take a closer look at the injury, but he doesn't.

Before I can inhale another breath, one arm dips beneath my knees while the other cradles my back. He lifts me in the air and pulls me to him, whispering, "Fuck, sunshine, I got you."

My heart stutters.

His words manage to eclipse the excruciating pain and blood loss, and *that's* what has the tears streaming down my face. Maybe it's a combination of everything, but maybe it's his words.

Maybe it's the way he just called me "sunshine" while whisking me away to the break room at lightning speed, holding onto me like a treasure.

I latch onto the back of his neck for steadiness as I continue to hold my injured hand at arm's length, watching with dread as the blood continues to spill out in rivulets of crimson.

"Breathe, okay? I got you," he echoes as we enter the break room.

Cal deposits me on one of the tables, pushing his way between my knees and snatching up my wrist. My breath catches when he reaches behind his back with his free hand and pulls his t-shirt over his head, quickly wrapping the fabric around my palm and holding tight.

I feel lightheaded. Dizzy. Queasy.

Safe.

I feel safe right now with Cal between my legs, putting pressure on my wound with the shirt off his back, his eyes full of brazen concern.

"Breathe, Lucy."

He repeats it again.

We stay in this position for a few heartbeats. Cal's face is so wrought with worry, I forget which one of us is in peril. He holds my hand with both of his, his grip firm and secure, and my breaths finally begin to steady before hysteria sinks me.

"Fuck, let me grab the first aid kit." He dips his forehead to mine for the tiniest moment, then moves back. "Hold this tight. Don't take any pressure off of it."

I nod, my eyes fluttering closed, then opening slowly.

My gaze lands on his bare chest, only inches away from me. There's a silver chain around his neck, a pendant dangling from it —it's a heart woven into a treble clef.

Before I can study it further, Cal is already gone, crossing the room behind me. I hear cabinets clapping open and shut as he searches for the kit, and I inhale a rickety breath while I clutch my cotton-sheathed hand.

I vaguely notice Jolene standing in the doorway, looking frazzled, asking if I'm okay, but I'm too woozy to respond.

I close my eyes again.

Breathe, Lucy.

Cal returns to my side, unraveling the t-shirt and examining the wound. He's talking to me, calming me down as he tends to my hand, but I'm already thrown back in time, stolen away by a memory...

. . .

"Breathe, Lucy."

Cal pulled me from the swimming pool.

I'm staring up at him, shivering, my lungs tight, chest achy.

I can't catch my breath.

He says it again, his handsome face shadowing the midday sun.
"Breathe, Lucy."

Commotion races around me, but all I see is him. All I hear is him. All I feel is his hand pressed to the middle of my chest, fingers splayed, centering me.

"Is she okay? Cal! Is she okay?"

Emma.

Emma and Cal, my rescuers.

Sirens blare in the distance. Someone called an ambulance.

But I already feel safe.

Cal is telling me to breathe, and Emma is holding my hand.

I'm okay.

I'm okay.

As long as they're here, I'll be okay.

I can breathe.

CHAPTER 11

The weeks fly by, and my hand is healing nicely. My stitches were removed on Friday, and I haven't had any numbness or other concerning symptoms, so after two weeks off work for medical leave, I'm finally heading back to the shop tomorrow.

To celebrate the fact that I didn't need an amputation—which I'd convinced myself was somehow fine because technology is so advanced now, I'd probably have received a super cool bionic hand that could double as a flamethrower like Tony Stark—Alyssa came by with a thin crust pizza from my favorite pizza parlor a few towns over.

And wine. Always wine.

"Nobody puts green olives on pizza," she says through a mouthful as we binge-watch true crime documentaries. "It's truly heinous."

"It's an option, so clearly, people *do* put green olives on pizza."

She huffs.

I used to like pepperoni before I became a vegetarian, so the salty olives—or even dill pickles if I'm feeling daring—serve as a tasty alternative, along with extra onions.

Alyssa doesn't agree, so she ordered a meat lovers calzone, but only took one bite before going straight to the wine.

Kiki is lying at our feet with her eyes bugged out, waiting for a scrap to fall, while Lemon snoozes in her dog bed across the living room, uninterested. Alyssa sneaks Kiki a piece of sausage, and I swat her hand away. "No feeding sausage to the sausage. She's already ten pounds overweight."

"Her face, though."

"I know. That's why she's overweight."

Puckering her lips, Alyssa shifts on the couch and draws her feet up onto the cushion. She reaches for her wine, chugging back a few swallows, leaving a cranberry kiss behind. "Speaking of sausage, your house is looking great."

I snort.

She always does that—starts a sentence with "speaking of" and then says something completely unrelated. Glancing around the cozy living area, I bob my head with agreement. It *is* looking homier lately. I made good use of my time off work, inviting my mother over to help me decorate. Embarrassingly, I'd been too busy to fully commit to interior design, so the walls were still sterile and empty. Snubbed for graver tasks, such as losing myself in pages made of ink and ashes.

A three-hour shopping extravaganza at Home Goods changed that, and now I'm sitting amid overpriced coral-hued pillows on an ivory sofa while my slipper-covered feet tap along the new sage and white area rug.

The walls still need fresh paint—maybe a sea-breeze blue—but they'll do for now. Mom hung an assortment of art prints and family photos since my hand was out of commission, while I broke out a box of hand-me-down trinkets to sprinkle throughout the space.

It's finally feeling like *home.*

Their home, my home.

They are interchangeable.

As Alyssa and I dive deep into the pros and cons of Benjamin Moore versus Behr paints, my cell phone pings from the side table beside me. I reach for it, my heart skipping when I see his name.

CAL:

How you holding up?

An organic smile lifts. Cal has been checking in on me every now and then over the past fourteen days, sending me texts like:

How's the hand?

Healing up okay?

Doing any better?

Which, in my mind, all sounded like: *I'm worried about you.*

Of course, I could be reading into that—after all, Cal doesn't strike me as the sensitive type.

I've caught glimpses of vulnerability and empathy; empathy for *me*. He's still closed-off, his disposition more prickly than plush, but nothing will ever erase the memories of that afternoon when he carried me in his arms and told me to breathe in that same, troubled voice from years ago. I'll never forget the worry lines etched into his face, bending his brows and crinkling his forehead. His eyes were glazed over, the darker brown rims charged with tension, the golden flecks twinkling with tenderness.

He drove me to the hospital in my car, then waited there until I was released, dropping me off at home and walking back to the shop for his bike.

Cal never once complained, and my heart soared.

It's still soaring.

And that's what will forever stand out about that day. Not the blood, or the fear, or the pain—just Cal and his soft edges.

Smile still in place, I type back a reply while Alyssa hovers over me, trying to peek at our messages.

ME:

> Much better! I got my stitches out on Friday and everything looks good. I'll be back tomorrow. I hope you haven't missed me too much. ;)

"Oh my God, you're flirting, Lucy. I knew you had it in you," Alyssa says. The subsequent whip of straw-blond hair tells me she's proud.

My face sours. "What? Did that sound like flirting?"

"Uh, yeah. You even added the wink emoji."

"Oh God...I didn't mean to. I was just being silly." The message shows "read," and I promptly blanch.

Alyssa settles back into the couch, shaking her head and swallowing down a few sips of wine. She likes red wine, opposed to my preference for white, paralleling our contrastive personalities. She's the sexy siren to my wholesome modesty. Deep down though, we both still love wine.

The Merlot swishes around her glass as she twirls the stem, matching her ruby-tipped fingers and red lips. "Why not? He's hot. You're hot. Flirting is appropriate—and rough, dirty sex is inevitable."

I stuff the phone between my thighs, too scared to see his response. My neck burns at her analysis, reminding me of the fire-raising moment Cal and I shared in the storage room when he looked me dead in the eyes and said God help the woman who broke his two-year bout of celibacy.

Not that I need the reminder.

His words have been on auto replay for two weeks, loud enough to wake the dead. The dead being my libido.

Worrying my lip between my teeth, I glance at her. "I won't lie and say I'm...*immune*," I admit softly, feeling the heat climb up my neck and commandeer my ears. "But...I'm not a rough, dirty sex kind of a girl, and that's probably what he likes."

She just laughs at me in that Alyssa way. Floaty and feminine with a touch of audacity. "Lucy, you *are* that girl. Every one of us is that girl with the right man."

I reach for my own wine glass and chug the whole thing. Then I blurt with my lips folded around the rim, "I'm a virgin."

Her head swings toward me so fast, she eats a piece of her hair. "*What?*"

"Yeah, I know. It's mortifying."

Extending a hand as if to stop me right there, a frown steals her sandy eyebrows. "Hey, no, that's not what I meant." She pulls her lips between her teeth and sits on the confession for a beat. "I just didn't know. I'm surprised because you're—"

"Twenty-two."

"Again, no," she sighs, tipping her head back. "I was going to say gorgeous. A straight-up ten."

Warmth blossoms in my cheeks, a fusion of guilt and timidity. While I've never bold-faced lied to her about my chastity, I *have* skirted around the subject whenever it's come up, possibly implying otherwise with ambiguous responses and quick subject changes. "Sorry I never told you," I tell her, reaching for a pillow. The pillow is bright and happy, free of disappointment. "You're this total sexpot, so I was embarrassed to admit the truth, and I didn't want you to feel like you couldn't share your spicy stories with me. I live for those, you know."

She rubs her lips together, then gives them a pop. "Is it a religion thing? Nerves?"

"Personal reasons, I guess."

"Okay," she nods. "I won't pry." In a contrast to her claim, she pries the pillow from my lap and points at my cell phone still tucked between my thighs. "However, I *will* pry in this department. Read his text."

I pull my legs apart, marginally, allowing the phone to slip deeper into hiding.

"Lucy!"

"Okay, okay," I relent, reaching into the dark cavern of my sweatpants and fishing out the phone. My gut bubbles with anxiety and inexperience as I spot the new notification.

One eye open, one snapped shut, I swipe at the screen.

CAL:

I have missed you. You miss me?

Omigodomigod.

Is he flirting? Is he drunk?

Either way, the juncture between my thighs throbs, my pulse revving with something entirely foreign to me. I'm not even sure what I should say, but my fingers have a mind of their own.

ME:

Yes.

Then I chuck my phone across the room, terror seizing me. "I don't know what I'm doing, Lys. I'm an awkward mess of a human being."

Alyssa looks far too giddy for such a dark moment, but then her tipped lips soften. "You're not a mess, babe. You have the biggest heart out of anyone I know. You're kind, generous, funny, and absolutely stunning. That's what *he* sees. That's what we all see."

I bury my face between my palms, hiding my fear, my misplaced insecurities, my soul-deep worry that sex equals love and love equals loss and loss equals being stripped of everything golden.

Loss gives the scatheless scars.

Loss is a vitality sucker.

People mostly just exist after loss and sometimes they don't even realize it. They stop noticing when the leaves change. One day, those leaves are green and vibrant, drinking in the dayspring, and the next moment they're rusty brown, and then they're dead.

And we don't notice.

Those leaves have always just looked dead.

I felt this way for years, so I understand it. It still lives in me as this little black hole I'm constantly filling with laughter and good people and daydreams.

But I get it, I do, and I refuse to be responsible for it.

"Thanks, Lys," I finally reply, adding her flurry of compliments to that black hole until it has no choice but to close up and put its teeth away.

I have a charmed life. A blessed life.

And the tangled, ugly roots of loss have no business leaching.

Alyssa falls asleep on my couch a while later, slipping into a wine coma and snoring into the palm of her hand. I smile at the image, considering snapping a photo of her dribble of drool, but choosing to give her grace. Instead, I drag myself from the sofa and put myself to bed, snatching my phone off the floor in the process.

Part of me wants to ignore that little notification bubble I know is waiting for me.

But the bigger part opens his message before my dreams whisk me away to endless summers in which the leaves never die.

CAL:

:)

There is bad luck, and then there is worse luck.

And then there is the kind of luck that can't even be cataloged.

Like a category six hurricane.

One would think that a severe hand laceration and two weeks out of work would be an adequate amount of suffering for one person, but the universe did not agree.

My house flooded.

My perfect new house flooded after the water heater burst sometime in the night after Alyssa slept off her Merlot and headed home. I made the discovery shortly before five a.m. when I woke up to let the dogs out and traipsed through inches of standing water in my fuzzy socks. Since the water heater is located in the small laundry room off the kitchen, which borders the living area, my entire main living space has been compromised.

Ruined, really.

I tried not to have a breakdown as I fed the dogs outside, forcing the sobs strangling my chest to morph into delirious laughter. My neighbor was sitting on his deck with a mug of coffee, sending peculiar glances in my direction, so I waved madly through the cry-laughter and stretched a smile so wide, I'm sure I looked maniacal.

He hasn't formally met me yet.

And now, he never will.

I decide to drag the dogs with me to work that morning because I can't leave them alone in this mess, and Mom hasn't answered my calls because her definition of retirement is sleeping in.

I'm in such a rush, and unwilling to trek through the flooded carpet to my bedroom that morning, that I pull a box marked

"Goodwill" out of my coat closet and throw on what I feel like qualifies as a presentable outfit. It's a white t-shirt with a sunshine design that says, *"What sunshine is to flowers, smiles are to humanity."* I pair it with stretchy leggings, knowing everything is a few years old, but they still seem to fit okay despite the shirt being a little on the snug side.

Combing my hair into a high ponytail with my fingers and smearing on lip balm, I head out the door.

Luckily, my mother calls me as I'm pulling into the parking lot. I breathe a sigh of relief and connect her through the Bluetooth.

"Lucy? Sweetheart? Are you at the hospital? I'm never sleeping in again," she rambles. "I've been reminding you to stop putting off your doctor appointment. Where are yo—"

"Mom, please, calm yourself. You're spiking my anxiety." This is why I shouldn't leave her voicemails consisting solely of, *"Call me as soon as you get this."* Mom is going on the fritz. "My house flooded. Can you call Uncle Dan and see if he can come by today?"

"The gutters were clogged, weren't they? I knew it."

"No, it hasn't rained in weeks. The water heater burst."

"Are you okay? And my furry grandbabies?"

"We're fine, but I might need a place to crash for a few days until Uncle Dan can get this taken care of. Do you mind?"

It's a silly question. She minds as much as she minds deep-tissue massages followed by mimosas on the beach while waiters that look like a young Pierce Brosnan bring her never-ending bowls of ceviche.

"I'll get the guest room ready. We can make those vegetarian porcupines you love for dinner. I'll see if I have the ingredients on hand."

"Thanks, Mom. Let me know what Uncle Dan says."

"I'll call him right now."

We say our goodbyes and disconnect, then I take a quick moment to convince myself that this is not the end of the world. This is fine. This is okay.

I wanted to replace the floors anyway.

This is a good thing.

New floors are good.

Skimming my fingers through my ponytail, I repeat this over and over until it sticks.

Yay! My house flooded! Best day ever!

The peptalk seems to lift my spirits, so I shuffle inside the shop with Kiki and Lemon, one-handed, and secure my smile into place, even though my dogs are already barking their heads off and pulling on the leashes so hard I almost face-plant.

"What the hell?" Cal is standing behind the desk when he spots me lumbering through the main door trying not to trip over two corgis that have no business being in an auto shop.

I was also so frazzled that I put my shoes on the wrong feet.

So, that's not helping.

"Good morning!" I breeze as Kiki makes a beeline for Cal, and Lemon hops up onto a waiting room chair and settles in like it's her new throne.

Dante and Kenny poke their heads out of the break room. "Are we doubling as a doggy daycare now?" Kenny wonders amusedly. "Shit. I'll bring my Malamute tomorrow. Bet he'll scare off all the asshole customers."

I wince. "My house flooded. I panicked."

Cal looks pissed, but he still crouches down to give Kiki the belly rubs she's begging for. My shameless animal literally plopped down at his feet, rolled onto her back, and spread her stubby legs for him in an instant.

"I'm really sorry," I continue, chewing on my thumbnail, then puffing my cheeks with air. I'm not sure what to expect from Cal today, considering it's the first time I've seen him since my impromptu hospital visit and our subsequent bordering-on-flirty text messages. Maybe if I didn't bust in here with a zoo, he wouldn't be looking like he wants to fire me. "I wasn't sure what else to do and had to think quick. I was hoping I could keep them in the break room. Their dog beds are in the car—I'll take them out for potty breaks and clean up any messes."

"It's fine," Cal grumbles, straightening before stalking toward me. He swipes off his burgundy beanie, ruffles his hair, then puts it back on. His face is blank, showing zero indication of the smiley face he sent me eight hours ago. "What's the damage?"

I pop my shoulders, trying not to let the feeling of blinding defeat pull me under. "To be determined. I'm hoping my uncle can take a look today—he's a contractor. All I know is that the kitchen and living room are totally unlivable at the moment, and my pretty new Home Goods rug looks like it was discovered at the bottom of the ocean during a deep-sea diving expedition."

"Come stay with me for a few days."

"Yeah, I—" *Wait, what*? Blinking a thousand times, I say, "Wait, what?"

Cal looks totally blasé, his demeanor nowhere close to matching the magnitude of his unexpected invitation. "I've got a spare room I hardly use. Fenced yard for the dogs."

"No...no, don't worry. That's too generous."

"It's practical."

I swallow, the idea of shacking up with Cal for an unknown number of days causing my left eyebrow to twitch. "I'm staying with my mom. It's all taken care of."

"Isn't she forty-five minutes away?"

"Yes."

"Not practical. I live a mile from the shop."

Scratching at my collarbone, my eyes skate around the room as I try to think of something to say. I feel blindsided by the offer. "I – I don't mind the long drive. Really. I'm up early, anyway, so it's not a big deal—"

"We'll swing by your place after work so you can grab clothes or whatever other shit you need. I have a kitten, so hope that's fine."

I start blinking crazily again. "You have a kitten?"

"Yeah. Cricket."

Cal has a kitten.

Cranky, unapproachable, tattoo-covered Cal has a kitten named Cricket.

My reproductive parts perk up with interest in the same way Kiki does when she spots a squirrel in the yard.

I'm so distracted by this new development that I completely miss my window to contest, and Cal takes my silence as surrender.

"You can follow me to my place after you grab your stuff.

We'll order in food."

He moves back toward the desk while I nibble on my lip, avoiding the knowing glances from Dante across the room. "Um, okay. Just give me a minute to call my mom and let her know the change of plans."

"Yep."

Gulping infinity times, I rush around to get my pets settled in the break room after Kenny grabbed the beds from my car and I filled plastic bowls with food and kibble. I pray they don't bark the whole time as I whisper sweet-nothings to them, mentally preparing for the conversation with my mother.

I decide not to overthink it and click on her name in my recent contacts. "Hey, Mom. Change of plans."

"Oh God, are you on your way to the hospital?"

My lips vibrate when I let out a sound of exasperation and pinch the bridge between my eyes. "No, I'm fine. But I actually won't be coming by after work because...um, Cal offered me his spare bedroom to stay in. It's only a mile from work, so it makes sense."

Silence answers me, eventually broken by a faint, "Oh?"

"Yes, but I'll definitely come by this weekend so we can make those porcupines. I was really looking forward to it."

"I didn't realize you two were intimately involved."

I almost drop the phone, my eyes bulging at the assessment. "What? How did you come to that conclusion?"

"I wasn't born yesterday, Lucy."

"Well, that's not the case. At all. Not even a little."

"Okay."

"Mother. It's not."

"*Okay*, sweetie. Just...keep me posted," she says, sighing into the receiver. "Your uncle will be over after his morning appointment today. I gave him my spare key."

Massaging my temple with two fingers, I nod, grateful for the subject shift. And for Uncle Dan. "Thanks, Mom. I love you."

"Love you most."

When I hang up and slide the phone into the waistband of my too-tight leggings, Cal is behind me looming in the doorway. I turn, feeling his eyes on me, and discover him leaning against the frame with his arms crossed and a subtle smirk on his face. "What?" I probe, my throat tight. He has a look like he's remembering the smiley face.

"She thinks we're sleeping together."

How?

How does he always do that?

He sees me start to fluster and cuts in. "Your mother always talks like she's trying to speak over a pod of sperm whales partaking in a fire drill. I heard."

Why?

Why did he have to say sperm?

I'm even more flustered when I reply, wiping my clammy palms along my backside and blowing my chaos ponytail out of my face. "Well, she's just nosy. You know this."

"Yeah, I do. Can't forget the time she practically broke down your bedroom door, convinced I was trying to sully your preteen innocence."

Even though that moment was humiliating, I can't help but bark out a laugh. "You were only helping me with my spelling bee words."

Cal bites his bottom lip, sliding it between his perfect teeth. "Right."

The look he shoots me sends a flurry of flutters down south, then he pulls up from the doorjamb and steps out.

I heave in a breath, unable to prevent the smile from tipping my lips.

Cal holds the notebook just out of reach, listing off words as he leans against my cotton candy pink headboard with a ballcap shadowing his features. "Leisure," he reads off.

"L-i-e-s-u-r-e."

"Wrong. E before I," he quips.

"What? It's always I before E except after C."

"That's a web of lies. Erase that from your brain."

"English is hard," I whine.

Shrugging his shoulders before squaring them, his eyes roam over the spiral notebook. They glance up at me, glinting with some-thing like mischief. "Have," he says.

I blink, confused, but I spell it anyway.

"You."

I spell it, still lost. These are not my spelling bee words, I'm sure of it. These were sight words when I was in second grade.

"Ever."

"Cal, what are you doing?"

"Spell it, Lucy."

"Ugh," I say, but I do.

"Been."

He's being infuriating and wasting time.

Still, I spell it.

Then he glances up again with only his glittering light brown eyes, long lashes tickling his brow line. He bites his lip in a strange way and says, "Kissed."

My heart slams against my ribs, my thirteen-year-old brain going haywire. I study him, seeing the question staring back at me.

Everything feels warm. My skin, my throat, my nerves.

Moistening my desert-dry lips, I squeak out the letters, one by one, watching as he lowers the notebook and scoots closer to me on the bed.

"K-i-s-s—"

My bedroom door barrels open, revealing my mother in her lavender bathrobe, pointing a disapproving finger in my direction as Cal and I jump to our feet like the mattress just caught on fire.

"Lucille Anne Hope!"

CHAPTER 12

10/04/12
"Fireflies"

The thing I miss most about summertime is the fireflies.

Fireflies, lightning bugs, glowworms.

Campfires are warm and bright, but they don't replace the magic of little lanterns lighting up the backyard when the moon crests. I sometimes make wishes on them. I sometimes catch them in glass jars. I sometimes name them because things without names are just things.

And I always miss them.

Tonight I curled up on my window bench and stared out through the glass, missing the fireflies...

So I named the stars instead.

Toodles,

Emma

I'm nervous when I pull into Cal's gravel driveway and the rocks smash beneath my tires like a fist around my lungs.

He parks his bike under the attached carport and removes his helmet, sliding his eyes to me through the windshield when I make no effort to exit my vehicle.

I need a minute.

I need a minute to drink in his landscaping and shutters and the front door that I never expected to be red. Red doors are welcoming, somehow, and Cal is...

Well, Cal is a gray door.

Cloudy and overcast, in dire need of sunshine.

Maybe the house just came with a red door, I decide, just like my house came with Emma. Maybe cheerful things simply have a way of finding people.

It's a tiny ranch-style house, similar to mine, but even smaller. The bricks are ruddy and brown as opposed to my honey-yellow bricks, and the shrubbery is overgrown with dying weeds and a singular wooden ghost decoration that sticks out of the wood chips. I recognize it. It's old and weathered, purchased from a pumpkin farm years ago when Emma spotted it and named it Mr. Boo-tiful.

God, he still has that?

My eyes water, knowing he probably snatched it from one of his mother's overflowing tubs of Halloween décor, and that he takes the time to display it every October.

I'm so lost in the sentiment that I don't notice Cal standing right outside my driver's side door, hands loosely planted on his hips, eyebrows arched in question.

I snap back to reality and kill the ignition.

The dogs go wild when I open the door, trampling over my lap and darting from the vehicle to circle Cal's ankles.

"Sorry, I spaced," I laugh lightly, reaching for my overnight bag stuffed with a few outfits, Halloween pajamas, toiletries, and a bottle of white wine I panic-grabbed from atop the refrigerator. I figured I might need it to get through this first night with less nerves than I usually have—which, admittedly, is still a lot.

Cal bends to collect both leashes before my animals take off down the sidewalk in search of squirrels and chipmunks to terrorize. "It's not exactly a bed and breakfast, but hopefully it'll do," he tells me, scratching at his mess of hatless hair. There's a pinch of humbleness that claims his eyes, as if the accommodations might not be up to my standards.

I don't hesitate to say, "It's perfect." He takes my bag from me with a nod, hoisting the strap over his big shoulder as I join him in the driveway.

"Come on, we'll get you settled," he says before sauntering ahead, arms full of my belongings.

When we step through the red door, I'm instantly ambushed by the smell of him. Earth and spice and a hint of amber floating off a bottle of diffuser sticks resting in the center of his coffee table.

My dogs take off when Cal unhooks their leashes, sniffing and discovering, and abandoning us in the entryway.

That's when I'm ambushed by something else entirely.

Something that blindsides me.

Tackles me.

Steals every stunned breath from my lips.

Cal already knows why I've locked up and drifted away with both hands clasped over my heart. Slipping out of his boots, he kicks them to the side like he's trying to kick the discovery I made out of my mind. "I don't want to talk about that."

"Cal..."

"I'm serious, Lucy. Dead serious. Forget about it."

I can't, I won't, I never will.

It's a piano.

Emma's old piano sits in the corner of his living room, nearly taking up the entire space, just as *she's* taken up the entirety of my soul since the day she dragged me over to their yard while Cal dribbled a basketball in the driveway. It's draped with thick black velvet, the cherrywood legs peeking beneath the fabric. Sheathed in dust, and likely not touched for years, it just sits there.

Idle and songless.

Unforgotten, still preserved, yet missing everything it's meant for.

Just existing.

He doesn't want to talk about it, but I don't care. I *need* to talk about it. "Do...do you play?" I murmur, my mind in a trance.

"No."

I peel my eyes away from the instrument and swing them over to the man. Cal is, as expected, stone-faced and close-grained. He looks at me though, finding my gaze through the dimly lit foyer and the thickening wall of tension.

Off my glossy stare, he lets out that long sigh I'm all too familiar with, then scrubs a palm up and down his face.

"I can't even look at it," he admits, tone softer. "But my house is so fucking small, it's all I see. Every day. And I can't stomach the thought of getting rid of it."

I'm nodding through each word because I understand, and I empathize, and I want him to keep talking.

"Mom had it for a while, but..." His jaw tics with trapped emotion. "She can't."

I swallow, still nodding, before I turn back to the veiled piano. When I lift my eyes a fraction, my attention lands on a framed art print hanging directly above it. It's a canvas of a midnight blue sky sprinkled with twinkle lights, a quote etched across the front:

Beautiful things never last,
and that's why fireflies flash.

The tears hit me hard.

A collision of love and loss—which is, ultimately, just a potent entanglement called grief.

I hear Cal walk forward, his footsteps lighter when he's sans his boots and armor. He's right behind me, his warm breath tickling the hairs on the back of my head as he whispers, "Don't, Lucy."

It's less demand, more defeat, but that only has my tears falling faster. I swipe at them, not wanting him to see me any less than the cheery ball of sunshine he's come to know, but my shoulders are trembling, giving me away.

"It's just some quote I found."

He says it like it's nothing, but it's not nothing.

It's so much more than nothing, and I'm crushed by the weight of everything it is, like there's a giant boulder strapped to my chest.

"I'm okay," I tell him, sniffling and swiping. "I'm fine."

A few heartbeats pass between us before I let the moment go, packing it away so the black hole doesn't get hungry. Cal never touches me, but he's so close, it feels like he does. I wonder if he wants to. I wonder if he wants to wrap his arms around me and draw me to his chest, holding me like I've always held onto him.

I'd let him.

I wouldn't pull away if he wanted to just hold me forever.

Instead, he releases a final sigh into my hair and steps back, forgoing an embrace for a distraction. "I, uh, don't have a ton of dinner options, but we can order in. Pizza, Chinese, whatever."

"Sure."

Sure, fine, okay.

We'll wade in the shallow end where nothing can nibble at our ankles.

We'll stay behind the yellow tape so we don't see things we can't unsee.

Slowly, I turn around, hoping my eyes aren't raw and puffy. Hoping the smile I've slapped on looks authentic. "What do *you* want?" I ask him, referencing his dinner request.

The melancholy in his eyes flickers into something more biddable. He crosses his arms, focus skipping over my shoulder before panning back to me. That's when a tiny little smirk blooms. "That's a loaded question."

Flush settles into my cheekbones as a glimmer lights up his face. Not quite a shimmer, but more than a gleam.

Since we're floating in the shallow water, I choose not to drown in his innuendo. "How about Thai food?"

"That works." Cal gives me a quick nod and pivots away, flip-

ping on a table lamp as he stalks through the living room and into
the adjoining kitchen where the dogs are sniffing around like
pirates on a treasure hunt. I follow behind him, tucking my now-
loose hair behind both ears. The mood has lightened, but it's far
from light, and I don't know what to do with myself. It's
different at work when I have job-related blather I can fall
back on.

Unless I'm talking about clitometers.

But here, it's personal.

Here, it feels...*intimate.*

There's history, and things unspoken, and a piano-shaped
elephant in the corner of the room, and there's also—

A kitten.

There's a kitten sitting on the countertop in his galley
kitchen, almost camouflaged by the cream laminate. I knew this,
yes, but amid all the heaviness, it managed to slip my mind.

Cal glances over his shoulder as he finally deposits my duffel
on his dining table. "Told you I had a kitten. She's still a little shy,
so don't take offense."

"Oh my God, she's precious."

And then—*and then*—Cal scoops her up, this itty-bitty ball
of ivory fur held snugly in his vein-lined, ink-spattered arms of
steel, and I swoon.

I actually, legitimately *swoon.*

"You're swooning," Cal says.

The kitten wiggles from his grip to climb his chest, stretching
her chocolate-speckled paws over his shoulder. My eyes are surely
shaped like animated hearts as I watch them interact. "I – I'm
sorry, I just...you didn't strike me as the type of guy who had—"

"A beating heart?" he provides in his typical deadpan way.
"Well, surprise, I do."

"That's...not what I meant," I grin, ducking my head.

"It is, but it's fair. I need to stop being an asshole, or you're
never gonna like me."

When I pop back up, Cal is staring at me like it was a question. There's a kitten digging its sharp little talons into the cords
of his neck, but he doesn't seem to notice—he's just watching
me. Waiting for an answer to the non-question.

I wet my lips and say, "I already like you."

It was supposed to sound sweet and reassuring, like, "hey, you're not an asshole," but it comes off like I just told him to tie me to his bedpost, strip me bare, and call me his very good girl.

Oh.

And now I'm imagining that scenario in vivid detail.

Cal inches closer, peeling Cricket off his shoulder as he levels me with a look that falls somewhere between playful and heated. "Yeah?"

His tone matches the look in his eyes, and I moisten my lips again, watching as he tracks the gesture before slowly sliding his gaze back up. Warmth trickles through me, twisting my nerves into a tingly feeling that has me squirming where I stand.

Our text messages from the night before spring to mind, and I start to fidget with the ends of my hair. "Your text last night..." I begin, gnawing on my lip, knowing I'm opening a can of worms or Pandora's box. Possibly my legs, but probably not. Something is opening; that's all I know. "You said you missed me while I was out on leave." I brave direct eye contact. "Did you really?"

He doesn't hesitate to nod, stuffing one hand into his pocket while the other holds Cricket underneath his arm. Then he says, his voice threaded with a deep timbre, "Yeah...I do."

I *do.*

Not *did.*

Cal misses me.

Those tingles race through me, lighting me up like a thousand enchanted fireflies as Cal moves out of the kitchen with a kitten tucked under his armpit and two corgis trying to climb his legs like a tree trunk.

He glances back at me standing frozen in his kitchen and mutters, "I'll pull up the menu for that Thai place off Broadway. What do you want?"

I smile and join him, even though I'm mentally racing toward my hidden stash of wine.

That's a loaded question.

I finished the wine.

I don't exactly regret the decision because I feel fantastic, but I'll probably regret the decision in the morning when I *don't* feel fantastic and am forced to replay every embarrassing, tipsy thing I did in front of Cal—who is sitting beside me on the couch, a few beers deep. He had a glass of wine, too, but I think it was only to prevent me from having it.

I hiccup.

His two long legs stretch out across the carpet as we attempt to watch a movie in his finished basement beside his collection of work-out equipment. I say "attempt" because I haven't caught a single minute of it. I'm too busy staring at Cal beside me, my cheek propped up by my fist, and a slap-happy grin on my face.

"What?" he finally asks, catching me ogling him.

I know I said I was staring, but I'm definitely ogling. Then I start to laugh. "Ogling," I snicker.

"Ogling?"

I giggle even harder, lurching forward, unable to catch my breath. "Oh my God. That is such a funny word." I'm wheezing when I lift back up with tears in my eyes. "Don't you think?"

"I think you had too much Riesling."

"No such thing," I pout.

"There is, actually. Why did you have three glasses?" He twists toward me on the couch, and our knees brush together.

I feel overstimulated, so the gesture causes my heart to thump harder. Clearing my throat, I admit, "You make me nervous, so I thought it would help."

His eyes narrow. "I still make you nervous? It's been two months."

"I know, but you just have this...*thing* about you."

"Clarify."

Inadvertently, I slide closer to him on the couch, noticing the way he resituates, stiffening slightly as the gap between us thins. When I drop my hand from my cheek, it plants itself atop his knee. Cal glances at my hand, then back up, shadows and embers coexisting in his eyes.

I'm feeling bold, thanks to the alcohol warming my blood. Normally, I'm too scared to even make eye contact with Cal, but now I'm actively touching him. He doesn't move away, and neither do I. "Well, you're sort of intense."

The muscles in his cheeks twitch as he skims my face. "Okay."

"And big."

"Okay," he parrots.

"And hard...hard to read, I guess."

And just like that, a half-smile lifts. "So...my *thing* is intense, big, and hard. Got it," he quips, swinging his gaze to my mouth for the tiniest second. "You're not wrong."

My brain registers his comment like its sludge trying to slither its way down a clogged drain. Then I start blinking wildly, my eyes popping. "Wait. Is this a penis thing?"

Cal lets out a burst of air that might be his version of a laugh, and ducks his head, shaking it back and forth.

"Is it?"

"Jesus, Lucy."

"No, but is it?"

Raising his chin, that little smile still lives within the corners of his mouth; a miraculous thing, like lightning bugs in the dead of winter. But it soon fades, replaced by something heavier. Something that has the tingles returning tenfold.

Something that makes me nervous.

Cal lifts an arm, placing his palm over the back of my hand— the one that still cups his denim-clad knee. A calloused thumb grazes over my knuckles, triggering a shot of arousal to my core.

I suck in a breath, zoning in our clasped hands. I wouldn't say I'm drunk, but I'm definitely buzzed, and the heat from our proximity could double as me being trapped inside a burning building.

No, maybe I *am* drunk. I'm drunk on the feel of his hand on mine.

"Lucy."

His voice is all deep timbre again, the pull of it drawing my eyes to his.

And then...he's *actually* pulling me.

In a blink, his hand is curled around my wrist, and I'm being rocketed into his lap like I weigh no more than a dandelion seed caught in the wind.

Oh my God.

I'm straddling him.

The wine daze has me nearly blacking out as my hands latch onto his shoulders for steadiness, so I don't collapse across his chest.

I can't look at him. I can't look at—

"Look at me."

A long finger tips my chin up until I have no other choice. I suck in a sharp breath. My nails dig into the tops of his shoulders, my chest heaving with the weight of something I don't understand. Cal leans into me, and my eyelids flutter closed, lashes fanning across my cheekbones until I feel his lips caress the shell of my ear.

"You should be nervous around me, Lucy," he rasps softly. Our pelvises are flush together, our heartbeats synchronized. "You're so fucking beautiful, it hurts."

I'm feathery, floaty, utterly weightless.

I'm sinking.

I'm nothing and everything, lost to what we were and what we could become.

I won't let him kiss me, though—I won't.

I can't.

Kissing is a gateway to all the things that will destroy me— destroy *him*.

Jessica's name tramples through my mind, haunting me, reminding me. She's my own personal ghost. I bet her story started with a kiss, too.

His warm, full lips graze down the edge of my jawline until he whispers, "I'm not going to kiss you."

Those words have my eyes popping back open with something that feels like disappointment. I know it's ridiculous because *he can't kiss me*, but the feeling is still raw and real.

I swallow.

"Not now," he explains. "Not when there's a chance you

might forget how good it's going to feel when my tongue is inside you."

Holy crap.

I tremble in his lap and manage to croak out, "See? Intense."

Half of his mouth lifts up. "Big," he adds.

Something like a steel pipe teases the juncture between my thighs and a shiver crawls down my back. But I can't seem to get that third, indecent adjective out. "Okay," I murmur instead. My tongue slicks over my lips as I nod in slow-motion. Then I blurt, "The wine wants to know why you haven't had sex in two years?"

Smirk still in place, Cal grips me around the waist with two impossibly strong hands and picks me up off his lap, placing me on the ground as we both rise from the couch. "A conversation for another night," he says, gradually releasing his hold on me. "Come on. I'll show you to the guest room so you can crash."

I feel like I might actually crash face-first over his kettlebell weights, so I reach for his forearm for balance as we make our way to the staircase.

Cricket is nowhere to be found when we ascend to the main level, but my dogs are quick to ambush us, trailing my heels while Cal guides me down the short hallway to one of the spare bedrooms. My duffel bag already sits in the center of the twin bed, housing a pair of embarrassing Halloween pajamas that are a surefire way to douse this flame crackling between us.

Nothing says, "*Take me now!*" like a giant pumpkin onesie.

"I'll let you change or whatever," Cal says, scratching at the back of his neck. "Sheets are all washed. I have an extra pillow if you need one."

Glancing around the quaint space, I smile, touched by the hospitality. "Thank you. I appreciate it," I tell him.

He gives me a quick sweep with his eyes, nodding. "You bet."

Then he turns to leave, closing the door behind him.

I drink in a deep breath to steady my balance, libido, and racing heart. Everything is in disarray. I'm not a huge drinker—usually just a glass of wine, or maybe two if Alyssa is instigating—so the three ultra-full glasses are sending me into a tailspin.

I was straddling Cal's lap.

Breathe, Lucy.

He wants to put his tongue inside me.

Breathe, Lucy!

God, I can't think about that. As soon as I'm sobered up, I'll have to tell him why we can only be friends, even though my body is still reacting to the feel of his hands on me, his lips against my ear, and his erection digging into my inner thigh.

Breathe, breathe, breathe.

Centering myself, I start digging through my overnight bag, searching for a distraction, and cringing when I pull out the onesie.

What was I thinking?

I guess I was going for comfort—as if I was heading up to Papa's bear cabin to play backgammon by the fireplace while the record player serenades us with Dean Martin's greatest hits.

Honestly, I have no idea what I'm doing.

I shake my head at myself and reach for the edging of my t-shirt, tugging it up my body in an attempt to replace it with the mortifying jack-o-lantern bodysuit.

Keyword: *attempt.*

I realize in a dizzying instant that it doesn't want to come off. Tugging and wriggling, I try to inch it up farther, but the damn thing won't budge. The shirt manages to get stuck around my breasts and shoulders, clearly two sizes too small.

It's fine.

This is fine, and there's no reason to panic.

I begin to sweat when I still can't get it off no matter how many times I twist my arms in a thousand different ways, and my heartrate escalates as I imagine myself trapped in this godforsaken state for all eternity. I should have burned the shirt the moment my boobs grew in.

Wishing I had taken my mother up on gymnastics lessons, I bend over and awkwardly shimmy, stretching my arms, and even sticking my foot in the center of the shirt to force it over my upper body.

It doesn't work, and the wine isn't helping my cause, so I immediately topple.

No. This isn't happening.

My ancestors have survived plagues, bears, and all those

diseases from *Oregon Trail*. I refuse to be wiped out by a fifty-percent polyester blend. But I consider letting that happen because the idea of just becoming a living, breathing clothes rack sounds more appealing than asking Cal for help.

Unfortunately, he must have heard my ass hit the floor, because he materializes through the door, to my utmost horror.

"What the fuck?"

"Nothing!" I yelp. I'm a misshapen, writhing pretzel on his guest room rug, and my grandma-bra is on full display. "Everything is fine."

"What the hell is happening?"

"I'm stuck in this shirt, but I got it." I huff and tug and twist. "I'll get it. Almost there. You can go."

Please go. I've already lost my dignity, so at least let me die in peace.

Cal does the opposite and moves toward me, reaching down to pull me to my feet and sit me on the bed. He just kind of stares at me for a few seconds, unblinking. "I don't even know what to say."

"Can you go? This is humiliating." My skin is sheened in sweat and decorated in pink splotches. My cheeks are fire engine red, and my hair looks like I was electrocuted a couple of times. "Cal, please."

"Christ...I'll go grab scissors."

He stalks out of the room before he sees my eyes bug out, the thought of anything sharp and pointy touching me causing me to panic further. When he returns a minute later, I'm near tears. "I'm sorry I'm such a disaster," I moan, blowing out a pathetic breath.

Cal's expression softens. "You say disaster, I say adventure. Turn around."

I do as he says, allowing the compliment to temper my climbing anxiety as he takes a seat beside me on the mattress.

Cool metal skims across my spine as Cal positions the scissors and carefully begins to snip at the fabric. "I see how attached you are to this shirt, so forgive the butchering I'm about to do."

A laugh slips. "Funny."

I try to keep as still as possible as he clips away, his unoccupied hand anchored at my waist. As he moves higher, his hand lifts, trailing up the length of my body until he's gathering my long mess of hair in a gentle fist and layering it over my shoulder to avoid potential chopping.

I shudder at the feel of his fingers gliding through my hair. For as rough as he comes across, his touch is gentle. Almost loving. Instinctively, I move into his hand, and instinctively, he keeps threading long fingers through my hair, over and over, until the shirt falls loose off my shoulders.

We both go still for a moment, his hand falling to my bicep, then skimming down to my elbow. I hear his breaths unsteady. I feel them heating the nape of my neck as his nose kisses the back of my head. I realize I'm sitting beside him in only a bra and leggings, right off the cusp of a lusty encounter on his basement couch. Tingles shoot and spark inside me as I anticipate his next move.

But all he does is inhale a deep breath, drop his hand, and stand.

"Get dressed and meet me on the deck." That's all he says before leaving me half bare on the bed, my shirt in shambles beside me.

I forgo the onesie, too wracked with embarrassment to add any more to it, and instead slip into a pair of skinny jeans and a sweater I had planned for tomorrow's work day.

When I tiptoe through the house and out the patio door a few minutes later, I discover Cal swinging languidly on a swing, front to back, back to front. Cricket is snoozing in his lap, a little ball of ivory and cream, while Kiki and Lemon are passed out on the wood planks near his feet. Kiki is sprawled out on her side, Lemon on her tummy with her snout tucked between both paws.

It's an image that won't ever leave me.

Picturesque and permanently ingrained.

I move forward, taking a seat beside him as he looks over at me with a half-finished beer tucked inside his palm. We don't say anything for a while. Only the sounds of a light breeze, our steady breaths, and wispy animal snores serve as a nighttime soundtrack.

Finally, I speak.

"You said I was an adventure," I note wistfully, sparing him a glance as I tug the sleeves of my sweater down over my palms. "I always thought the same thing about you. We'd get into so much trouble together, but it never felt like chaos. It was always...*fun*. Exciting. Those last few years before—" Emotion snags in the back of my throat, and I swallow it down. "Those were the best years of my life."

Cal makes a humming noise, rocking us forward and back with the soles of his shoes as he gazes out over the chain-link fence. "I think that's the difference between a disaster and an adventure," he says. "It's the people you experience them with."

Smiling, I nod slowly, soaking up his answer.

I can't help but inch closer to him until our shoulders brush together, my chest tight with the whispering of ancient memories. The remnants of my wardrobe malfunction fall away, as does the lingering heat of our lap encounter.

I just feel warm.

Content.

Safe.

Nostalgia grips me when I catch his eyes fixed on the star-studded sky. "Emma used to name the stars," I tell him, resting my head against his shoulder. I worry Cal will pull back, maybe leave me alone on the deck at the mention of his sister, but he doesn't.

He glances down at me, his face bathed in half shadow, half moon. "Let's name them, then."

A startled, overjoyed breath bursts from my lips, and my ensuing smile is organic, eyes misty. "Okay."

We name as many as possible while I curl up beside him on the patio swing and soon fall asleep. With my temple held up by the breadth of his shoulder, I drift into hazy dreams beneath the stars.

They aren't fireflies...

But they still give us a little light.

CHAPTER 13

It's a golden morning when I awake amid soft quilts and cool sheets. Cal's guest room drinks the daylight pouring in through the lone window beside my bed that serves as a much more tolerable alarm clock to the obnoxious jingle that came with my cell phone.

I dig the heels of my palms into my eyes and rub the sleep away before surveying the sun-drunk room. It's sparsely decorated and hardly furnished, but the bed is comfortable, and the pillows are top tier. They're the feathery down pillows that lull me to sleep the moment my head meets them.

I have an extra pillow if you need it.

I smile at his words. He wasn't just being casually hospitable —he was remembering. I always used to sleep with two pillows; never one, never three. It needed to be two, or I'd be restless and sleepless all night. With the amount of sleepovers shared between Emma and me, Cal became very aware of my strict pillow requirements.

Does he remember everything about me?

Like how I'd always put my shoes on the wrong feet?

Like my aversion to horror movies and how he'd force me to watch them while holding my hands away from my eyes during a scary scene, so I had no choice but to giggle and squeal?

Like my love for the Christmas season and how I'd always wear a light-up jingle bell necklace every day in December?

Like my addiction to lime-flavored things, such as Jell-O and Skittles? I used to pick out the green candies and pop them into my mouth all at once. Honestly, I'm pretty sure the last time I felt truly betrayed was when I discovered the green Skittles had been changed from lime to green apple.

I wonder if he remembers those things in the same way I remember everything about him.

Sighing through my yawn, I rip the covers off and glance at the time on my phone.

7:02 a.m.

My eyes round at the notion that I managed to sleep in for once in my life. I'm almost always up by five, like clockwork. I start scrambling, throwing on the pair of jeans I'd discarded after meandering inside at some point around eleven last night, opting to sleep in only an oversized t-shirt instead of the onesie. I pull a cinnamon-brown sweater over my head and smooth back the fly-aways before venturing across the hall to the singular bathroom to freshen up.

When I finally make my way into the main living area, Cal is perched at the kitchen table with a mug of coffee.

He's scrolling through his phone when he mutters without looking up, "Morning."

"Good morning," I breeze, glancing around the space for my dogs. It's not long before I hear them barking outside in the yard, then spot them hopping along the fence line trying to intimidate some poor squirrel. *Adorable heathens.* "Sorry I'm up so late. That bed was delightfully comfortable."

Cal lifts his chin, giving me a quick onceover. "Good."

Fidgeting near the step where living room meets dining room, I glance at the bowl of cereal in front of him sitting beside a half-gallon jug of chocolate milk.

A smile blooms. "You still do that."

"What?" he frowns, drawing the spoon to his mouth.

"Eat your cereal with chocolate milk."

His eyes dart to the box of Rice Krispies, then to the milk, then back to me. "It's delicious. Try it."

"Pass, but thank you. How many cereal combinations have you tried?"

"Close to all of them. This one is the best, followed by Cheerios. Corn Flakes are pretty solid, too."

My nose scrunches up. "Have you tried it with the fruity ones?"

"Yeah, they taste like citrus-fudge ass. Don't recommend."

Laughter spills out of me as I stroll forward, climbing the one step that separates the two rooms. I look around for Cricket, but she must be hiding. Hopefully, she gets used to me soon.

"I'm not really sure what to do with a person who doesn't drink coffee, but I have orange juice," Cal says through a mouthful of cereal. "Muffins are on the counter."

Sure enough, a plastic container filled with four banana-nut muffins stare back at me. I'm certain they weren't there yesterday. "Did you run out to get these?"

"Yeah," he says, taking a sip from his mug that reads, *"I'm a mechanic, not a fucking magician."* "Couldn't sleep, so I made a stop. I got a few things for dinner tonight in case your house isn't livable yet. You can stay as long as you need."

As he rises to his feet and closes the top of the cereal box, I stand stock-still near the counter with my wide eyes glued to him. My expression goes slack and soft, my heart glowing with affection. "That was really sweet, Cal. Thank you." Off his curt nod, I turn to open the muffin container, then ask curiously, "Why couldn't you sleep?"

He doesn't hesitate. Not even the slightest falter. "Because I couldn't stop thinking about you straddling my lap last night, or about that kiss I regret not taking."

My glowing heart ignites to inferno-level and nearly detonates inside my chest. Instead of reaching for a muffin, I grip the edge of the countertop instead, my back to him.

I have no idea how he manages to exude such a striking juxtaposition of relaxed intensity, but it never ceases to rip the air right out of my lungs. "Oh," I squeak out. "Really?"

"Yeah. What about you?"

"M-me?" My breath is a-quiver, my limbs shaky. "Did I sleep?"

He sighs from behind me, rustling something at the table. "No, I know you slept. Did you dream about the kiss I know you wanted as much as I did?"

Cal is still all casual dynamite, and I close my eyes as if I can't bear to look at his words. "We...we can't do that."

This has him faltering. A few silent beats pass before he says, "No?"

"I – I mean, it's not a good idea."

"Why? Because I'm your boss?"

I swallow, dipping my chin to my chest. I'm not sure how to tell him how inexperienced I am at nearly twenty-three years old. I don't know how to explain my deep, dark fears when it comes to intimacy, or fill him in on a girl I used to know named Jessica.

I have no idea how to confess that kissing him would be the tipping point to love.

And love?

Love has teeth.

Love will eat us both alive.

"It's not that. Well, that's part of it, I guess, but it's more than that, too. I just..." I squeeze my eyes tighter, confusion and indecision rattling my bones. I feel lost; out of my element. My words are scattered and unprepared. All I can manage is: "I can't."

I wait for his reply while anxiety crawls through me, but he doesn't say anything.

Not right away.

Cal finally comes up behind me, caging me in with one arm on my left, one on my right. His hands curl around the countertop beside mine, and his breath tickles my ear when he leans forward. "I know when a woman is interested, so I'm not going to pretend to understand your reasons," he murmurs, his broad chest flush against my spine. Swallowing me up. "But I'll respect them. If that's what you want."

All I can do is nod. I'm not sure which part I'm nodding at, but I'm afraid if I speak, I'll say all the wrong things. Everything I shouldn't say. I'll tell him that I *do* want him to kiss me, to love me, and to let that love sink its teeth into me, chew me up, and spit me out.

It's worth it for even the smallest bite.

Just a taste.

Truthfully, I don't know if Cal could ever love me—maybe he's only looking for a quick tryst. Someone to break his two-year dry spell. Sex, and only sex. But I know my own heart, and it's a heart that will undoubtedly fall in love with him as it already did once before, back when I believed Emma was the stars and Cal was the moon.

I loved them both.

My adventure people.

But there's a fine line between adventure and disaster, and I'm terrified I'll become lost in the blur.

"Thank you again for the muffins," I say quietly, cowardly. I glance down at his hands dwarfing mine, his thumbs dusting my pinkies. "We should get ready for work."

He makes something like a grumbling sound, dropping his forehead to the crown of my head for a split second before pulling away. "Right."

Cal stays out of my way for the rest of the morning, avoiding eye contact. Avoiding any contact. He doesn't say much when I let my dogs in and prattle on about how I rescued them from *Forever Young*, or when I inquire about where Cricket came from.

All he mumbles is, "Found her in a parking lot."

I can't tell if he's angry, or frustrated, or both, or maybe he's just resorting back to the Cal from two months ago because it's safer that way. I can't blame him for it, and I never meant to give him mixed signals. The signals inside of me just happen to *be* mixed.

And I'm not sure what to do about that.

Either way, we leave his house shortly before eight-thirty, me in my car and Cal on his bike, and the thrum of his engine vibrates through me like his words did in his kitchen:

Did you dream about the kiss I know you wanted as much as I did?

The truth is, I did dream about it.

I probably always will.

My mood brightens the moment I see the pile of boxes sitting outside the front door to the shop.

The t-shirts!

Cal steps around them, pushing through the entrance. "I'll grab those. Pull up the client list for the day," he says in his usual gruff tone before flipping on the lights.

I pick up one of the boxes anyway, shuffling inside with a smile. "The t-shirts are here," I exclaim in time with the jingle bells.

Cal just huffs and pulls a beanie out of his back pocket, situating it over dark windswept hair. Then he starts carrying in the rest of the boxes while I tear open mine.

I wouldn't say Cal was *against* me ordering t-shirts for the crew—and for selling to the clientele—but he was certainly *resistant*. It might have been the too-many hours I put into selecting a design and slogan, skipping through the bays with my handy notepad and surveying the guys for their opinions. It could have been the fact that Cal is allergic to the color yellow, which was, of course, my color of choice.

"Yellow is obnoxiously happy," he said to me, his tone bordering on disgust. "Pick a different color."

Spoiler alert: I didn't.

Ultimately, it's probably because Cal is resistant to most things, so the odds of him disagreeing or complaining about something are decidedly high.

Grin in full swing, I sift through the tissue paper and bubble wrap and dig down deep for the individually wrapped t-shirts to inspect my creation. When I pull one out, I'm beaming from ear to ear. "These look amazing!" I squeal, unfolding it and holding it across my chest to display.

Cal hardly spares it a full-second glance. "It's yellow," he gripes.

It's yellow and perfect.

"Cal's Corner" is scrawled across the top in bubbly letters, and a little wrench symbol rests just beneath it. Then, under that, is the slogan that won by a majority vote.

"Putting a Wrench In Your Day"

My grin broadens.

I love it so much, and I don't even care that—

Wait.

Pulling the shirt away from me, I drag it right up to my face and squint, rereading the slogan over and over, until realization dawns.

No.

No!

There's a typo. An awful, horrible typo, and Cal is going to kill me. Or fire me. Or both, but not in that order.

Maybe.

No, no, no.

He must notice something is amiss when I make a croaking sound and shove the t-shirt back into the box, folding it up like it never existed at all.

"What?" he says from behind the desk.

"Nothing."

"What is it?"

"I'll pull up the schedule for the day like you asked. You can get to work now. Bye." My redirecting skills need work, I know this, but I'm flustered and don't know what to do, so I shoo him away from the desk and take over the computer. "Oh, look, Roy has an eleven o'clock. Great."

"So does your boyfriend."

The t-shirts become nothing but a blip when I register his statement. Blinking half a dozen times, I turn toward him, my brows pinched together. "What? Who?"

"That bartender you were making eyes at after your show. The one who leaves you love notes."

"Nash? He's..." I shake my head, completely thrown. "He's not my boyfriend."

"No?"

"No."

Cal studies me hard for a few seconds, as if he's trying to unveil the lie that doesn't exist. "I figured he was."

"Well, he's not. I'm not into him like that. How do you even know it's him?"

Blowing out a breath, he looks away, stuffing both hands into his pockets. "He called to make an appointment yesterday while you were on break. Asked if you were working. I don't know many guys named Nash, so I put two and two together."

"Oh," I mutter, swiping the hair out of my eyes. "Okay. Maybe no other shops had availability."

"Or maybe no other shops had you." His eyebrow arcs.

I blush, not knowing what to say. It's true I told Nash about my new job position at Cal's Corner, and it's true he said he'd stop by to see me some time, but I thought he was just making conversation. Trying to be nice. I didn't think he'd *actually* show up.

Cal notices me flustering and pivots back to the t-shirts.

No, that's worse!

"So, what's wrong with the shirts?" he wonders, folding both arms over his navy muscle tee.

"Nothing."

"Lucy."

I untuck my hair, so it covers my reddening cheeks and just shake my head, clicking away at the keyboard. "Roy has an air filter problem again? How many times can that guy—"

"Lucy."

"It's fine, Cal. It's not a big deal. Just don't look at them."

Off that dubious instruction, he immediately lets out a sigh and saunters over to the box, pulling the tabs back open. I wince with every creak of plastic, waiting for his wrath.

And then—

"What the hell, Lucy?"

"I'm sorry, okay? I don't know what happened." My face is burning with shame. I positively *begged* Cal to let me design these shirts, and I failed.

I'm failing at everything.

I'm flailing while failing.

I'm a flailure.

"It looks like I operate a brothel," he snaps, releasing a half-sigh, half-growl. Cal tosses the shirt down before storming away, shaking his head as he makes his way to the service area. "Fix that."

"I will! Promise!" I call back, but he's already out of earshot, and the door slams shut.

Then I collapse onto the desk, forehead to forearms, cursing the printing company while simultaneously wondering if they did it on purpose just for laughs.

"Putting a Wench In Your Day"

I decide to put one of the t-shirts on, despite the mortifying typo. After calling the printing company, they offered to send out a batch of brand new shirts at no cost, and said to donate the faulty ones. I'm not sure what strangers out there would want to wear a shirt with the word "wench" on it, but maybe somebody. There's got to be somebody. Either way, I'm taking one as a souvenir, because after thinking on it for a few hours, it's actually fine. It's funny, even.

Plus, Roy Allanson legitimately *guffawed* when he read it aloud, and that was *after* he was made aware of his eight-hundred dollar bill.

He ended up buying three of them.

The guys laughed, too, all of them changing into the t-shirts and calling the error "brilliant" and "hilarious."

All of them except for Cal.

The curmudgeon.

I've hardly seen him since this morning, only brushing past him once in the break room when I went to retrieve my cheddar and honey sandwich and snack cup of lime Jell-O. He mumbled something about ordering new brake pads, and that was it. Radio silence ever since.

It's now ten-past-three, which is when Nash walks in to pick up his Chevy Blazer. I didn't get a chance to say hi this morning because Cal cornered him in the parking lot before he could even attempt to veer toward the entrance.

"Lucy," Nash greets, triggering the jingle bells as he steps inside the lobby. He wanders up to the front desk, mussing his hair, looking shy and cute.

I grin brightly. "Hey, you. Car trouble?"

"Oil change," he shrugs.

"Oh, wow. You made quite the trek. Don't you live out by the wine bar?" I pull up his invoice on the computer, and sure enough, all he got was an oil change.

"I do, but I told you I'd stop by. How are you liking it here?"

"I like it a lot, actually. The guys are great."

Swiping at his honeyed hair again, he peeks over at the garage area before stepping closer. "That was the guy from the show a few weeks ago, right?"

I blink through a nod, fiddling with the ends of my sweater sleeves.

"Are you guys...together?"

Clearly, there is something in the water today. Nash thinks I'm with Cal; Cal thinks I'm with Nash. Alyssa thinks I should bang them both. But, in reality, the only long-term relationship I'm in is with my dogs.

And carbs.

I shake my head, forcing a laugh as I break eye contact. "No, no. We're just friends. We grew up together." He gives me an odd look, a little ambiguous, so I keep going. "We're not even really friends, I don't think. He's not overly friendly. I mean, he is when he wants to be, but he doesn't usually want to be, so—"

"I think I got it," Nash cuts in with a chuckle, fishing out his wallet. "What's the damage?"

The emotional damage I cause myself by being myself?

Infinite.

The oil change?

"It'll be one-hundred-and-twenty dollars and fifty-five cents."

"Great."

As Nash sifts through the wallet for cash, the service door plows open, and Cal appears, wiping his grease-stained hands along his faded blue jeans. He comes up beside me and glances at the computer screen, not saying a word. All he does is hover, standing over me like a menacing shadow.

Then he swivels toward Nash with a glare and presses forward on the desk, palms down.

Clearing his throat, Nash hands me a wad of bills as he flicks his eyes between us. "So, uh, Lucy," he begins.

"Yeah?" I plaster a smile onto my face as I count the money, but I can't seem to count with Cal so close and so terrifyingly silent, so I end up recounting it five times before popping it in the drawer, still unsure if I did the math right.

Nash coughs into his fist, and then, "I was wondering if maybe you wanted to—"

"She doesn't want to," Cal interrupts.

Oh my God.

Cheeks heating, I immediately elbow Cal in the ribs, but he doesn't flinch. He's a brick wall. "What? Cal, go away."

Nash frowns. "She doesn't? And why is that?"

"Because I'm sleeping with her, that's why."

I go pallid.

My neck does a one-eighty *Exorcist* twist toward Cal as my already pink cheeks morph into fuchsia.

"Um." Nash scratches the back of his head, shifting between feet. "Beg your pardon?"

Cal crosses two big arms over his oil-stained t-shirt, his expression blasé. "I'm fucking her," he repeats. "Regularly. Aggressively."

"Cal!"

I'm mortified.

I'm leagues beyond mortified.

I'm not sure if there's a word for leagues beyond mortified, but it's probably dead.

I'm dead.

"I see," Nash says as his eyes flit back and forth between me and Cal. "My mistake."

"No, no..." I try, still futilely jabbing my elbow into Cal. "Nash, we're not—"

"All good. I'll take the receipt and head out. See you Friday." He smiles, but it's strained.

I'm so frazzled, I accidentally hand him a bake sale flyer decorated in smiley-faced scones that I grabbed on my lunch break, instead of his receipt. And because the moment couldn't possibly get any more awkward, he glances at it, happily accepts it, and turns around slowly to leave.

When the door shuts with a cheery farewell, I tent my hands and press them to my chin. I think I might hyperventilate.

"Breathe, Lucy. You look pale."

This—*this*—has my eyes pinging back open as I fling myself around in a circle to gape at Cal. "*What* was that?"

"What?"

I blink at him like I'm about to have a stroke. "Cal. You just humiliated me in front of—"

"A guy you said you weren't interested in. I did you a favor."

"You told him we were having aggressive sex."

"So?" He leans on the desk with one hand, shrugging, completely cool and collected. Acting like nothing even happened. "I gave you an out. You're welcome."

"An *out*?"

"Yeah, an out with him," he says. "Or an in with me. Whichever."

That smirk reappears, the one I've grown to crave, the one that makes me question my eternal vow of celibacy. And I can't help the rush of tingles to my nether regions, or the heart palpitations, or the belly flutters that feel like buzzing hummingbird wings as my mind instinctively races with images of taking Cal up on his...*in*.

Stop it, Lucy. He's being a brute.

But Cal notices the way my eyes flare, paired with my brief moment of hesitation, and his smirk broadens. Scrubbing a hand over his jaw, he saunters backward, away from the desk. "Your floors done yet?"

Tucking my lips between my teeth, I shake my head.

My uncle texted me saying he needed one more day.

Cal gives me a nod and turns around to head back toward the garage. "Good. See you for dinner."

And then he's gone, leaving me shaken and conflicted, but

ultimately fumbling for my cell phone inside my purse and making a split-second decision to call my mother.

"Lucy? Everything okay?" Mom wonders on the other end of the line.

I swallow and drink in a deep breath. "Yep, everything's great. How about those porcupines tonight?"

CHAPTER 14

The little Instagram icon that pops up on my notification bar has me doing a double-take. I hardly use the app, as I hardly use much of social media at all. It's too isolating, which is interesting, given its purpose is to connect and unite. My personal feed is limited to about a dozen posts over the past few years, consisting mostly of animals and nature.

There's a singular photo of me that Alyssa took one rainy, wine-inspired evening last spring when inhibitions were low, and spirits were high. It's a darker photo—more laughter lit than moonlit—and it's not exactly flattering with my wet hair plastered to both sides of my face as I close my eyes and scrunch up my nose through a slap-happy grin. Raindrops float along my lashes, a result of the downpour we were dancing in on Alyssa's condominium terrace.

It's one of those candid photos; the kind you couldn't recreate even if you tried. I ended up slapping on a black-and-white filter and uploading it to my feed, less because I wanted to and more because Alyssa begged me to show off her blossoming talent for cell phone photography with a tag and full credit. *But...* I'm glad I posted it. I pull it up sometimes when I need the reminder that everything is okay, I'm still breathing, and life is good.

And now, the photo has a new "like" from an account that recently followed me.

Curious, I click on the handle named **_oilandink**, which looks to be a newer account with a picture of a motorcycle as the profile image. One photo is posted to the feed, dated a little over a week ago, and I recognize it instantly.

It's a slightly blurry shot of two corgis and a sweet kitten all curled up together on a small cat bed. They are a ball of sable and cream, squished and content, and my heart races with pure adoration.

The picture is paired with a simple caption of a smiley-face emoji.

I give the photo a "like" and follow him back from my own account titled **everythinglime**. Then I investigate further, noting he has fifteen followers, but he only follows two of them back.

There's one comment under the photo that reads, "*Omggg Cal! I didn't know you had puppers and a kitty!*" along with a slew of cat-shaped heart-eyes emojis—to which he responded with, "*Dogs aren't mine.*"

I stare at the picture for a long time. Longer than necessary. Longer than I should, considering I'm on the clock and Cal is sauntering up behind me from his office mumbling something under his breath.

"Can't find that invoice folder," he says as he approaches.

Robotically, I reach for the folder lying beside me on the desk and hold it up. "You have an Instagram account."

"Am I viral yet?" he deadpans, snatching the manilla folder from my hand.

A smile pulls. "I didn't know you took that picture. It's so sweet." I brave a glance at him as I close out the app and toss the phone back into my purse.

Cal flips through the loose papers in the folder, brows bent with what could be either deep thought or irritation. The sleeves of his gunmetal-hued shirt are hacked off at the shoulders, highlighting big biceps and a canvas of ink stained with what looks like fuel oil.

He lifts his chin, eyeing me for a beat before sifting through more receipts.

Off his silence, I continue. "I didn't realize Cricket had warmed up to my dogs. Maybe she'll warm up to me, too, one day. I guess that would require us spending more time together..."

"Hm," is all he says.

It's more of an acknowledgement, really, less actual response.

When he pivots away from me, I blurt, "What are you doing tonight?" I don't think it through, because if I'd thought it through, I probably would have considered the fact that personal time with Cal outside of work is a dangerous, blurry line that I've been trying to avoid ever since our intimate rendezvous on his basement couch that hasn't been mentioned since the day I ditched his dinner invitation in exchange for visiting my mother.

I was a coward, I know.

I mean...I *think* I was a coward. Truthfully, I'm not sure if running from something you wholeheartedly believe to be an erroneous choice, while wholeheartedly wanting it anyway, is more cowardice or courage.

Either way, Cal took my running as rejection, which I suppose is understandable—even though I wasn't rejecting *him*, per se, but the thought of crossing that dangerous, blurry line with him.

What doesn't seem fair is the fact that he's hardly spoken to me all week unless he's barking orders or scolding me for something I may or may not have done.

And I miss him terribly.

Cal pauses his retreat, releasing a sigh as he scratches at the stubble on his cheek. "Why?"

"Well, there's this fall carnival going on all weekend—Harvest Fest. I was wondering if maybe you wanted to go," I swallow. "You know, with me."

He levels me with a look that says more than words.

The last time we went to a carnival together was with Emma. We'd been so young and carefree, popping tufts of pink and blue cotton candy into our mouths, eating churros until our bellies ached, and laughing atop the Ferris wheel, untouchable and unscathed.

We were high on life.

Buzzing with adventure.

Blissfully in love with everything under the stars. Everything the sun touched, and everything the moon kissed. In love with each other.

It was the weekend before Memorial Day.

The weekend before—

"I've got plans," he finally says.

Oh. I tinker with a loose wave of hair before flipping it over my shoulder. "Oh, sure, no problem. What are you up to? Anything exciting?"

"A date."

A date.

A date.

Anxiety nibbles at my insides, and then those teeth turn into sharp fangs and take a painful bite. I try to school my expression, keep it from wilting and dying as if the bite were poisonous, but Cal must notice a piece of me goes missing. Gets chewed right off.

Most men would most likely relish in such a reaction and poke further. Another jab.

A "*take that.*"

But Cal looks down at his dirty boots, then back up, and a softness glitters in his eyes as he shakes his head. "Sorry. I didn't mean it like that," he tells me, squaring his jaw. "I'm grabbing a drink with Jolene at Mallory's. Just catching up."

I'm not sure if that makes me feel entirely better, but the fact that he noticed the dark cloud fog my eyes and tried to temper the storm, does trigger the smallest of smiles. "Of course. Have fun."

"Yeah...you, too."

Cal gives me a nod, dragging his eyes over me, up and down, before turning away again.

I stop him.

I stop him because I didn't say everything I wanted to say.

"I guess I just..." Emotion sticks in the back of my throat, and

I feel silly for it. But it sticks there anyway, and I worry my lip between my teeth, averting my eyes as Cal comes to a stop one more time with his back to me. Then I breathe in deep and say on the exhale, "I just miss you."

I watch him stiffen to stone. The planks of his back ripple as he flexes a hand at his side, splaying his fingers before making a fist.

He doesn't look at me. Just stares at the floor and says, "I'm starting to realize...you can't miss something you never had."

And with that, he stalks away, disappearing into his office with the folder.

I feel even sillier when hot tears blur my vision, but all I can think, all I want to say is...

I did have you, Cal. I had you for eight beautiful years.

I'm sitting on the couch picking at a salad that evening, my stomach too knotted to enjoy much of it. As I flip through channels in an off-the-shoulder, ultra-fuzzy sweater—because fuzzy sweaters are the fashion choice for pain—my phone pings with a text message. Lemon's nose pops up from my lap as I wedge my hand between the cushions to locate it after purposely stuffing it there.

Blowing a piece of hair out of my face, I swipe at the screen.

CAL:

I'm outside.

It takes a moment for me to process his message.

My thumbs hover over the keypad as my eyes ping-pong back and forth between the two words. Then I jump to my feet, smooth down my uncombed hair, and race to the front window to peek through the blinds. Sure enough, Cal is standing outside my house, leaning against his motorcycle in a nutbrown leather bomber jacket and dark blue jeans, his arms crossed. Sans a hat, his hair is all windblown waves and disheveled sex appeal as he sweeps his fingers through it, occasionally glancing at the phone in his opposite hand. Sundown paints him in a muted gold and peach hue, softening his crags and chipped edges.

I gulp.

Fluffing my hair, I swerve to the front door and crack it open, catching his gaze across the lawn. "Cal."

His name vanishes within the draft that blows through, but he hears my question anyway.

"We're going to that harvest thing," he says, straightening from the bike and tucking his hands in the pockets of his coat. "Grab your stuff. I'll wait."

"But, I thought—"

"Grab your stuff, Lucy."

I'd say he doesn't need to tell me twice, but he clearly did, so I sprint into action, double checking water bowls, frantically fixing my mascara smudges, dancing through a cloud of pear and sugar-cane mist, and swapping my dog-hair leggings out for white-washed skinny jeans. Slipping into a pair of suede lace-up boots, I snag my purse off the wall hook and race out of the house, curving toward my Volkswagen.

"I'll drive," Cal says, taking one stride toward me and holding out the helmet. "It's not far."

I'm surprised when hesitation doesn't grip me like it did that first time, voided by the tingle of anticipation. I nod through a smile and join him at the bike as he gears up for the ride. Popping the helmet over my head, Cal turns to help me with the chin strap again.

I shiver when a calloused thumb grazes the line of my jaw. "So, um…what happened to your plans with Jolene?"

"Something better came up."

His tone is easygoing, like there was no other answer, but the way my heart picks up speed is anything but. "Was she disappointed?" I wonder.

I would be. I'd be dreadfully disappointed in a lonely, Cal-less evening—proven by my night of old sitcoms and fuzzy-sweater wallowing.

All he says is, "Nope."

Then I straddle the seat and scoot forward, twining both arms around him and clasping my palms at his abdomen. Similar to last time, he reaches behind him one-handed to tug me closer, only he grabs more ass than thigh.

And similar to last time, I lose a breath and try not to tremble.

"You good?"

"I'm good," I say, reiterating it with a squeeze.

We take off, and I'm lost to the engine purr, the autumn breeze filled with bonfire smoke and remnants of the afternoon rainfall, and the oaky notes of his cologne. His hair flies everywhere as if to mimic my heart, and I have to press my hands together even harder to avoid doing something stupid like letting go and dragging my fingers through it.

There's no taming it right now.

It's a ten-minute ride to the festival, and we park at the far end of the muddy lot as the scent of deep-fried everything tries to overpower the scent of him. Cal hops off the bike and takes the helmet from me to secure it.

We both hesitate, our eyes tangling, and I feel unprepared for the moment. Memories come careening back like a waterfall of lost time. I have to remind myself that I'm not that thirteen-year-old little girl whimsically in love with the boy next door, and that Emma isn't lacing her arm through mine to haul me toward the ticket booth with laughter in her eyes.

Instead, Cal rests his hand on the small of my back and guides me forward. It's enough to ease the sudden rush of melancholy. It's enough to make me smile.

"Thanks for doing this," I tell him, glancing up as we weave through the crowd. It's the final weekend before Halloween, so it's brimful of people eating taffy apples, pushing strollers through lumps of dying grass, and sipping plastic cups of cider.

He spears me with a look. "You say it like I felt obligated."

"Didn't you?"

"No. I wanted to."

I know he's not lying because I don't think Cal makes a habit out of doing things he doesn't want to do. The people-pleaser in me struggles to relate, but it gives me a surge of comfort, nevertheless.

"Where to first?" he asks, digging through his pockets for a piece of chewing gum.

I watch him unwrap the tiny yellow rectangle and pop it in his mouth. "That's nicotine gum, right?"

"Yeah," he nods as he chews. "I smoked for way too fucking long. I smoked to prevent myself from reaching for a bottle of pills, until I decided they were both shitty habits."

My heart stutters.

They aren't a lot of words, but he says a lot with them.

It makes me wonder about our lost years, our severed friendship, his struggles and weaknesses. Nothing about Cal screams *weak*—nothing about him strikes me as vulnerable.

But I know he has his demons, and they look a lot like mine.

It's fascinating how two people burned from the same experience can come out on the other side with completely different scars.

Normally, I'd pry into that confession and try to pull it apart, layer by layer, but the music in the air is light and the mood burdenless. So, I swallow down my interrogation and change the subject. "Well, let's grab something to eat first, then we can check out the rides."

"I still owe you one of those stuffed animal things. What was it? A hamster?"

Oh my God.

I'm not sure whether to laugh or cry, so the sound I make sounds like a weird mix of both. "A mouse," I correct him.

It was giant and hot pink, and had a belly decorated in rainbow stars. Emma saw it first and named it Pinky. Once it had a name, it had to have a home.

Cal tried *all night* to win that mouse for me, perching himself at the basketball free throw station, while furiously throwing balls into a swiftly moving net. He was a freshman basketball star, after all, so the fact that he couldn't make enough baskets to win me the toy had him downright *enraged*.

Emma and I both eventually dragged him away from the

game before he imploded, forcing him onto the Ferris wheel to cool down.

And *that* turned out to be a moment that will live inside of me forever.

We got stuck.

Right at the top, right among the stars, with Emma squealing in the bucket below us.

I still see her staring up at us with a galaxy of freckles on her nose and dark hair flying around her face as the wind nearly choked us.

"Kiss her, you chicken!"

I jolt back to the present moment when Cal's fingers lightly graze my elbow. "Where'd you go?"

The Ferris wheel lights become blurry, and I realize tears are sneaking up on me.

Not here, not now.

Shaking my head, I force a big smile and avert my attention from the wheel. "Thinking about how many basketballs it'll take for you to win me a prize this time," I tell him.

Cal knows exactly where I went, but he doesn't poke. Looking over my shoulder at the row of carnival games, he cracks his knuckles. "Can't say I haven't been preparing for this moment of redemption."

"It's haunted you, hasn't it?"

"In the worst way."

I giggle. "First, deep-fried Oreos, then we can sell our souls for a dollar-store plushie."

We amble up to the food vendor and step in line as the breeze picks up. In my rush out the door, I didn't bother to grab a jacket, and the balmy sixty-degree day has plummeted into the low fifties. Swiping at the goosebumps prickling beneath my sweater sleeves, Cal doesn't hesitate to slide out of his jacket and wrap it around my shoulders.

"You forgot your coat," he states the obvious.

I'm immediately warmed, but it's less because of the added layer and more because of the way Cal steps into me, carefully helping my arms into the armholes before sliding his hands down the length of them. He wavers briefly when our fingers brush, like he's thinking about linking them together, but he clears his throat and inches back instead.

"Thank you," I say with sincerity, swallowed up by the leather and lingering aroma of earth and oak. "Aren't you cold?"

"I'm fine. Looks better on you anyway." His eyes travel over me, then he turns to face the front of the line.

A long-sleeved Henley hides beneath the jacket. It's all black, simple, with three buttons at the top, sending a shot of heat through me. I hardly see Cal wear anything but sleeveless t-shirts and oil stains.

The heat could also stem from the way the shirt hugs every bulging muscle in his arms, and I'm flashing back to how I felt in his lap when those huge, careful arms were wrapped around me.

Suddenly, the jacket is stifling and I'm overheating.

As I shift uncomfortably inside of it, Cal orders us the Oreos and two cups of spiked cider, and I take both with shaky fingers.

"Cider will warm you up," he tells me.

"Great. Thank you." I notice the pendant on his necklace chain outlined through the front of his shirt and clear my throat as we stroll away from the line. "I like your necklace," I say, licking a finger. "It's a heart woven into a treble clef, right?"

He glances at me as we walk side by side. "Yeah, I had it custom-made years ago."

My mind races with memories of teaching Cal how to play guitar on my bedroom floor, and of watching his fingers press piano keys with Emma in the finished basement while I sang *I Will Follow You Into the Dark* by Death Cab for Cutie. "Do you still like music?"

It feels like a ridiculous question.

Who doesn't like music?

But Cal takes a long time to answer, biting into his Oreo and chewing while he thinks it over. "I like your music," he says. "You're good. Really fucking good."

I grin brightly and blush. "Maybe we could play or sing together some time."

"Probably not." He answers quickly, dismissively, then takes a big swig of his cider. "Let's do the games. Ferris wheel last."

Sipping on my own, I nod. "Sure." The wheel both beckons

and deters me as we pass, and the shrieks from riders have my heart teetering in time with the swinging buckets. "Have you been to a carnival since...?"

My voice trails off when his eyes flash. Still, he answers after another draw of cider. "No."

"Me, either."

Swallowing back the rest of his beverage, he tosses the empty cup into a passing trash can, and then reaches over to palm the back of my neck, squeezing gently. It's an affectionate gesture that has me chugging my own cider until a telltale buzz mingles with the buzz of Cal.

Adventure swims through my bloodstream, revving my pulse.

He gives me a small smile, then drags his hand down my spine, only releasing me to saunter ahead. "Come on. I see some pink, fuzzy shit up ahead with your name on it."

I skip up alongside him, grinning ear to ear. We play a few games, shooting water guns, whacking timeworn mole heads with hammers, and tossing balls at bullseyes. We don't win anything, but it feels like every second that ticks by is a tiny victory.

Laughing, I even swerve the water gun in his direction, squirting the front of his shirt. He retaliates with gusto until my hair is matted to my cheek and water trickles down my neck and underneath my sweater.

He laughs, too.

He *laughs*.

And I'm convinced that laughter from that one person you don't expect it from is like a symphony. The perfect marrying of chords and notes; a composition that causes the heart to dance.

My heart is dancing.

Cal makes two separate pitstops to order us more cider and a handful of ride tickets, and as an hour rolls by, I'm positively vibrating.

I'm still sipping on my third cider when Cal hands me a piece of chewing gum. I eye it warily. "Hmm. I don't know."

"It'll give you a little buzz, especially after you eat or drink something. Up to you."

I'm feeling frisky, so I take the gum and slowly chew.

It tastes like there's a wasp family caught in my throat, so I cough and splutter. "This is awful. How do you chew this all the time?"

"I'm used to it."

His smirk brightens, reaching his eyes, and his eyebrows even turn up with a touch of playfulness. *God*, I could get used to this side of him. This walls-down, delightfully vulnerable version of Cal Bishop I was beginning to think I'd merely made up and written into a song.

Sure enough, my eyes dilate to giant saucers when the nicotine buzz ignites. I'm giddy, wound, high on everything. I link my arm through his and drag him over to the basketball game I know he's been eyeballing. "Ready for this?"

"Well, fuck, sunshine." A big hand scrubs down his face. "No pressure or anything."

My grip on his arm tightens in time with the knot in my belly. That tingly, warm knot travels lower and lower as the childhood nickname ripples through me. I play it cool, looking up at him with my glazed nicotine eyes. "Nervous?"

"A little." Cal slips from my arm-link and does that hand-to-neck grab again. He lingers this time, massaging my nape and dragging his fingers over my scalp. "Think I got this?"

My balance wavers, and I sag against him as we move into the line.

As long as you've got me.

Almost as if he hears my internal dialogue, he wraps an arm around me, tugging me closer, his fingers grazing down my bare shoulder where the jacket slipped. The cider is making him bolder, the nostalgia making him looser. He keeps his hold on me as we inch forward, like we're a happy couple out on a date. Sound fades out, dwindling into a drone of background noise, and I can't help my eyes from fluttering closed as I breathe him in.

I allow him to fill that black hole that hides inside me until there's nothing left for it to take.

When it's Cal's turn at the hoop, he's tossed a basketball by a young brunette, and I swear he *does* look nervous. Almost like this moment means more to him than winning an overpriced teddy bear. He takes a deep breath and throws the ball. I watch as it coasts through the air, teases the rim, then bounces back out.

He curses under his breath and tries again.

Miss.

Another miss.

Then he makes one, but it's not enough to win a prize.

Cal fishes more change out of his wallet, handing the teenager manning the game a twenty. "Another," he clips.

She throws him a ball. He makes it.

Then he misses.

Cal mutters profanities into the night, throwing balls at lightning speed, his form getting sloppier as aggravation takes over.

"Cal, it's fine. I don't need anything," I say gently, pressing my palm to his twitching bicep. "Let's go on the Ferris wheel."

"You're getting a fucking prize if I have to spend my entire paycheck on this rigged-ass game."

My eyes catch with the young attendant, who pulses her eyebrows at me like she's impressed with Cal's dedication.

Another twenty is pulled from his wallet, in exchange for more balls.

I swear he's sweating. It's fifty-two degrees outside, but there's a sheen reflecting off his hairline from the game lights as he lifts the ball slightly over his head and positions it with his opposite hand.

Swish.

Another one goes in.

Swish.

My heart races with childlike adrenaline. I feel like I'm sitting on the bleachers at one of Cal's old high school games; like that wintry night in December when there were three seconds left on the clock and a teammate tossed him the ball as he stood perched at the three-point line, and everyone in the crowd went silent.

He made the shot, just like he makes it now.

Swish.

Cal turns to look at me as the ball glides through the net, in the same way he looked at me then, when he found me through the sea of people on those aluminum benches and thrust his arms to the sky in victory. I'd jumped up and down, grabbing Emma's hand, whooping and whistling until my cheeks ached. He'd pointed at me—or at Emma—but his eyes were on me, that I knew.

"That's my big brother!" Emma had hollered through cupped hands, her ponytail whipping me in the face as we bounced up and down.

That's my everything, I had thought.

I couldn't say it because what did a thirteen-year-old know about everything? But I *thought* it, and I'm still thinking it, wondering if I ever stopped.

The game blares victorious with a winning shot, the multicolored siren flashing blue and emerald. Claps ring out through the long line behind us as the attendant pops up from her stool to fetch a prize. "Which one do you want?"

Cal smooths back his chaotic hair, dark tufts curling behind his ears. "You got a mouse?"

"A mouse?" Her nose crinkles. "Fresh out of mice. I have sharks, panda bears, and some sloths."

I slide my lip between my teeth, surveying the toys. Nothing is pink, but the panda is cute. Its eyes look sad, one ear droopier than the other. Something about it has me pointing with a smile. "That one."

Cal frowns. "That one looks sick. Its ear is falling off."

"It's the one I want."

The young girl shrugs and reaches for a long hook, snatching up the panda bear. She hands it to me as she glances at Cal. "Nice job. Lucky lady."

In that moment, I *do* feel lucky.

I feel like the luckiest girl in the world.

We're both still damp from the water gun fight as we leave the line and I tuck the panda to my chest. I'm also still buzzing, a combination of cider, adrenaline, nicotine, and the soft look Cal throws me as we curve toward the rides. "This means a lot," I tell him, peering up at him through my lashes. "Really. Thank you." I squeeze the panda tighter with both arms, my smile misty.

He scratches at the stubble along his jaw and returns his attention straight ahead. "You gonna name it?"

"Yes. Pinky."

"It's black and white."

That doesn't matter; Emma already named it. And maybe it's not a mouse, and maybe it's not pink, and maybe we're grown adults now and she's not here, but she still named it. I pop my shoulders, glancing down at the wads of gum stuck to the pavement. "She looks like a Pinky."

He doesn't argue, and silence stretches between us.

It's not the awkward kind that I'm quick to repel. It's lighter, kinder, comfortable. It doesn't need to be filled—it just needs to be savored.

It's the kind of silence that has Cal reaching for my hand, the one I dropped to my side. He says nothing as his knuckles graze mine, gentle at first, just a kiss, and then his pinky finger extends to link with my own. My feet stagger, my legs crisscrossing. His hand is cool from the late autumn air, but his touch is warm. Still silent, he weaves the rest of our fingers together until our palms are clasped and intertwined.

Cal is holding my hand.

I'm not his, but I have his hand, and I have a little panda pressed to my heart, and I have this night, even if the nights don't last forever.

Right now, I have everything, and all that ever really matters is right now.

He remains silent as we wind through the passersby, dodging double strollers and sugar-infused toddlers high on cotton candy. At one point, instead of letting go, Cal grips me tighter and arches our hands through the air and over a young girl's head as she tries to plow through our arm barrier like a game of Red Rover. As the girl vanishes behind us, Cal and I pull back together like two magnets and nearly trip over each other's feet.

And then, somehow, we find ourselves in line for the Ferris wheel.

Of course we do.

The line isn't too long, and we get stopped right at the gate, waiting for the next ride. Cal is still holding my hand like it's completely natural, entirely instinctive, leaning back against a rail and staring up at the starlit wheel.

I'm only staring at him.

Of course I am.

"Excuse me."

Somebody tugs at my jacket, and I turn around.

I blink, nearly fainting. The school-aged girl looks so much like Emma that my esophagus withers up like a dying orchid, and I can't breathe.

Maybe I'm hallucinating. It could be the cider, possibly the gum. Maybe my brain is so mixed-up, caught between then and now, that I'm imagining her.

"Do you have any extra tickets? I dropped mine," she says, wrinkling her freckle-smattered nose.

I wonder if Cal notices the resemblance. He releases my hand to dig through his pocket, fishing out a fistful of red tickets. "Yeah, here. We only need two."

Her eyes brighten like copper pennies, and she snatches the tickets with a toothy grin.

I almost expect her to say, "*Toodles!*" as she spins on her heel, ponytail whipping around her, but all she says is, "Thanks, mister!"

My chest is tight, a noose around my neck. Tears burn behind my eyes, and I'm forced to circle away from Cal, my back to him, while I rein in my confusion and erratic heart.

"You okay?"

He's so close that his words warm the back of my head, his chest inches from my spine. One hand curls around my hip, a gentle reminder that he's there.

All I can do is nod.

Cal lowers his lips to my ear and whispers, "Breathe, Lucy."

His words seize me from the reverie, anchoring me. My eyes close. He's telling me he knows, he understands, but it's okay. I'm okay.

I'm okay.

I nod again, leaning backward until both of his arms envelop my waist. That's when my resolve wavers and my fears beg to be expunged. I try to focus on Jessica and all the reasons I've committed myself to a lifetime of solitude, but it's hard when his arms are around me and his heartbeats heat my back, tempting me with a different path. I want to love him from afar so I can't break him, but he's too close. He's already tucked inside my unsafe hands, and I'm going to drop him.

God, I'll drop him, and he'll shatter.

"Tickets." The ride attendant opens the gate, extending a palm toward us.

Cal pulls away to give him our tickets, releasing me before I can let him slip. Pulling in a deep breath, I follow him onto the ride, and we slide into one of the empty buckets, thighs smashing together as the bar comes down.

"Been a long time since I've been on this thing," he mutters, face aimed straight ahead. "Didn't think I'd ever be here again, to be honest."

I allow a smile. "Getting stuck on a ride doesn't exactly entice someone to do it again."

"Yeah. But sometimes I wish..." Cal's eyes narrow, squinting at nothing in particular. "Sometimes I wish we never got unstuck, you know?"

The ride comes to life before I can even process his words. Those words rise up inside of me as *we* rise, lifting off the ground and into the sky.

For a moment, I pretend that his wish did come true. We never unstuck, never unglued. Time stopped at the top of the Ferris wheel when Cal looked down at me, his hair pitch dark but his eyes moonlit. Flirtation sparked. Adventure crackled.

Emma giggled and chanted from one bucket beneath us: *"Kiss her, you chicken!"*

He did.

He did.

An inky, midnight sky stretches out before us, equally suffocating and cathartic. Suffocating because I'm choking on stars and unanswered wishes—*suffocating*, because how can a sky look so vast and endless, and yet she's not here?

Cathartic because I feel her anyway.

I grip the safety bar with one white-knuckled hand while my other holds onto Pinky the panda. We rise and rise and rise, just like this feeling swimming between us, but the trouble with rising is there is always a fall. Sometimes it's with grace, and sometimes it's devastating.

You just never know.

Nothing makes a person crazier than emotion trapped with nowhere to go, so I turn to Cal as we tip over the top and descend back down. "I missed you so much," I confess, squeezing the toy in my hand to avoid reaching for him. "Why did you leave me? Why didn't you try to find me?"

Pain skates across his face. Real, awful pain, like my words are little blades stabbing at his chest. He closes his eyes for a brief moment before turning to look at me. "I didn't have a choice. We moved, Lucy. I was just a kid."

"But...*after*," I probe. "After you grew up. I made a Facebook and an Instagram account, just so you could reach out to me, but you never did."

"I didn't have a choice."

He says it again, just as certain, just as tortured. I hate his answer because he *did* have a choice. Cal didn't choose me. "That's not true," I whisper, turning away. I focus on the sea of people below me instead of the lie in his eyes.

I hear him exhale a long sigh, his knee bumping against mine, but he doesn't say anything.

Maybe I should be grateful that he never tried to track me down. It's not like anything can happen between us, and it's so painfully evident how easily it could.

The wheel dips, then catapults us right back up. My belly knots, recalling how the ride came to a grinding halt last time with Cal and I stuck at the very top. I'd been terrified, digging my fingernails into his knee while my heart jack-knifed inside my chest. Emma hadn't been scared at all. She was the fearless one. Instead, she bounced in her bucket, letting it swing precariously on its hinges as she squealed with a rush of excitement.

For a moment, I expect the wheel to get stuck again as we round the final spin and Cal's voice thunders through me. "It's not that I didn't want to," he says. "I just couldn't."

Swallowing, I peek over at him while we careen up over the top. I hold my breath as if we're about to stall among the stars with our lips locked together.

Our eyes meet when we crest. I wonder if he's thinking about it, too; maybe even wishing for it. Everything feels easier up here. Lighter, weightless.

But the ride doesn't stall, and Cal doesn't kiss me. Emma doesn't materialize out of nowhere, and we don't time travel into the past to rearrange history like a science fiction story.

We just step off the ride and walk away.

My feet carry me farther ahead of him, almost like I'm trying to escape the heavy hum of nothingness that just transpired.

"Lucy, wait."

I pick at the floppy ear on my panda bear and clench my jaw, hearing his footsteps come up beside me. I'm not angry. I'm not even upset.

I don't know what I am, but the cider already filtered through me, and the gum buzz is long gone. And Cal isn't smiling anymore.

I think I'm just tired.

"Lucy," he repeats.

I slow my pace, and that's when I hear him mutter under his breath, "*Fuck it.*" His feet stall in my peripheral vision as he reaches for my wrist, pulling me to a stop, his eyes finding mine.

Cal swallows, his Adam's apple bobbing, irises reflecting neon and indigo against the Ferris wheel lights. "Come home with me."

Come home with me.

He wants to spend more time together.

The dimming light inside of me switches back on, and a smile twitches on my mouth. I don't even hesitate. "Okay."

"Yeah?" Blinking a few times, he swallows again, as if he wasn't expecting me to say yes. He staggers back, silent for a beat, just staring at me. "You want to?"

"Sure," I nod. "I'd like that."

The truth is, I don't want the night to end on a sour note. I want to savor the sweetness of handholding and hard cider and water gun fights. Maybe he'll forget that I ever brought up the past and hurled my impossible questions at him.

Cal is still gazing at me through narrowed eyes. Then he nods his head slowly, the ghost of a smile lifting on his mouth. "All right."

"All right."

His smile grows the moment mine does.

Then he takes my hand and drags me from the festival, his steps hurried, grip eager. I can't help but glance up at the spinning Ferris wheel as we race past it toward the parking lot, the sound of young laughter ringing in my ears.

My mind must be playing tricks on me, or maybe it's the little girl who asked us for tickets, but I swear—I *swear* I see her.

I see Emma swinging her bucket from side to side, pumping a victorious fist in the air as she smiles down at me, backlit by a sea of stars.

CHAPTER 15

C al takes my hand as he leads me through his red front door. I remember when I was in junior high, I'd paint my fingernails red to appear older. My mom had a deep cherry color called "Vixen" that I'd sneak from her makeup drawer whenever I was going to visit Cal during that last year—the year of thirteen when I finally decided that boys weren't gross and kissing them sounded appealing.

Kissing *him* sounded appealing.

They were painted red atop the Ferris wheel that night when Cal pressed his lips to mine for the first and only time.

"Come on, it's perfect," Emma said, her face brightening with expectation beneath the moon. "It's so romantic up here among the stars."

"Maybe it would be if you didn't name them all after your boy band crushes," Cal teased.

She stuck out her tongue at him, then pumped her fist in the air. "Kiss her, you chicken!"

My vixen nails had been digging into his kneecap, making me come across like a terrified little girl instead of the blossoming young woman I was attempting to be.

Still, he kissed me. Sweet, short, just the tip of his tongue poking out to trace my bottom lip before he pulled away and left me forever in love with him.

I sigh as I step through the threshold and watch as Cricket dives off the couch to hide underneath it. I'm determined to win her over one of these days. Maybe tonight while Cal and I curl up to watch a movie downstairs and avoid talking about Ferris wheels and cotton candy kisses and a little girl with fireflies in her eyes.

Cal moves in behind me as I traipse across his hardwood floors and set down my panda bear, my not-red fingertips grazing along the top of the sofa. We didn't say much on the drive over, considering any words would have been swallowed up by the growl of his engine, but whenever we stationed at a stoplight, he'd touch me. He'd reach behind him and palm my outer thigh, causing me to lean into him as far as the helmet would allow.

I hear the front door snap shut behind me as I glance around the dimly lit living room that smells like smoky amber. "So, what did you want to—"

My question is cut short when his hands grip my waist, and I freeze.

"I should probably offer you a drink or something, but I can't fucking wait."

He gathers handfuls of my hair, layering it over one shoulder while his lips tilt down to scatter kisses along the other. My sweater dips lower, giving him more skin to drag his mouth over.

Oh my God.

"Do you still taste like bubblegum?" The tip of his nose glides up the arc of my neck until his teeth find my earlobe. He nibbles on it. "I bet you do."

Instantly, there's a lake in my underwear.

I'd be a literal statue if my body wasn't suddenly trembling and leaning back against his chest on instinct.

Cal's breath warms the sensitive skin just below my ear as one hand curls around my hip, and the other continues to hold my hair to the side, his grip on it tightening. "You still smell like pears," he whispers raggedly, his fingers inching up my sweater to skim my lower belly. "Fruity and sweet. So fucking gorgeous."

A little moan falls out of me. I've never been touched like this, talked to like this, which is partly humiliating, but mostly addicting.

Jessica, Jessica, Jessica.

Her name stampedes through my mind with steel hooves, and I spin around to face him. "What...what are you doing?"

His eyes are dark and hooded as he stares down at me, both hands now around my waist, under my sweater. "What do you think I'm doing?"

"I..." I lift my hands to clutch his shirt as my body sways and teeters. "A-are you going to kiss me?"

"I'm going to do a lot more than kiss you." Bending down, his rough stubble tickles the side of my cheek as he murmurs against my ear, "I'm going to destroy you, Lucy. In the best fucking way."

I can't breathe. I can't move. I can't even keep myself upright as I fall into him, my forehead pressed against the breadth of his chest. "Oh," I squeak out. "You...you want me?"

"What the hell do you think?" He reaches down for my hand and tugs it to the hard bulge straining his jeans.

I almost die on the spot when I grip his erection. Hard, massive, terrifying. I've never touched a penis before, not ever. Not clothed, not bare, not even a pretend penis, like a dildo.

"You want me?" he counters, kissing the top of my head, still holding my hand against him.

I nod because I do, and that's the truth, but all my fears are bubbling to the surface, and I'm scared. So, so scared. "I wasn't...I don't..." My breathing is unsteady, my body wracked with tremors. Fear, lust, confusion, inexperience.

Cal pulls back a few inches to look down at me. "What's wrong?"

Shaking my head, I wet my lips and close my eyes, my hand falling away from him. "I just..."

"Talk to me. Something's wrong."

I can't look at him as the silence thickens between us, but I nearly topple forward when he steps away, his grip on me loosening.

"You don't want to," he says.

"No, I do, but I—"

"You look like you're going to throw up."

Mortification rockets through me, heating my already flushed cheeks. I feel like a pathetic teenager. Gathering enough courage to open my eyes, I peek up at him as I wring my sweater between my hands. "I just...I wasn't expecting this."

Cal looks confused. His brows furrow between his eyes, gaze scanning my face like he's searching for something. "Did you think I brought you here to play Yahtzee?"

I swallow. "Well, not Yahtzee, specifically. Monopoly crossed my mind. Maybe Scrabble."

"Christ." He makes a sound like a laugh, but it's not a laugh. Blowing out a breath, he runs a hand through his hair. "You can't be that naïve."

His words have me cowering back a little, flooding me with embarrassment.

"Sorry," he mutters off my deer-in-headlights expression. Scrubbing a hand down his face, he looks off to the side. "I just thought it was pretty clear when I asked you to come home with me."

I realize he's right—I *am* naïve. In retrospect, it should have been obvious by the heat in his eyes, the way he was touching me on the bike, how he'd already tried to kiss me on his couch not long ago. But I told him we couldn't, and I thought that was it. He's hardly spoken to me since that night. "If you were anyone else, I might have considered that."

"Anyone else," he echoes drily. His eyes draw back up to mine. "Gee, thanks, Lucy. It's great to know I'm the absolute last person on the planet you would consider sleeping with."

"No, God, that's...that's not what I meant." Flustered, I drag my fingertips through my hair, pulling it back as I try to pinpoint the right words. "You're the last person I was expecting to *ask me* that. I thought you were mad at me after we got off the ride. It just...it didn't even cross my mind."

"I'm not mad at you. I've never been mad at you." Cricket sneaks out from underneath the couch and starts circling his ankles. "It's more than that," he decides, looking me over, head to toe. "What are you afraid of?"

"I'm scared to cross a line," I admit.

"Lines are drawn for protection. And this?" He flicks a finger between us. "Nothing is going to hurt you here. It's supposed to be fun."

Fun. Maybe for most people it would be fun, but I'm not most people, and I don't know how to tell him about Jessica, or about my health complications, without confessing the whole truth and scaring him away for good.

I just got him back.

Desperate for a new angle to latch onto, I tell him, "I don't want to be your one-night stand, Cal. That's not me."

"I wasn't planning on limiting it to one night."

My throat closes up. "You mean, you want...a relationship?"

"No," he says simply.

I blink up at him, processing his response.

He wants to be friends with benefits.

A fuck buddy.

That's not me, either. I want all or nothing, and if I can't have it all, I'll have to settle for nothing. I'm vaguely aware of Cricket slinking toward me to sniff my boots, so I reach down to pet her, half distracted by the man in front of me. As I'm fumbling for a response to Cal's implication that he wants to turn our budding friendship into a noncommittal sexual fling, I accidentally miss Cricket's head and poke her in the eye with my finger.

She swats at me, slashing a claw across my knuckles, then scampers back to her safe haven under the sofa.

I jolt upright and glance down at the blood seeping from the scratch. It's not bad, but it's bad enough to bleed, and apparently, I'm prone to hand injuries whenever I'm around Cal.

"Shit, she get you?" Cal moves forward in two big strides, grabbing my hand to survey the damage. "Damn. Sorry, she's still cagey."

"It was my fault," I confess, hissing through my teeth when it starts to sting. "I know better. I've worked with animals for years. God, I'm sorry."

"Stop apologizing for everything. Let me see." He pulls my knuckles to his face, grazing a thumb over them in time with his eyes. "Doesn't look bad. I've got some Band-Aids in the kitchen."

Cal doesn't let go of my hand as we journey into the

adjoining kitchen, then surprises me by cinching my waist and lifting me up to the countertop. He plants me there, reaching over my head to grab a plastic tub of first aid supplies out of the upper cabinet.

I lean to the side to switch on the faucet next to me, sluicing the wound with warm water and soap. It burns, and I know I'll have to keep an eye on it for infection—cat injuries can turn serious quickly. After patting the area with a dry towel, I lift back up, with Cal between my knees, while he peels apart a bandage. "I know you said not to apologize, but I feel bad," I admit, watching his long fingers tinker with the delicate wrapping.

"You do always manage to keep things interesting," he says, eyes lowered.

"I bet you're wishing you didn't cancel plans with Jolene, huh?"

He looks up. "That's not what I said."

"But you're thinking it?"

"No. I'm exactly where I want to be."

"Tending to my self-induced cat wound and not getting laid," I muster through a half laugh, half sulk. Self-deprecation bleeds through my words. "Sounds like a party."

"If I wanted to get laid, Lucy, it wouldn't be difficult. I'm with you because I want to be, whether you're in my bed or not."

My cheeks redden as he takes my hand back and places the bandage over the scratch. I chew my lip. "It's not that I don't want to be."

His palm is warm and big as it cradles mine, his thumb brushing over my knuckles again, lingering. "I know. That's why this is confusing the fuck out of me."

Guilt seizes me. The last thing I want is to confuse him, or lead him on, but I don't know how to explain that this is for his own good without telling him why. I *should* tell him why. God knows he'll find out eventually, whether with words or with something even worse—but the confession catches fire on my tongue and turns to ash.

Cal inches closer between my thighs, his torso flush with my pelvis, my hand still tucked inside his. His presence is dominating, but his touch is gentle. Soothing. "There's a lot you don't know about me," I say softly, soot in my throat.

He glances at me with only his eyes. "So tell me."

"I can't."

"Tell me." Moving even closer, his hand trails from mine and glides up the length of my arm until he's palming my neck. "Tell me why your body is begging for me, but this mouth is telling me no." His thumb moves over to my mouth, dragging down my bottom lip.

My breath hitches, a gasp expelling. Tingles spark down low, dampening my panties as my legs tighten around his middle. When our foreheads press together and I think he's going to kiss me, I give him my partial truth. "I'm a virgin." I watch his expression falter, his half-lidded eyes blinking as realization dawns. I swallow, embarrassed. "I've never even kissed...except you. Only that night at the carnival. On the Ferris wheel," I tell him. "That's it."

A long, treacherous beat passes.

His hold on my neck strengthens, his jaw clenched and taut. Body stiffening, he presses closer, until I feel more than muscle going rigid.

He's hard. He still wants me.

"Fuck," he whispers right against my lips, eyes closing briefly as he releases a strained breath. "How?"

It's a reasonable question, but I was hoping he wouldn't ask it. I want to dart my gaze away, but the look in his eyes has me in a chokehold. "I – I don't know. I haven't wanted to. It hasn't felt right." Lifting my hands to his waist, I finger his belt loops, wondering why he hasn't pulled away yet. "Have I scared you away?"

He lifts his forehead from mine, jaw ticking. "Are you kidding me? Fuck if that doesn't make me want you more," he says raggedly. "But I get it. And I'll back off."

Isn't that what I want?

It is, it should be, but my chest still pangs with disappointment. "Is it a burden?"

"A burden?" His eyebrows twist up like the question is

absurd. "Fuck no. It's an honor. An honor I probably don't deserve."

"Why not?" I murmur.

Glancing off to the side, Cal lets out a breath and takes a step back, leaving the warm juncture between my legs. He cracks his knuckles and moves in beside me, leaning against the counter. "Because I'm not that guy. You held onto something important for years, and you should give it to someone who'll treat you right. Who'll give you everything that goes along with a gift like that." The cords in his neck dilate as he looks down at his boots. "But...if you want to give it to me anyway, I'm not going to say no. I'm not that guy either. Just make sure, if that's the case, you think about it long and hard because I can't promise you the things I know you're going to crave afterward."

Our eyes meet. Heat thrums through me, and my heartrate kicks up. There's something thrilling and empowering in the notion that he wouldn't say no to taking my virginity if I begged him to.

And yet, there's something incredibly sad in the notion that he also feels unworthy of it.

If I didn't plan on dying a virgin, he'd be the *only* one worthy of it.

I jump down and step toward him, my chest tight, legs wobbly. Both of his hands grip the edge of the countertop, as if he's forcibly trying to keep them off of me. "You said you weren't looking for a relationship. Is that what you're referring to?"

"Yes."

I wet my lips, trying to understand. "You...want to sleep around? You don't want to be committed to one person?" If that's the case, then he's absolutely right. I could never accept that, which means I could never sleep with him.

"It's not about being exclusive," he says. "It's about expectation."

"What do you mean?"

"I mean, I don't know fuck-all about being a good partner." Cal pops up from the counter and moves around me, pacing the small galley kitchen. "I like my space, I like being alone. I'm overly protective to the point where it's pretty fucking toxic, and

I own that. I'll break a man's face if he even *looks* at my woman. I don't like talking about my goddamn feelings, I don't have a big family to fawn over you, or many friends to take you out with, and I don't want to be tied down to anybody. A relationship is not conducive to my lifestyle, or to the way I see my future playing out."

Sadness trickles through me. A deep mourning. I think back to a night beneath the stars, camping in my backyard, when Cal told me he wanted to marry me one day. I was only eight years old at the time, and Cal was ten, but I've never forgotten it. It felt like a real proposal. It felt like our destiny had been written in those stars.

Heaving in a tapered breath, I stare at his back as he stands a few feet away running a hand through his dark hair. It glows with a tungsten sheen under the muted overhead light. "You wanted a different future when we were kids. You wanted all the things you say you don't want now."

"Yeah, well, shit changes, Lucy." His words are sharp, tone acidic. "I wanted a lot of things back then. A basketball scholarship. A higher allowance. A fucking puppy."

"You wanted to marry me."

Cal whips around. "I was just a damn kid. Everything changed the moment Emma walked out that door. *Everything.*"

His eyes flare. They darken when her name echoes off the plaster walls and our splintered hearts. The kitchen feels smaller, narrower, and the air scarce. Ducking his chin to his chest, he flexes both hands at his sides, reeling in his brush with emotion.

Then he steps forward, meeting my wide, glossy stare, my hip perched against the oven for balance.

"Look, if you want to be friends, I'll be your friend—as much of a friend as I can be." Cal continues to stalk toward me, gaze leveled with mine. "If you want me to fuck you," he rasps, focus dipping to my mouth, then swinging back up, "I'll fuck you. I'll worship every inch of you."

My heartbeat quickens again, skin flushing hot. My pulse is in my throat, his words digging into my chest.

I want him, I do. But—

"But I won't love you."

I stagger back, grateful to be propped up by something. I know I'd fall. I'd crumble.

"And that's what a girl like you really wants, isn't it?" he presses. "To be loved. Adored. That's what you deserve."

Lips trembling, I face him through the dim, yellow light. "You think you know what I want? What I deserve?"

"Yes." After a few quiet beats, Cal reaches into his back pocket and pulls out his cell phone. He thumbs through it, landing on something and studying it for a moment before turning the screen toward me. "This is how I know."

It's my Instagram picture.

Me, laughing in the rain, my hair stuck to my face as a sliver of moonlight reflects off my smile.

I swallow, lifting my eyes to him.

"This is how I see you, Lucy," he tells me soberly. "Weightless. Free. In love with life, untethered from hardship. Perfect in every way." Dropping the phone to his side, he looks off over my shoulder at the small window above the sink. His eyes narrow with thought, with memory. "This is how I've always seen you."

When his eyes flick back to me, I swear they're glazed over, glimmering with sentiment. He's not immune to this—to *me*. I find my voice. "I'm not untethered from hardship, Cal. It lives inside of me every day, just like yours does. I simply choose to overcome it. I choose to be happy because being sad spoils the little time we have here," I tell him. "And you're right. If I sleep with you, I'll feel something. I'll feel everything. More than you think you're capable of feeling." His lips thin, body tensing. "That's what you're telling me, right? That you'll make love to me and feel nothing?"

He falters. The crease between his eyes untwists, and he doesn't respond.

I get my answer then, and I know, without a doubt, he's not immune; he's not immune at all.

He's afraid—and that's something I can understand.

We marinate in the things said and unsaid before Cal rubs a hand over his face and sighs. "I can take you home if you want. Or you can stay in the guest room. Up to you."

All I manage is a weak nod.

"I'm gonna hop in the shower. Let me know what you want to do."

I nod again, our eyes tangling for a split second before he dips his head, pivots around, and disappears out of the kitchen.

A rush of tears flood me when he's out of sight. I turn and press my palms to the countertop, leaning forward as his words pulse through me like a doleful song.

I won't love you.

Cal carved a hole between us. A canyon. Two jagged cliffs, too far apart to jump without slipping and free-falling into nothingness.

And so I know what I have to do.

I'll take these broken bones and build a bridge.

CHAPTER 16

2/16/13

"Sad Songs"

Mom asked me if any songs made me sad.
I'd never thought about it before, but now that I
am thinking about it, the answer is yes. There's a
song that came out a couple of years ago called
If I Die Young by The Band Perry. It's probably my favorite song, but it also makes me really
sad inside. I played it on Pandora today, thinking
about how I'd feel if my brother or Lucy died
young. I started crying. There's a line that says,
"what I never did is done." It makes me want
to do everything. Kiss boys, jump out of airplanes,
play the piano in front of thousands of people, go
to music school, eat ice cream for breakfast every
day. You know, just in case.

I played the song for Lucy last night and told her she wasn't allowed to die young.

She cried.

Toodles,

Emma

The little panda sits beside me on stage, perched amid my sea of tips; a good luck charm of sorts. I'm almost positive I have double the tips I normally receive during a Friday night show, and it's probably because of Pinky.

I strum the strings of my guitar, my knee-high boots propped along the rung of the stool. "Any requests tonight?" I ask into the microphone, draped in golden bar glow, missing the setting sun that was recently stolen by daylight savings time.

Alyssa sits at a large round table, joined by my friend Gemma from the animal sanctuary, and her fiancé, Knox. Alyssa cups her hands around her mouth and shouts, "*Gangsta's Paradise!*"

Laughing, I blush. "We'll save that for our karaoke shenanigans tomorrow night," I say back, producing a flurry of chuckles from the crowd.

I just finished playing *Got My Mind Set On You* by George Harrison, which went over incredibly well for my first live attempt. I reveled in the way the audience clapped and sang along, bouncing in their chairs and stools while tossing ten-dollar bills into my guitar case. The mood calls for something slower now, a little more somber, so I page through my set list and begin to play the first few chords of *Fields of Gold* by Sting.

That's when someone calls out, "*If I Die Young.*"

Reflexively, I freeze. Ice slithers through my veins, and I'm certain I go whiter than snow. For a moment, I'm standing at that podium beneath a dove gray sky and sad clouds, while a guitar shakes in my hands, my tears mimicking the drizzle I know is coming.

I couldn't play it then, just as I can't play it now.

It's the *only* song I can't play.

I'm not sure if it's fate or design or wild misfortune, but that's when the door whips open and he's standing there.

Cal.

He's dressed in a jet-black beanie sheathed in a sprinkle of the season's first snowfall, the leather bomber jacket I can still smell on my fuzzy sweater, dark jeans, and a look in his eyes that melts the frost in my bones the second he looks up at me.

I'm flustered but relieved. Nervous but inherently soothed.

Pretending I didn't hear the song request, I dive back into Sting and close my eyes, centering myself to the stage. To the music. To him.

It's been just under two weeks since I spent the night in his guest room, having not felt right about making him drive me home after I'd agreed to come over. I slept soundly, the same way I had the first time I slept over. We danced around each other in his kitchen the next morning, neither of us bringing up the prior evening's conversation and heady truths, and we danced around each other at work over the next two weeks, skirting and sidestepping, careful to avoid any dangerous rhythm. His feelings were made fairly clear. Mine were less clear.

Ultimately, the clearest takeaway has been that friendship is the safest option for both of us—even though I questioned that takeaway when I awoke Sunday morning in his guest bed with a familiar panda bear resting beside me. I'd left it on the couch when we got back from the festival, yet somehow, Pinky found her way onto my pillow.

Cal put her there.

So, yes, I'm questioning everything, but I'm forcing myself to choke back any hidden meanings and focus on the probability that it was just a token of friendship.

The start of a bridge.

His bridge.

Having him as my friend again is enough for now, and I hope and pray it always will be.

When I wrap up the set and voice my thanks to the resounding applause, I take a minute to put my guitar away and collect the tips before winding over to my table of friends in a rust-brown corduroy skirt and long-sleeved pinstripe blouse tucked into the waistline. My boots click atop the tile floor as I move, and I glance up at Cal who pushes up from the wall he was perched at near the back of the room. Alyssa calls out to me first.

"And she crushed it, as usual," she chimes with a flash of teeth, holding up her empty wine glass.

I smile, my focus shared between the table and Cal stalking toward me. "It's easy to perform well when I have the best audience."

"Yeah, no shit," she says, voice dipping. "Your sexy-as-sin boss was undressing you with his eyes the whole time."

My heart palpitates. Alyssa hasn't even met Cal yet, but she's seen his picture. And he's the kind of man she won't soon forget, even if her acquaintance was limited to a low quality internet article. I hum an awkward laugh as Cal stops just short of the table, looking fidgety. "One sec," I tell them, pivoting away.

He stuffs his hands into his pockets, glancing around the room before settling on me. "Hey."

"Hi," I beam.

I'm vaguely aware of him saying something—probably akin to "good show" or "nice job"—but the only thing I really hear is the echo of his words from two weeks ago:

I'm going to destroy you, Lucy. In the best fucking way.

Maybe he didn't mean *destroy*, but somewhat ruin. Marginally maim. The way he said it made it sound tempting either way, so it's been difficult to concentrate on things other than my brush with a seemingly good kind of destruction.

I don't know what that means, exactly, but my ovaries do.

They know.

"Did you want to come sit with us?" I offer, fiddling with the button on my skirt.

His eyes skate over me, from my legs cased in umber boots, to my long waves of hair hanging over both shoulders. He clears his throat. "I just wanted to stop by. For support."

"You can still show support at the table," I try, hinting a smile. "I want you to meet my friends."

Thinning his lips, he darts his eyes away again, then shrugs a little. "Yeah. Sure."

Alyssa is already twisted around in her chair, drinking him like he's her second glass of Merlot. Gemma and Knox give him a wave as he saunters over looking completely out of his element. It's strange to see Cal act nervous—that's usually *my* forte.

"Cal, these are my friends, Alyssa, Gemma, and Knox. And this is Cal—my boss."

Gemma's nose wrinkles. "Have we met before? You look really familiar."

He shakes his head. "Don't think so."

"Oh my God, it's so great to finally meet you," Alyssa pipes up, standing to shake his hand. "Lucy never stops talking about you."

My face flames. *Never* stops? She lives to mortify me. "Lys," I scold.

"I'm just teasing. Sometimes she talks about dog neuters and muffins. Anyway, I've been dying to meet you, but Lucy says you're kind of a recluse."

I zone in on the way she's *still* shaking his hand.

"Just busy," he says, his tone clipped. His hand falls away to tug the beanie off his head, revealing a mess of shaggy hair. "But I try to make it to these things when I have time. She's talented."

Our eyes catch, and a kaleidoscope of butterflies take flight in my belly. "Well, thanks," I say, pulling out two empty chairs for us. We take a seat. "It's nice to have familiar faces in the crowd."

Knox sips a craft beer as he trails his hand up and down Gemma's back, toying with her auburn ponytail. He's a country boy at heart, dressed in a plaid shirt and gaucho boots, his sandy hair pulled back into a man bun. "Lucy says she works at an auto shop with you. Do you own it?"

"Yeah," Cal says, shifting in his chair as he pulls a piece of gum from his coat pocket. "My dad owned it first. I took over."

"Family business. I like that."

Alyssa nods to the glass of wine sitting in front of me. "Riesling is for you. No note this time."

That's not surprising. While Nash has been nothing but nice to me, his napkin notes stopped right around the time Cal told him about all of the aggressive sex we weren't having. I blush. "Great." I turn to Cal. "Did you want a drink? I can grab something for you."

"I'll go with you."

He's out of his seat before I even make a move to stand, and I'm met with Alyssa's wiggling implication eyebrows. The blush travels to my ears as I tuck my hair behind them. "I'll be right back." Cal is already at the bar, trying to get the attention of the second bartender who is not Nash. "Sorry to throw you to the wolves like that. I know you're not much of an extrovert."

"It's fine."

"I really appreciate you coming out tonight," I continue. "Thank you."

After ordering a bourbon on the rocks, he flicks his attention to me. "You don't need to thank me for supporting you. We're friends."

The word *friends* sounds less like *friends* and more like *regrettably not sleeping together*. I swallow down a lump in my throat and repress the urge to order something stronger than wine. When Nash catches my eyes from behind the bar, the urge heightens.

"Hey, Lucy. Great show tonight," he says, refraining from Cal eye contact. "Can I get you something?"

"I have my wine. Thank you for that, by the way. I feel like I owe you for all the complimentary glasses over the past year."

"Nah. It's the least I can do for all the business you bring in." He winks.

For a moment, he seems to forget that Cal is standing beside me like a hulking bodyguard with a murderous gleam in his eyes.

I'll break a man's face if he even looks at my woman.

I'm not his woman, not even close, and yet it still looks like he wants to break Nash's face.

I pull my hair over one shoulder and play with the split ends. "This is my favorite night of the week. I'm happy to be invited."

Rapping his knuckles on the counter, he quirks a smile before spinning away to tend to more customers. Cal grumbles.

"What?" I glance up.

"Nothing."

"You growled or something."

"I didn't growl. He's just not my favorite person."

My nose crinkles. "You don't know him."

"I know enough. Come on." Scooping up his glass, he takes a sip before turning back toward the table and sliding into his chair that looks to have magically scooted closer to Alyssa's chair.

When I plop down into my own, Alyssa chirps, "Gemma was just telling us about her wedding next month. I still don't have a date. Does that make me pathetic?" She twirls a strand of sunny hair around her finger, deep in thought.

"If you're pathetic, I'm pathetic. I don't have a date either," I shrug.

Her eyes squint. "Yes, you do."

"I do?"

She elbows Cal right in the bicep, but he doesn't flinch. He never flinches. I squirm in my seat, reaching for my wine glass.

"You're more than welcome to come," Gemma adds, glancing at Cal, sensing the evident invitation. "I put Lucy down for two just in case she wanted to bring a friend."

I look up at him through my lashes, but he's staring down into his floating ice cubes. "Did you want to go?" I wonder, cursing the timidity in my voice. It's not like it's a *date* or anything. Friends go to weddings together all the time. Probably. "It's December tenth."

His lips twitch. "Yeah, I'll go."

Somehow, all I hear is "*no that sounds awful please never speak to me again and you're also fired,*" so I keep rambling. "I'm sure you have plans, or want to relax after a long work week, so it's totally fine that you don't want to—"

"Lucy. I said I'll be your date."

I blink.

Gemma perks up, reaching for Knox's hand atop the table. "Oh, that's great! We'd love to have you there. It's sort of a country-Christmas theme, if you can picture it. Knox grew up in Lexington, so we wanted to integrate his southern roots, and I'm sort of obsessed with the Christmas season. Lucy and I are already crocheting little holiday sweaters for the animals at the sanctuary, and..." She trails off, her head tilting to the side as she studies Cal. "Wait, is that where I've seen you? Have you stopped by the shelter?"

A gulp of wine gets stuck in my throat at her question, and I force it down, shaking my head. "No, no...I haven't really told him much about it." I turn toward him, watching as he twirls his glass between his fingers. "You should come by sometime, though —it's an amazing place. It's right off Richardson Street, near the train tracks. All the pets are older. Seniors. It's a great cause."

"Hm," he says. "Sounds nice."

Alyssa smiles up at Nash when he stops by to refill her wine, her fingernails matching the deep Merlot. "Speaking of senior pets," she sighs, filling her cheeks with air. "Thanksgiving is in less than two weeks. This year is flying by."

The realization sends a wave of anxiety sweeping through me. I've been so caught up in work, music, the sanctuary, and Cal, that I lost track of time. Mom usually starts sending me turkey memes right about now, which is my reminder to start prepping the menu.

We've kept it simple since Dad died a few years back. My Aunt Millie and Uncle Dan usually join us with my cousins and their twin girls, but last year, the extended family came down with the flu, so it was just Mom and me. I can't help but wonder what Cal does for the holidays. He mentioned he didn't have a big family, and I don't recall too many relatives coming over when we were growing up. Holidays were often spent together—the Hopes and the Bishops.

That tradition died years ago, so what does he do now?

Does he spend it with his mother?

Does he spend it...*alone*?

My heart withers at the thought of Cal eating Thanksgiving dinner all by himself in his empty house, just him and a squirrely kitten.

I squeeze my wine glass. "What are your plans?" I ask him when the other three start discussing the pros and cons of doing a wedding "first look" as they scroll Pinterest for photography ideas.

"Plans?" he murmurs, lips folded around the rim of his glass. "For Thanksgiving."

Bleakness claims his eyes as he swallows. "I don't really celebrate."

"You don't? How come?"

"Do I look like a guy who's bursting with holiday spirit?"

I decide not to mention the Halloween ghost decoration I saw poking out from his wood chips last month. "I mean, not exactly, but everyone does *something*. What about your mom?"

"I order takeout and watch football. My mother heads up to Green Bay most years to visit her parents."

"That sounds...lonely." Peering down into my wine glass, I swipe at the lip gloss smudge with my thumb. My fears were dead-on—Cal spends Thanksgiving alone. Probably Christmas, too. As embarrassing as it is to get choked up over something like this, I can't help the prickle of tears. "It makes me sad."

"I like being alone," he reasons. "I told you that."

When I glance up at him, eyes shimmering with unshed tears, his brows crease, like he can't believe I'm getting emotional. "Spend Thanksgiving with us this year. Mom and I cook everything from scratch. There will be plenty of food."

There's a wavering softness in his expression that he tries to wash away by scrubbing a hand over his face. He scratches at his jaw, looking off to the side. "That's not necessary. I'm good."

"Please."

Our eyes meet again. Hesitation lingers, hovering between us, but it's fleeting. He shakes his head. "I appreciate the invitation, but no. I said I'm fine."

I'm about to insist, tell him about the turkey Mom cooks on the little charcoal grill in the garage, just like Dad used to, and fill him in on my favorite fixings like sweet potatoes, cranberry sauce, and my too-easy green bean casserole that basically consists of processed cheese and creamed soup—but I'm stopped short when a familiar face catches my eye, strolling by our table, hand-in-hand with someone who isn't Jessica.

He spots me immediately, doing a double-take. "Lucy?"

My chair teeters on its rear legs when I pull to a stand, almost tipping. "Greg. Hi."

Memories flood me, adding to the tears I'd hardly begun to blink away. Alyssa swivels around, her eyes popping with recognition.

"It's been a long time," Greg says, clearing his throat as his eyes flicker with shadows of the past. The woman on his arm smiles, a little warily, likely wondering why the tension in the room thickens into black tar. "How are you?"

"I'm good. I'm really good," I breathe out, glancing down at Cal, who is still seated but shifting in his chair with apprehension. "Do you come here a lot?"

"No, actually, first time. Angie recommended it..." He trails off when the brunette tightens her grip on his upper arm, her knuckles going white. Greg clears his throat. "Sorry, this is my girlfriend, Angie. Ang, this is Lucy—she used to be friends with..." He trails off again, and this time, the trail feels endless. Destination-less. Sun-stripped, full of dust and tumbleweeds. "Us," he finally opts for.

I'm latching onto something for balance, and I think it's the chairback, but I soon realize it's Cal's shoulder when his hand lifts to graze along the back of my knuckles like a calming tether. The weight on my chest loosens. I'm reeled back to sunlit skies and fresh air that doesn't make me choke. "It's nice to meet you," I say to the woman with violet-rimmed glasses and big brown eyes. She looks nothing like Jessica, who had white-blond hair, even lighter than Alyssa's, and irises painted with the jewel-blue hues of the sea. Angie nods tightly, uncomfortable. "Sorry, it's been a long time since I've seen Greg. A few years."

"No worries." She nods at my guitar case propped beside my chair. "Are you playing tonight? We were hoping to catch some live music."

"Oh, I did," I bob my head. "Unfortunately, I just wrapped up. I'll be here next week at seven."

Greg's eyes round. "You play? I mean...you play live? Like a paid gig?"

"Yep, for over a year now. I love it."

"Wow, that's..." He swipes a hand through his chestnut hair, falling away for a moment. Disappearing. Losing himself along that desert trail. "Jess would be so proud."

The air in my lungs whooshes out of me like I just stepped into a polar vortex, strangled by a glacial draft. Her name makes me woozy. Lightheaded and tipsy. My fingers dig into the expanse of Cal's shoulder, and he instinctively grips me tighter. My eyes water as I force a smile. "It's...great to see you, Greg. And so nice to meet you, Angie. I, um...I should get going, though. I have to work in the morning."

"I'll walk you out," Cal adds, rising from his chair and abandoning his partially-sipped drink. He bends to pick up my guitar case, alleviating part of my weight. "Good to meet you all."

Greg holds my gaze for a heavy beat before nodding and turning away, leading Angie to the bar. When I look down at Alyssa, she's spearing me with sympathy, mouthing, "*Call me*," before I wave my goodbyes to the group and slip away from the table.

I'm through the door before Cal can even catch up, and when I rush out into the bitter November night, I *do* choke. I *am* strangled, but it's more than the cold. So much more.

"Lucy." Cal comes up behind me, my guitar case dangling from his hand. "You good?"

My car is parallel parked behind Cal's bike on the downtown street, so I race toward it, not necessarily away from him, but away from everything else. "Sure. Of course. Thank you for grabbing that." I spin around to reach for my guitar, but he pulls it back. "I'm fine, Cal. Really."

"You look like you saw a ghost."

I'm certain my face goes as white as the ghost I wish I saw. I falter, my eyes lifting to Cal as he takes a few steps closer, his breath falling out of him in little chalky plumes. Lamplight blankets him in gold and citrine, brightening his hair like a halo, and for a moment I wonder if he's an angel.

My angel.

Words are on the tip of my tongue. The right words. The truth about Jessica and Greg and all the secrets that live inside my black hole. Instead, something else entirely escapes from my lips. "Do you have any sad songs?"

He frowns, but it's not his typical scowl. It's pensive, thoughtful. "What?"

I lick my lips, glancing out at the quiet street lined with idle cars. All I hear are my heartbeats pounding like a bass drum inside my chest. "Sad songs," I repeat. "You know, the ones you hear that make you want to cry, or dive under a warm blanket to forget. The ones that you can't sing, or even hum, because you'll choke on them. Songs that follow you around like a burial hymn."

His expression darkens. The streetlamp flickers above us as he looks down at the sidewalk cracks, then back up. "Yeah," he mutters softly. Cal sets my guitar case at my feet before inching away. "All of them."

My chest squeezes. I watch as he inhales a deep breath and pulls the beanie from his back pocket, slipping it over his head.

"Text me when you get home," he adds before walking backward. "So I know you made it okay."

I nod, swallowing hard. "It's not far."

"Text me. Please." Holding my gaze for another beat, he turns around and stalks toward his bike, swinging his leg over the seat before starting the engine.

I stand there for a moment, shivering as the snowfall picks up, watching his taillights fade into the night. I close my eyes, thinking of Jessica. Thinking of Emma. Thinking of all the things I try so hard not to think about.

Somewhere, bar noise livens with rowdy patrons, laughter, and an upbeat song. Something bouncy and light. Dance music.

A happy song.

But...all I feel is sad.

CHAPTER 17

I t's no surprise I'm standing on his front stoop on Thanksgiving day with a potted orchid in my hands and a pompom wool hat shielding my ears from the sting of an impending Wisconsin winter.

He sure seems surprised, though.

Cal towers before me in sweatpants and a t-shirt, his hand curled around his front door. "What are you doing here?"

"Happy Thanksgiving!" I chirp, holding out the lemony orchid. I chose yellow to symbolize friendship and new beginnings. "Get dressed. Mom's been up since the crack of dawn grilling the turkey."

Sweeping his eyes over me, he blinks when our gazes meet. "I already told you, I like being alone."

"Too bad."

Shock steals his expression, arcing his brows to his hairline, as if he'd been expecting me to instantly cower and trudge back to my car with my tail between my legs.

Nope—not today. Today, there will be no moping.

There will be no sad songs.

"Lucy, I'm good," he sighs, leaning against the door frame, looking weary. There are dark circles under his eyes, and his hair is messier than his usual standard for messy. Glancing away, he steps back into the foyer and clears his throat. "Tell your mom I said hi. And happy Thanksgiving."

He shuts the door in my face.

He shuts the door in my face!

My stomach churns, and my cheeks flame, despite the thirty-degree temperature. I stand there like a pillar for a moment, ramrod straight, processing his rejection, only to be met with the door reopening with a smirk dancing across Cal's mouth. I blink up at him, snapping back to reality. "I can't believe you did that."

"I'm messing with you," he grins, folding his arms. "You think you left me any other choice but to go to Thanksgiving with you?"

"Yes, Cal. The door slamming on me definitely had me thinking you went with another choice."

"You brought me a fucking flower. I'm not a total asshole." Moving aside, he ushers me through the doorway. "Hang tight while I change. For the record, I'm not staying long, and I'm not happy about it."

I let out a deep breath, relaxing on the exhale. "I'll make sure you're happy about it. I made you banana bread. And pumpkin bread. And three pies."

His interest piques. "Fuck, really?"

"Yes, really. And you can bring Cricket, too. Mom is dying to meet her."

The smirk on his face softens into something else. Something sweeter. "All right."

Our gazes hold tight, sending flutters to my heart and to much lower, much more dangerous places. I glance down at my boots and step inside, letting him close the door behind me. "Well, thanks for tagging along. I thought I might have to drag you there."

"You can still drag me. I'd encourage it."

Flirtation laces his words, and I can't hide my blush. Hopefully, he'll think it's from the chill outside. I move farther into the living area and set the orchid down on his coffee table, beside the diffuser. When I look back over at him, he's massaging the nape of his neck, the gesture causing his t-shirt to ride up his abdomen and expose rippled planks of bronzed skin.

A smattering of dark hair peeks out from atop heather gray sweatpants, heating my cheeks to a concerning level. I attempt to shift my attention to the wall before he notices, but I'm too late.

He grins again, eyes close to twinkling. "Give me five minutes. Cricket was in the kitchen earlier if you think you can avoid another hand injury."

"I'll keep my mittens on, just in case." I wiggle my fingers at him before he nods, and then treks down the short hallway to his bedroom.

Five minutes later, we're out the door.

Cal tries to take his bike to follow separately, but I convince him that Cricket would be more comfortable riding with him in my car. Truthfully, my motives are mostly selfish. If he rides with me, he can't leave early, and there's nothing I want more than to spend a whole Thanksgiving with Cal and show him what it's like to be surrounded by warmth and laughter on a holiday, instead of being alone on his couch with plastic containers of takeout food.

I'm convinced he'll never want to leave.

When we pull into my mother's long gravel driveway, I stall the car in front of the cape cod-style home with snow-white siding and black shutters. Her door is also red, which might be why I associate red doors with all things cheery and welcoming. We're greeted by a wreath woven with cardinal and burnt orange autumn leaves with a little turkey decoration dangling in the center of it.

"Nice house," Cal murmurs as we step up onto the porch with Cricket tucked underneath his arm. "You move here after...?"

After.

I swallow back the instant swell of emotion. "Yes. We moved not long after you moved. I lived here for almost ten years, but it never truly felt like *home*...you know?"

He scratches at his newly combed hair, glancing around at the architecture and the sprinkling of fall décor. "Yeah, I know."

"My parents tried, but I've come to realize that home isn't just four walls and a roof," I say softly as we linger in front of the screen door. "The memories here aren't as palpable. This isn't the house I dream about when I go to sleep at night."

Before he can respond, Mom's voice blares from the other side of the threshold, which is decidedly for the best. "Come in!" she calls, drowned out by a clamoring of barking and stampeding claws across hardwood floors. The dogs are going wild, sensing our arrival. My mother took them home with her the night before, after stopping by to help me prep side dishes, consisting of parmesan mashed potatoes, dressing with cranberries and diced apples, and a plethora of desserts.

"Anyway," I clear my throat, forcing the melancholy aside. Today isn't the day for wallowing in the past. "Come on in."

My long, burgundy peasant skirt kisses the holiday floor mat as we make our way inside, greeted by the sweet, spicy scent of cinnamon and nutmeg mingling with savory butter and brine. Lemon paces in a circle near our feet while Kiki dives at Cal's ankles. Cricket squirms from his grip, overwhelmed and more skittish than ever, dashing away to hide beneath the loveseat.

"Oh, Callahan," Mom beams, skipping out from the kitchen with a dishrag between her hands and a festive apron tied around her waist. "I'm so happy you came along. I was hoping you would. Dana couldn't make it?"

I slip out of my boots and cropped jacket, watching Cal tousle his hair before sticking his hands in his pockets. He dressed up for the occasion. A long-sleeved sienna button-down is tucked into unwrinkled khakis, which, admittedly, is a sight to see. Even his hair is spritzed with some sort of taming product. And he smells sinful.

"She's in Green Bay visiting her parents," he says to my mother, in the same way he said it to me. Detached, moderately uncomfortable. "I'll tell her you said hi."

Dana Bishop has been an elusive topic between us since our reunion this past August. He hardly talks about her, which doesn't surprise me considering his allergy to discussing family and personal matters—but still, I'm curious as to how my second mother growing up has been doing all these years. Cal gets a faraway look in his eyes whenever her name has come up.

Just like he has right now.

Curling my fingers around his stiff bicep, I gently pull him forward, toward the kitchen. He relaxes beneath my touch. "Come on. You're making pumpkin ravioli with me."

"Am I?"

"Yep. I don't eat turkey, so that's my main dish. Mom prepped the dough this morning, so I left you the fun part of turning it into raviolis while I whip up the sage-butter sauce."

"Sounds fancy. You make it all from scratch?" He glances down at me, one side of his mouth tilted up as we stroll through the foyer, still arm-in-arm.

"Does that surprise you?" My tone is flirtatious, my flash of teeth doing nothing to counter it.

His grin widens, just marginally. "I can't promise my raviolis will be up to your standards, but I'm willing to be put to work."

Warm candlelight and soft music greet us as we amble into the open kitchen. Mom has her back turned while she scrubs a dinner plate beneath the faucet, humming along to the Christmas music she always turns on at five a.m. every Thanksgiving. It's tradition, just like I hope Cal making raviolis with me will become a new tradition.

As Cal stares at the pasta press like it's a medieval torture device, Mom begins the interrogation I'd hoped wasn't coming. "So, Callahan, tell me what you've been up to these past few years. Lucy has been talking about you nonstop, but I haven't gotten all the details. How long have you been working at the auto shop?"

Nonstop?

Apparently, my mother has been taking notes from Alyssa on How To Mortify Lucy In Front Of Her Boss. I cringe, cheeks turning pink, and release his arm.

"Two years," he says as I put a notable gap between us and shuffle over to the cabinets for a saucepan. "We moved just over the border into Illinois before I came back and bought the shop from the previous owner."

"Your father would be proud," Mom tells him, toweling off the dish. "Did you go to college?"

"No. Worked with some buddies right out of high school as a

bike mechanic. We made custom motorcycles; fixed them up, too. I saved every penny to put toward the shop."

My belly twists. I didn't know that, but I suppose I never asked. Pulling a few sticks of butter out of the fridge, I glance over at him as he fiddles with the pasta press. "You did?"

"Yeah. Mom still lives in Illinois, in a town called Spring Grove. I don't see her much. She's a bit..." He stiffens a little, leaning forward on the counter. "She keeps to herself."

Curiosity blankets me, but I don't want to pry. Not now—not when Cal is in my mother's kitchen on Thanksgiving day with Christmas music and the makings of a fragile kinship wafting around us. As I pluck the butter from the wrapping, I attempt to sound subtle as I say to Mom, "How's the turkey doing? Should you check on it?"

She's on to me, of course. I've been a lot of things in this life, but subtle has never been one of them.

"You know, you're right. Millie and Dan should be here soon. Unfortunately, your cousins are celebrating with the other side of the family today, so it'll just be the five of us," she explains. "Why don't you teach Callahan how to use that?"

"Just Cal," he tells her.

He will never be "just Cal" to my mother.

Graciously, she leaves us, but not without a wink in my direction, which is *also* not subtle. I'm most certainly my mother's daughter. I roll up the sleeves of my cardigan and glide over to Cal, who's still staring down at the pasta maker and sheets of premade dough with a crease between his eyes. "The barrage of questions would never end, so I figured you might want some wine or spiked eggnog before we roll into round two," I breeze, reaching for the ravioli stamp tray.

"Your mercy has been noted. How the hell do I use this thing?"

I smile. "First, you have to flatten the dough, then we pass it through the machine until it's the perfect thickness. Once it's pressed, we use this tray to make the ravioli shapes." I sidle up to him, catching a whiff of his cologne that makes me borderline delirious. Snatching up the rolling pin, I flatten the dough into a circle, swiping a loose strand of hair out of my face. "Like this.

It's pretty easy. The hard part was getting the dough to be the perfect consistency."

"Yeah," he murmurs. "Looks good."

When I glance up, he's staring at me and not the dough. Cal lifts his thumb to graze along my cheekbone, sending a shot of heat through me.

"You've got some flour on your cheek."

"Mmm. Common kitchen hazard." He's so close, too close, as we both weave the dough through the machine, our fingers brushing and teasing. "You don't cook much?"

"Nah," he says, collecting the dough as it slides out the bottom. "I'm a takeout man. Frozen dinners when I'm feeling frisky. Dad was always the chef in the family, so after he passed —" he falters for a moment, throat bobbing, "—Mom never really took over in that department. Any culinary potential I might have had died with him."

His words are blue, bleeding with sorrow, coincidentally spoken in time with Elvis' *Blue Christmas*—one of my least favorite holiday jingles. And that's because it's less of a jingle, and more of a psalm. "It's never too late to learn. I can teach you if you want."

He helps crank the dough through a second time, sparing me a quick glance. "I'm too busy. Thanks, though."

I nod, solemnly. I know Cal is busy, but no busier than me; no busier than a lot of people. Part of me wonders if he's too busy being in a permanent state of just existing to put any effort into the little things that would help him come alive again.

Once the pasta is thin enough, we stamp it into ravioli shapes. We work together, side by side, mostly in silence as our inner thoughts take over the conversation. Laughter sneaks in once or twice, lightening the mood, and we fall into an easy routine of shaping, filling, pressing, boiling. His squares are uneven, his technique unrefined, but I take note of his misshapen raviolis and secretly plan to steal them for my own plate. To me, they are perfect.

When the pasta is cooked through and simmering in the saucepan, Cal looks over at me, his expression spotlighted by the muted window light. He looks proud, fulfilled.

Unweighted and content.

And it makes me want to wrap my arms around him and claim him as my own, just like I'm going to claim his perfectly imperfect raviolis.

Instead, I dig up his prior declaration and let it echo through me, over and over, until I'm forced to believe it.

I won't love you, I won't love you, I won't love you.

And I refuse to call it fate; I refuse to call it luck—but I suppose it's for the best that I can't love him either.

The difference is…I say *can't.*

He says won't.

Dinner wraps up by six p.m., everyone full on food and wine. A gentle flurry of snowflakes falls from a newly darkened sky, sheathing the ground in pure white. Aunt Millie shuffles around the dining room, cleaning the table and popping dishes into the sink while Mom and I unwrap the ungodly amount of dessert selections. Cal and Uncle Dan are absorbed in a sports-related conversation, and I'm grateful the subjects of discussion were by all means light. The only time that lightness was compromised was when my uncle started talking about moving me into Cal's old house, reminiscing the last time he'd seen it, when it was thriving with fertile rose bushes and children dancing through sprinklers in the front lawn. I was quick to divert, pivoting back to politics.

I'm confident we were the only dinner table tonight in which the topic of politics was less destructive than memories.

"Are you going to play some songs for us, sweetheart?" Mom touches my shoulder, giving it a squeeze. "It's one of my favorite things about holiday gatherings."

Instinct has me looking over my shoulder at Cal, who seems to have checked out of Uncle Dan's conversation, and has his gaze pinned on me from across the room. I clear my throat, pulling plastic wrap off the loaf of banana bread. "I didn't bring my guitar."

"Use your father's. It's in my closet."

I suppose I could. It's not that I don't want to—I love playing for my family—but knowing Cal will be watching the intimate performance has my nerves winding into a queasy knot. I'm afraid emotion will get the better of me. "Okay, sure. I can play a song or two."

"Wonderful. Go tune up while I get the dessert ready." She swipes her palm up and down my back affectionately.

When I return from the upstairs bedroom with a guitar tucked in my trembling hands and an anxious flutter in my chest, I spot Cal digging into the banana bread I made especially for him. I glance at the dining table, noting he's the only one who took a slice, leaving the abhorrent end piece for someone else. A smile pulls.

"So, we're going to get a private Imogen performance, huh?" he asks through a bite, watching as I float down the staircase and move toward him. He's seated on the loveseat with Cricket pressed against his thigh, while the rest of the family fills their plates with pie in the adjacent room.

"Just Lucy tonight," I tell him, smile widening. "I'll admit, I'm a little nervous."

"Yeah? How come?"

I fold my lips together. "You know why."

"Ah." He nods, swallowing down a forkful. "I've seen you play before."

"I know, but this feels more...intimate." The word thickens between us as his eyes slide over me, glinting with gold against the dim lighting and flickering candle flames. "It's different at the wine bar. The atmosphere isn't the same, and I can zone out easier."

"You think I'm going to judge you?"

"No, I think you're going to see me. All of me."

I'm not sure where the declaration comes from, but my cheeks burn when the words slice through the buoyant mood that had been simmering between us all day. Just like that, I sink.

The waters turn dark and turbulent with an unexpected storm, yanking me under.

Dangling the guitar at my side, I use my unoccupied hand to sweep my hair back. "I just mean—"

"I know what you mean," he says, tone grave, fork poking at the lump of half-eaten bread. "You say it like it's a negative thing."

"It's a vulnerable thing. I don't want you to see me as anything but that girl in the picture. Happy, burdenless, alive," I confess, taking tentative steps toward him. "I'm afraid I'll sing, and you'll uncover all my buried pieces. The things I don't want you to see."

He swallows. "Would that be so bad?"

Would it?

Vulnerability is a gateway to attachment. Once someone unearths all your scratched, damaged bits, there's no hiding them away again. They're just there, out in the open, every flaw and defect on display. You lose a sense of control—and whether that's a good thing or a bad thing, depends on the person doing the unearthing.

It depends on how much you trust them with your imperfections.

"I don't know," I admit, nibbling my lip.

Cal sets his plate down on the side table, pulling Cricket into his lap. Leaning back against the loveseat, he shrugs. "One way to find out. Play me something."

"What? Right now?"

"Sure. Sing me a song you don't normally play when you're performing."

A song instantly comes to mind, but I'm gripped with hesitation.

Playing *just* for Cal, for *only* Cal, has my heart hammering in my chest. My ears are ringing, skin buzzing. My equilibrium feels wobbly. Singing this song for him will either have him running the other way, or it will connect us even more deeply, and I'm not sure which option I prefer.

The truth is, I like us the way we are. Safe, uncomplicated, tiptoeing just outside the edges of heartbreak.

And yet, my feet pace forward until I'm seated across from him in Dad's favorite worn recliner. It rocks beneath my weight, still lingering with the scent of leather and smoky tobacco as I move into position and place my fingers on the strings. I close my eyes and tune the guitar, feeling him watching me. Studying me from a few feet away, though he might as well be right on top of me.

Unearthing me.

Heaving in a rickety breath, I center myself.

And then, I sing.

It's a song called *Can't Go Back* by Rosi Golan. I've never played it live before because it's not overly well-known to the public—or maybe because it's *too* well-known to me. It takes me someplace else. The melody is melancholic, a little soulful, nostalgic, and glum. Reminiscent of things severed, of things long gone. A past we can't get back.

But it's beautiful, too. Raw with humanity, steeped in emotion.

I let it all bleed out of me in painful rivulets of hope and regret. I sing for Cal, I sing for me, I sing for Emma and Jessica, for my father, for his father, and for all the things we can't get back but can't let go.

I didn't want to cry, but I knew I would.

When the last note is strum, my cheeks are damp with tears. I inhale a long breath, my eyes fluttering open. Cal is bent forward on the loveseat, elbows to his knees, hands steepled and pressed against his chin. He's staring at me. *Staring* at me, like he's in a trance, like he choked down every chord and now he's drunk on them.

I blink through wet lashes. My mother is standing to my left, her hands clasped across her heart. She's also crying quiet tears, her smile love-laced, while the rest of my family gathers around her. Uncle Dan is first to clap, a sound that has me jolting in my seat, back to reality, away from the past. Everyone joins in the applause except for Cal. He's still staring at me, hands now cupped together at his mouth while his brows furrow into a deep crease. It looks like he's deciding if he wants to run away or kiss me, both options stealing us from the comfortable safe haven we were sheltering in three minutes ago.

Clearing my throat, I force a smile. First at him, then at my family. "Thank you. Sorry I got a little misty-eyed," I laugh lightly. "That song means a lot to me."

"You sing beautifully, Lucy," my uncle says. "Straight from the heart."

"Just like your father did," Mom adds, wiping her tear stains on the sleeve of her blouse. "I know he saw that, sweetie. He's smiling so brightly right now."

My heart squeezes. Aunt Millie blows me a kiss before spinning around to finish piling her pie with whipped cream, while my uncle follows behind her. Life returns to its standard state of blissful chaos while I continue to strum guitar strings, and Cal continues to watch me like I've bewitched him somehow.

After a few moments of plucking aimless chords, I prop the guitar against the wall and rise to my feet. "I'm going to get some air," I murmur, observing the way he follows my movements with only his eyes. Part of him is here, but part of him is somewhere else. He says nothing. "I'll be right back."

I traipse over to the foyer and slip into my boots, coat, and beige mittens, then slink out the front door. The lawn is sheathed in immaculate white, glittering under the lone streetlamp. It's so quiet tonight. Mom lives off an unpopulated road, tucked way back in a wooded lot, making the world feel soundless. I wrap my arms around myself, the air bitter but calm. There's no angry draft or howling wind; only a still, peaceful serenity.

As I gaze up at the skyful of stars twinkling down on me like fireflies at midnight, a weightless feeling fills my chest. That strange sense of déjà vu sweeps through me again, like it did not long ago when I left the sanctuary early to help Cal with inventory. The day I cut my hand.

The day he called me "sunshine" for the first time in years.

It's a feeling of familiarity tied to nothing specific, like a lost memory I can't seem to locate.

A warm, nostalgic tickle.

And in that moment, with my nose kissing the blue-black sky

and my favorite song still vibrating through me, I decide that it's Emma.

She's speaking to me.

She's hugging me.

She's with me.

"It's freezing out here."

Cal's voice has me spinning around in the few inches of snow, almost slipping. A beanie is pulled over his ears, a winter coat zipped halfway up his torso. His eyes are also aimed skyward, hands in his pockets, and he stands as still as a millpond a few feet away from me. "I'm not cold," I answer back. It's the truth. The air is cold, but I am not.

He glances at me. "I liked your song."

"It looked like it made you sad," I say softly, quirking a smile to counter the mood.

A plume of breath hits the icy air as he exhales, eyes narrowing at the sky. "Yeah," he agrees. "But in a good way. Sort of like you do."

"I make you sad in a good way?" My nose crinkles at the opposition of it.

"Something like that."

I'm not sure what to make of the sentiment, but it doesn't sound like an insult, so I nod my head and follow his gaze toward the darkened skyline. Silence stretches between us, both of us lost in the stillness of the night. It feels good to just be still sometimes.

I close my eyes, blackening my vision until all I can *do* is be still.

No sound, no sight, no taste.

Just the earthy aroma of terpene-scented snowfall, and the feel of a crisp November freezing my ears and turning my nose pink.

"The last time it snowed on Thanksgiving was that final year with them," Cal murmurs, sounding a foot closer than he once was. "It's been a decade since my dad was bundled up in the garage watching a football game after sneaking Mom's appetizers from the fridge."

I keep my eyes closed, but I feel the warm prickle of tears try to break free, nonetheless. A watery smile blooms as I recall that

Thanksgiving ten years ago. We celebrated at Cal and Emma's house, and his mother was *livid* when she noticed the charcuterie board was half eaten by the time we'd arrived. Alan Bishop had been banished to the garage. It was a good-natured punishment, mostly, and eventually, we all sat together at their grand dining room table to feast. The table was the one grand thing in their small house—now my house—taking up the entire space.

It was the one grand thing, aside from the love I felt there.

Before I can add my thoughts, Cal speaks first.

"I had no idea that six months later, the sound of my dad cheering on the game would be replaced with discovering him slumped over the wheel in that same garage, dead from carbon monoxide poisoning."

Sound comes careening back like a ten-car pileup. It's a collision of screams and wails, shattering glass, squealing tires, and crushing metal.

My eyes pop open, balance teetering in the snow. A sharp breath escapes me like an airbag just deployed, puncturing my chest. "Cal..." All I can say is his name, and nothing more.

His expression doesn't wilt as he continues to stare blankly at the sky that now looks more black than blue. "I'm glad you brought me here today."

Is he, though?

All it seems to have done is remind him of everything he's lost.

I shake my head, pivoting toward him. "I didn't mean to trigger bad memories. I just...I wanted..."

"You wanted to make me happy, and I am."

"You don't look happy," I note gravely, stepping closer to him.

He shrugs a little, not with defeat but with a semblance of certainty. "What does happiness look like to you?"

I go to speak, then seal my lips. What *does* it look like? What does happiness look like after inconceivable loss? It doesn't look the same as it used to, that's for sure.

Cal finally looks away from the sky to face me, a smile cresting. It's faint, but it's not forced. It looks genuine. It looks as happy as it can be.

And then, in a blink, before I even know what's happening, he falls backward in the snow.

I move forward. "Cal...?"

"We made snow angels that night," he tells me, extending his arms and widening his legs. "Emma pulled me down into the snow, laughing in the way only she could laugh. So fucking honest, like her joy was a tangible thing."

I choke out my own laugh, recalling how annoyed Cal was to get his clothes wet. "You hated it. You were miserable," I tease gently, wanting to join him but unable to move. I'm frozen to the ground like the winter frost.

"I hated it until I couldn't hate it anymore. She had that way about her, you know?" His arms move up and down, legs side to side, leaving a giant angel-shaped imprint underneath him. "Just like you do."

Finally, I urge my legs to move, to carry me toward him until I fall beside him in the snow. A startled laugh-cry falls out of me when my hair dampens with snowflakes. I move my arms and legs in tandem with his, and I wonder what we look like right now, two grown adults playing in the snow like children. Heartbreak entangled with innocence. A meshing of pain and hope.

We glance at each other at the same time. We're far enough apart that our arms don't knock together, but close enough that I can see his eyes shimmering with all the same things I'm feeling. I laugh when he kicks a chunk of snow at me, and he laughs when I retaliate. We're smiling, joyful, reminiscing but moving forward all at once.

And then he rolls over until he's looming above me.

My breath hitches.

The cold of the snow melts by way of his warmth as he removes a loose strand of hair from my lip gloss. A shiver sneaks down my back. "I'm glad you're here," I tell him.

I'm glad I found my way back to you.

Cal swallows, his eyes skating over my face, holding on my mouth. He lifts a hand to cradle my neck, thumb skimming my jaw, and leans in.

I think he's about to press his lips to mine—to take that kiss we've been strategically evading—but he thinks better of it.

He thinks better of it because he said he won't love me.

Instead, with his hand curled around the side of my neck, he bends to place a kiss on my hairline. Soft and sweet. Cal lingers, dragging his lips an inch lower to brush a second kiss to my forehead. My eyes flutter closed, my heartbeats skidding erratically like bald tires in the snow. My breathing shallows. His chest is pressed to mine, his fingers twining through my hair. I want nothing more than to lift my chin and steal that kiss I shouldn't take. He'd let me, I know he would. He's waiting for me to make the first move, to let him know I'm willing to risk it all. I could kiss him beneath the stars, just like that first time, and I'd find my way into his bed by night's end.

One night of bliss in exchange for a lifetime of heartbreak.

Somehow, it's tempting.

Cal's lips trail to my ear, his grip on my neck tightening. "You're thinking about it, aren't you?"

I expel a shaky breath. "About what?"

"Giving in. Letting me take you home, letting me sink into you."

Involuntarily, my legs part wider, answering for me. I squeeze the front of his button-down, but I'm not sure if it's a way to pull him closer or push him away. I'm always finding myself floundering in between the two, wondering which way I'll inevitably fall.

All it takes is for me to think about Greg walking into that wine bar, sans Jessica.

"I can't. I shouldn't," I say, my tone laced with despair. "I'm sorry."

His eyes close through a nod. "Yeah." Cal drinks in a deep breath before he rolls off of me, then sits up. "For the best."

We remain idle for a moment, laughter from inside the house floating out through the thin walls, trespassing on our solitude. "We, um...should get back inside. I'm sure Mom has been spying through the drapes." I try to add levity where there is none.

Dipping his head, he nods again. "Yep. The dogs probably finished off my banana bread." Cal's attempt also falls flat.

Avoiding eye contact, we both rise to our feet, and I glance down at our creations.

Two angels are pressed into the fallen snow, while I'm certain another watches from above.

The image pinches my chest and grips my heart. My gaze pans over to Cal who isn't looking at the grass-tipped angel designs, but glancing up at the sky one last time. He falters before walking away and moving toward the front door, slipping inside.

I look back down at the snow angels.

Side by side; one big, one small, softly illuminated by starlight and the glow of the streetlamp. Cal's has a smudge through it from where he rolled over for an almost-kiss.

I can't help but smile.

He told me I made him sad in a good way, and I didn't know what that meant. Now, I think I know. I think I get it.

Things that make us sad aren't all bad.

Sometimes, sad things serve as a gentle reminder that we still feel.

CHAPTER 18

I chose red.

I'm draped in the most vibrant shade of ruby, from the stain on my lips to the "Vixen" nail polish on my fingertips. My dress is long and form-fitting, the neckline lower than I'm normally comfortable with, given my scar is on full display, and my hair is down and curled, set in place with a misting of hairspray.

The mirror is my friend tonight as I twist from side to side, fisting a cream-hued clutch at my hip.

"You're an absolute smokeshow, bestie," Alyssa calls from behind me, her voice muffled by the roar of the hair dryer. "I give it five hours."

I blink, pivoting around from the hallway mirror to glance at her standing at my bathroom sink. "Five hours?"

The dryer shuts off. "Until your virginity has been voraciously claimed."

A shiver rolls through me. I'm not sure how I feel about the word *voraciously*, or about losing my virginity to Cal for that matter, but I can't help my skin from trying to match the shade of my dress. "You're relentless," I chuckle awkwardly.

"I know," she quips, tugging down the hem of her black minidress. "Oh! Speaking of virginity, I was thinking we could all go out for drinks after the wedding. Maybe some karaoke."

"Hmm. Maybe." Truthfully, I'm not feeling up for that tonight. I'm too nervous about the prospect of being Cal's date for the evening, that all I can focus on is how I'm going to end the night with my virtue still intact.

And if that's even what I want.

A knock at the front door has my dogs barking, their paws sliding across the floor as they race to the front of the house. My heart skips. We're all riding together in my car since Alyssa is going stag and wants to take advantage of the open bar. I have no problem being the DD.

Fiddling with a stubborn curl in front of the mirror, I call out, "Come in!"

I hear the door creak open, and I shuffle down the hallway to greet him in the foyer.

My heart lurches when I spot Cal looking as dapper as I've ever seen him. It leaps like it's trying to reach him somehow. Like it wants to plow through his chest and dance with his. Dressed up in a coal-gray dress shirt and black slacks, hair slicked and tamed with product, and his goatee trimmed to a shadow of stubble, he looks like he stepped straight out of a Men's Wearhouse ad. He's fiddling with the button of his barrel cuff when his head pops up.

He does the epitome of a double-take when he spots me standing at the base of the hallway. "Jesus Christ."

I flush from head to toe. Cal doesn't even pretend to be unaffected by the effort I put into my appearance, and the fire in his eyes is almost enough to burn down my steeliest walls. Gulping hard, I fidget under his stare and duck my head. "Sometimes I clean up okay," I laugh lightly, flattening the skirt of my dress with clammy palms.

The veins in his neck pulse, his pupils blown. "A girl as sweet as you shouldn't look like sin," he murmurs, voice full of grit. "Brings me to my goddamn knees."

I glance up, eyes widening, breath catching in my throat. I'm not even sure how to respond to that. Maybe I should force a weird laugh, or maybe I should run away. Maybe I should thank him.

Maybe I should strip.

Mercifully, Alyssa sweeps up behind me, smacking my butt as she passes. "Isn't she stunning? A next-level hottie."

Cal hardly spares my friend a glance as she moves into the living room to retrieve her purse and high heels. His eyes are locked, loaded, trailing me from bottom to top in a slow pull. All he manages is a throaty, "Yeah."

I go with the weird laugh. "Ha...ha," I mutter awkwardly, wringing my hands together. "You look great yourself. Really great."

He doesn't reply. Just stares at me, drinking me in.

"Everyone ready?" I look around, my chest feeling fuzzy and tight.

Me, Cal, Alyssa, my willpower to stay fully clothed all evening.

Alyssa chirps an eager "yes," and then we all pile out the door. When Cal's hand presses to the arch of my lower back, then makes a languid dip to my backside and lingers, heat blooms all over, sheathing me in white-hot surrender.

My willpower doesn't stand a chance.

It's the embodiment of a dream wedding. The ballroom is sprinkled with pinecone centerpieces, tasteful red flannel, warm candlelight, and mason jars filled with sprigs of greenery and holly berries. Rustic winter charm welcomes us to the reception as I glide through the double doors with Cal's hand pressed to the expanse of skin exposed through my backless dress.

The music is soft, the laughter loud. Gemma and Knox's friends and relatives mingle in small circles while a flurry of waiters pop in with trays of hors d'oeuvres and champagne flutes. My eyes pan to a giant Christmas tree that stands in the far corner, decorated in red and gold ornaments, and tinsel glinting beneath grand chandeliers. It takes my breath away.

After locating our table number, Cal guides me to table seven off to the left, where Alyssa is already sitting and chatting with someone I don't recognize. He snags two glasses of champagne on the trek over, and I take it, sending him a grateful smile. Even though there's an open bar tonight, I don't plan on drinking more than one glass of champagne—mostly because I'm driving.

Also because the last time I drank more than a glass of wine in front of Cal, I straddled him. And then I got stuck in a t-shirt on his guest room floor.

"Lucy!" Alyssa waves us over with her bacon-wrapped date. "God, that ceremony had me bawling. Those *vows*," she says when we approach, collapsing against her chairback. "Tell me you cried."

"I cried." I take a seat in the chair Cal pulls out for me, smiling my thanks as he situates to my right. "It was beautiful. Makes me want to have a winter wedding someday." My heart pangs with remorse because I know I'll never have a winter wedding someday.

Cal takes a sip of his champagne. "Your birthday is coming up," he states.

Glancing at him, I rest my chin in my hand and stretch a smile. "You remembered my birthday?"

"Of course. It's the same day as Christmas."

I suppose that makes it pretty convenient to remember, but I can't help the tickle of warmth that rushes through me, regardless. "We should spend it together this year," I suggest.

His eyes narrow thoughtfully. "You want to spend your favorite holiday, and your birthday, with your boss?"

"We both know you're more than just my boss, Cal."

That's the truth; he knows it, and I know it. The precise definition of our relationship is decidedly ambiguous, but still— we're *more*.

More than co-workers.

More than acquaintances.

More than friends, even.

More than what we can become.

And when Cal takes another sip of champagne and glances away with a small nod, wrapping an arm around the back of my chair, his fingers tickling my bare shoulder, the flimsy thread of friendship dangles between us even more precariously. I already feel the snap of it. A tether giving way to the ultimate ruin.

Goosebumps case my arms, causing me to fidget in my seat while subconsciously scooting closer to the man on my right. In turn, he holds me a little tighter.

Alyssa perks up from across the table, pushing her empty cocktail plate aside. "Are you going to be my dance partner tonight?" She wiggles her perfectly shaded eyebrows at me.

I pop my chin up and smile deviously. "Think we can put in a request with the band?"

"This isn't karaoke, Lucy. It's a wedding." Then she matches my smile with her own. "But yes."

And just like that, we're two best friends sharing a moment, breaking out into Lady Gaga's greatest hit—in our humble opinion—*Bad Romance*. As she raises an arm skyward and does spirit fingers on the way down, singing, *"I don't wanna be frieeeends,"* Cal's eyes meet with mine with a notable twinkle, and I'm drowning in a puddle of half-laughter, half-love.

Truth be told, there's no better place to be.

When we come down from the best-friend high, I'm still giggling when the woman beside Alyssa sends a warm smile in my direction, her gaze ping-ponging between me and Cal.

"How long have you two been together?" the stranger in an emerald dress to match her eyes wonders, fingering her champagne glass.

Cal speaks up first. "We're not together."

And yet, he doesn't bother to remove his arm. I swear he even pulls me closer.

The woman nods, her gaze sparkling peculiarly. "Oh, my bad. That was so presumptuous," she chuckles, looking away.

"We're friends. Good friends," I add, leaning to my right because I can't help it. I can't help leaning into him, just as I can't help breathing. Breathing is an innate part of me, and so is Cal. "How do you know the bride and groom?"

I make small talk to avoid the big talk. And while the woman introduces herself as Leslie and prattles on about high school friendships and college sororities, I realize my hand finds its way to Cal's thigh underneath the white tablecloth. Then, it becomes the only thing I realize. It's the only thing in this room I'm wholly aware of—my hand on Cal's thigh.

Paired with the way he doesn't move away, doesn't even flinch.

Mingling with the way his breathing shallows ever so slightly, and the way his fingertips trail down my upper arm, then glide back up to tinker with the strap of my dress.

Braided with the way we're shoulder-to-shoulder now, pressed together at this giant round table like there's nowhere else to go.

I could go anywhere, sit anywhere, move a dozen seats away, but the thought alone is the equivalent to slicing off my right hand.

There's nowhere else I'd rather be.

And then dinner is served, and speeches are given, and tears are shed, but somehow, nothing registers. My plate of pasta is a blur in front of me. Voices and laughter are muddled, bleeding into the sound of my ear-splitting heart-beats. Dance music filters through the ballroom, pulling guests from their chairs, but I am glued to the man beside me. His palm moves up my shoulder to massage my neck while he eats his chicken dish one-handed, and all I can taste as I draw the fork to my mouth is the acidity of what's to come.

Because I want this.

I want this.

"You've hardly touched your food," Cal notes as he chews, glancing down at my plate. His hand still rubs my neck, fingers tickling my hair. "Not hungry?"

I choke down a bite. "Not really." My fork clinks against the plate when I set it down, just as my cell phone pings from inside my clutch. I fish around for it as Cal finally removes his arm, and then glance at the text message from Alyssa who is giving me a Cheshire grin from across the table.

ALYSSA:

I have condoms in my purse. Do you need one?

I'm positive my complexion goes whiter than the linen table-cloth. I hadn't fully swallowed down my mouthful of noodles, so they slither down my throat like worms in the mud, almost choking me. I text her back.

ME:

I don't know. Maybe.

I can't believe I'm considering it.

The room feels stifling. An actual furnace.

I catch the way her eyes pop at my response as her thumbs skip over the keypad in reply.

ALYSSA:

Holy shit. Bathroom break.

The text is followed by the legs of her chair screeching across the sandstone-colored tile. Mine follow. Turning to Cal, I toss my napkin to the tabletop and flip my hair over my shoulder. "I'll be right back. Are you good?"

He nods, attention shifting from me to Alyssa, then back to me. "I'm good. Are you?"

"Yep. Sure, of course. Definitely. Just running to the washroom. You know, to...pee."

His tongue rolls along his teeth. "Kay."

I bolt.

Alyssa is hot on my heels as we wind our way to the bathrooms. "Oh my God," she whisper-yells from behind me.

"Please don't make it a thing," I plead, beyond flustered.

"But it *is* a thing. It's definitely a thing."

When we're safely inside the women's restroom, the door whips closed, and we stand face-to-face. I place both palms to my neck and inhale a quivering breath. "What do I do?" I wheeze.

"Are you asking me how to have sex?"

"I think so."

Grinning, she slides her index finger through the circle she made with her opposite hand, then pumps it in and out a few times. "It's not a Power Point presentation, but you get the gist."

"Not that part," I practically choke. "The other stuff. Everything else."

She drops her arms to her sides with a pitying sigh, her smile softening. "You just go with it, Lucy. Don't overthink anything. Cal seems like the 'take charge' type, so I'm sure he'll steer you around the curves." She hesitates, head cocking. "Wait, does he know you're a virgin?"

I gulp, swallowing hard. "Yes, I told him."

"And he's cool? Some guys are weird about it."

"I think so. He said it made him want me even more."

She starts fanning herself. "Stick a fork in me. Okay. Well, it's going to be amazing and perfect, got it? Don't worry. Don't stress." Reaching for her purse, Alyssa shoves her hand inside and pulls out a foil-wrapped square. "Here, take this just in case."

I stare at it like it's the peak of Mount Chimborazo and she told me to start climbing. Blinking at the condom, I take it with shaky fingers and bury it inside my clutch, zipping it up. "Thanks."

I'm not entirely sure I'll be able to go through with it for the same reasons I haven't been able to up until this point. But, I'm not sure how much longer I can avoid it, either. We feel imminent. Fated. Two live wires dodging and deflecting until the only thing left to do is combust.

Alyssa grips my shoulders and leans in close, her smile wide. "I've been waiting for this moment," she tells me. "*You* being in charge of the spicy stories for once."

The heaviness falls away for a moment, and I release a laugh. "I do owe you."

"You do." She pulls me in for a hug. "You have to tell me everything. Every tawdry detail."

We pull apart, and I take a moment to fluff my hair in the mirror and apply a smear of bubblegum lip balm over my faded red lip stain, my inhibitions floating off into the deep end.

No more shallow water.

Alyssa drags me from the bathroom a few minutes later, straight onto the dance floor. An upbeat song is playing— Whitney Houston's *I Wanna Dance With Somebody*. Typically, I wouldn't be nearly intoxicated enough to let loose, but since I'm drunk on something else, I zone out and let the music mix with adrenaline, the rhythm fusing with the prospect of turning indecision into resolve. Our bodies twist and writhe, hands in the air, our carefully coiffed hair flying in every direction. Gemma and Knox join us, along with Leslie and a few other spirited strangers, and we all go wild beneath multicolored strobes and gleaming chandeliers.

The song gradually morphs into something softer, something low-key and romantic, and Gemma and Knox pull together for a slow dance while Alyssa and Leslie tipsily dance with each other.

Before I can sneak away from the blooming romance in the air, Cal is beside me, a hand curling around my waist. I fly around to face him, sheened in a light sweat. My smile brightens. "Are we dancing?" I ask as we fall into an organic rhythm.

He smiles back. "Aren't we always?"

I melt against his chest as his arms envelop me, sighing into his dress shirt. My hands travel upward, latching onto his biceps while we undulate to a dreamy country song. "I suppose we are," I murmur. I'm not sure he can hear my muffled response, but he pulls me tighter anyway.

His hand strokes up and down my spine, gently fisting my hair, before repeating the motion. Our feet are hardly moving. We just sway. Our bodies feel like a single entity as we rock ever so slightly, and my eyes close as I breathe him in. Earthy musk, bourbon cologne, oaky notes. Masculine, overpowering, potentially lethal.

Cal's heartbeats thrum against my ear as I press my cheek to his chest. He inhales a flimsy breath that mimics my own as a child shakes a jingle bell bracelet at a nearby table.

"Want to know why I have those jingle bells at the shop?"

My breath all but stops as I open my eyes and wait.

The jingle bells shake again.

"Every time that door would open, I'd think of you."

A wall of tears blanket my vision. I squeeze him tighter for fear of falling; for fear of truly *falling*. "Really?" I squeak out.

He nods, his chin resting atop my head. "Yeah, really. You used to wear a jingle bell necklace for every day in December. I'd be doing homework in my bedroom, and those little bells would chime each time you'd pace the room, run down the hallway, or have a dance party with Emma. Always made me smile."

I can't cry. I won't cry.

Cal just admitted that he's thought about me, all while I've lived in a lonely reality of thinking he'd forgotten me. I force back the deadly waves of emotion threatening to yank me under and bury my face into his chest. I feel his heartbeats kick up, and he bends down to gather me closer still, nuzzling his stubble against the sensitive curve of my neck.

"I know I said I was going to back off," he murmurs right into my ear. "But I assure you...this is me using an unbearable amount of restraint."

Me, too.

Me goddamn too.

I'm only partly aware of the song ending and guests jumping into livelier dance moves as the beat picks up, but we continue to hold each other for a few more minutes, swaying, remembering, wanting. Wanting more than what I've allowed.

Finally, I inch away, gazing up at the lust-laced look in his eyes. "Want to get some air?" I nod my head to the glass double doors that lead out onto a terrace.

"Sure."

He takes my hand and grabs his coat, and we weave through the thrashing bodies to find our reprieve on the other side of the doors. A few guests are bundled up, puffing on cigarettes and laughing through the smoke, so we make our way farther into the night, away from the ballroom. The reception is being held in a botanic garden, and there's a trail leading to landscaped gardens of dahlias and winterizing roses. The snow has mostly melted, but patches of white are still sprinkled into dirt and green grass.

The temperature has warmed to the upper forties, but I forgot my jacket inside, and my body shivers against the cold.

Cal notices and starts pulling off his coat. "You're freezing." Wrapping me in the warm leather, he brushes his hands up and down my arms to subdue the chill. "Why did you want to come out here?"

He asks it like he's fishing for more because he knows it's more.

He wants to know the real reason I wanted to get him alone.

I stumble over my truth as we stand idle among the winter

blooms, not a soul in sight. Glancing up at the night sky twinkling with stars, I let out a breath. "It's peaceful out here."

"Yeah," he nods, still warming me through the jacket with his touch. "It is."

I swallow. "You really have those jingle bells on the door because of me?"

"Yes." His jaw clenches, eyes skimming my reaction. "You think I forgot about you, but I never did. I never intended to."

"Why...why didn't you look for me?"

"I did. One time." Grinding his teeth together, he bends to rest his forehead against mine. "The day I got my driver's license, I drove up to your old house, but you'd already moved. I took it as a sign to leave the past in the past," he says gravely. "Besides...I knew this would happen."

"Knew what?" I probe, voice shaky.

"You know what."

He says it like it would be a devastating thing—and he's right, I reckon. Only, he doesn't know *why* he's right. Cal has no practical reason to be scared of this.

I pull back, knowing I have to tell him the truth.

I have to tell him everything before we take this any further.

My speech is unplanned, a mess of words and sad confessions jumbled in my mind, and I need a minute to think it through. It has to be right. It has to be careful and gentle and *right*.

I turn away from him to gather my thoughts.

And that's when his fingers snake around my wrist, tugging me back to him. In a single, furious heartbeat, I'm pulled against his chest as his hands reach out to cup both sides of my face.

He bends down, opens my mouth with his, and slides his tongue inside.

Instantly, I moan.

His tongue is inside me, trespassing on my confession until it flees from my lips.

He's kissing me.

Kissing me.

It's nothing like our first kiss, so innocent and tame.

This is all tongue and heat and pure need.

The tinderbox inside of me, once filled with flint and twigs and dying leaves, has been ignited. I'm a firestorm, a sea of flames.

I reach out and latch onto his shoulders to steady myself. One of his hands moves to cradle the back of my head, fingers fisting my hair and scraping my scalp. He groans into my mouth, tongue plunging in and out of me, desperate and wild. Cal twists my head to the side, angling our kiss to delve deeper. My own tongue meets his thrusts like I've done it a thousand times before, skimming across the roof of his mouth and pulling more groans out of him.

He walks me backward. Stumbling over my feet, he keeps me upright, wrapping an arm behind my back, not breaking the kiss. I'm pressed up against a trellis, his hard erection digging into my belly. It sends a rush of moisture to my underwear, and I grind into him on instinct.

"*Fuck*," he rasps, pulling back and breathing heavily. His hand is still in my hair, squeezing and tugging. "Fuck, Lucy."

"Cal..." I arc against him, aching to relieve the pressure between my legs. My skin is flushed and hot, my heartbeats thundering. I hold him tight, my head tipped back against the wood trellis.

"I know you're a virgin, I know you're scared, but I know you want this as much as I do." He kisses me again, pulling my bottom lip between his teeth until I mewl. "It's all I can think about."

I nod, light-headed. The juncture between my thighs heats and throbs as if his mouth is already on me.

"I'll get us a hotel room," he husks, mouth trailing to my neck. "Tonight. Right now. Privacy, cool sheets, champagne. I promise I'll make it so fucking good for you."

Desire sluices me, and I can hardly function enough to remain standing. Cal drags a hand down my body, squeezing my hip, then moves it lower. Before I even know what's happening, his fingers are inching up my dress, grazing along my inner thigh.

"I'm dying to touch you," he says, his lips resting against my mouth. We pant in time with each other, sharp wisps of breaths warming and wanting. "I'm desperate to feel what I'm doing to you."

I nod again because I can't find words. My vocal cords have withered away to ash.

"Fuck," he repeats at my silent consent, lifting his hand all the way up my thigh until his fingers are pushing my silk panties to the side. When he comes in contact with the hot pool of desire drenching the fabric, he physically reacts to it. His face twists with lust, his eyebrows pinching together, lips parting against mine as he groans, "Goddamn. You're soaked for me."

His fingertips tease me gently until one slips inside, causing me to gasp and nearly collapse.

"I got you," he pants, "I got you." Cal slides a finger in and out of me, holding me up by the waist with his other hand as I shamelessly writhe against him. "Does that feel good?"

When he rubs my clit with the underside of his palm, I feel like I might actually black out. Somehow, I manage to moan out a tapered, "Yes."

"No one's ever touched you like this before?"

"No."

"Just me?"

All I can do is nod, stabbing my bottom lip with my teeth.

"Say it," he orders, grit in his throat.

I moan again, falling apart. "Just you."

"Jesus, Lucy..." He kisses me, deeply, messily, the slippery sound of him fingering me echoing through the quiet night. Pulling away to rasp against my lips, he says, "I'm a split-fucking-second away from taking you right here."

Reality punctures me. My heart kicks up speed, knowing I need to clear my head long enough to tell him the truth. "Cal... before we do this, I – I have to tell you—"

"You don't."

"Please," I practically cry. "I have to."

"Unless you're telling me no, there's literally nothing you can say that will keep me from fucking you senseless tonight."

He dives back into me, trailing wet kisses along my neck, pumping his finger in and out of me, and it's then that I blurt out, "I'm dying."

Just like that, he freezes.

His finger stills inside of me.

A ghastly, eerie quiet replaces the sound of our desire, and I squeeze my eyes shut, horrified by the words that just spilled out of me.

I can't believe I said that.

I can't believe I said it *like* that.

A few more beats of excruciating silence pass between us as Cal pulls his hand away and inches back, the loss of him pinging my eyelids back open.

We stare at each other.

We stare, chests heaving, gazes locked.

And then I watch him go pale before my eyes.

Completely ashen.

He makes a sound like he's choking, and I swear he's dying right along with me.

"I – I have a congenital heart defect," I quickly explain off his shell-shock. "It's called Tetralogy of Fallot—or TOF. I was born with it, and...there's no cure. I'm okay, for now, but my heart has an expiration date, and it's going to be a lot sooner than yours. I can't...I don't want to hurt you, Cal." I start to cry, helplessly, suffocating on every word. Fat tears roll down my cheeks like sad, falling raindrops. "I've been trying to avoid this because you've already lost so much."

His eyes are glazed over, unblinking. Cal just stares at me, shaking his head a little, like he's trying to process everything I said—or, maybe he didn't hear a word of it.

All he heard was:

I'm dying.

A sound like heartbreak is an avalanche to my ears.

It's one of those ugly sounds. The kind that pours out of someone who just witnessed something horrible. It's involuntary, like smiling or breathing—only, there's no dignity in it.

When rivulets of tears pool along my upper lip, I lick them away with my tongue, tasting the salt.

That sound poured out of me.

His heartbreak is my heartbreak.

"Cal...please, say something," I beg, my knees bouncing beneath me as I hug myself from the sting in the air.

He doesn't. He says nothing.

All he does is look away and grip his hair with both hands, fisting it as he takes another step back. Then another. And another.

When he glances at me one last time, his expression is tortured, dazed.

Riddled with disbelief.

Then, before I can say another word, he storms away.

He leaves me halfway collapsed against the trellis until I *actually* collapse. I fall to my knees in the grit and dirt, landing in a melting patch of snow, rubble and ice digging into my kneecaps. My face falls into my palms as my body shakes with sobs.

I tried so hard to shelter my heart from love. I tried to hide it, protect it, keep it safe. I buried it out of reach, too scared to let anyone hold it.

But I forgot to fireproof it.

And as everything around me burns, it cowers inside my chest, begging to be spared.

CHAPTER 19

I wind through the blur of dancing bodies, my vision obscured by tears. Pink dresses, teal suits, a bride in snowy white. Red and ivory bouquets. Technicolor strobe lights.

Everything might as well be gray.

There's a film of grief over my eyes.

I'm vaguely aware of a familiar face attached to a bob of blond hair beelining toward me as I push my way through the crowd, but I pretend not to see her.

"Lucy?" Alyssa jumps in front of me, blocking my attempt to make a hasty retreat off the dance floor. "Whoa, babe, what happened?"

"I – I'm fine," I fluster, swiping two fingers under both eyes. "I just need to find Cal."

She takes me by the shoulders and gives me a full sweep. "Your dress is torn at the knees, your hair is a mess, and your eyes are all puffy. You look like you just had your heart broken."

Deflating, my bottom lip wobbles as I duck my head. Is this what a broken heart looks like? A tattered dress, hair in disarray, and swollen eyes? All I can see is the mask of pure blindside on Cal's face. That's what heartbreak looks like to me.

Perhaps it's different for everyone.

I realize I don't know how to tell Alyssa about what just transpired because she's also not privy to the truth about my heart condition. My attempt to keep the ones I love in the dark, convinced it was the only way to live in the light, has backfired. I feel like a deceiver. A double-crosser. My good intentions have turned rotten, and my stomach curdles amid the blowback.

I lift my chin, squaring my shoulders. "I'll tell you everything, Lys, but I need to find Cal first. Did he pass through here a few minutes ago?"

She shakes her head. "I'm not sure, I was too caught up in dancing. Did he reject you? Please tell me no."

"No," I tell her. "It's not like that. I'll be back in a bit, okay?"

Alyssa nods, dropping her hands from my shoulders and stepping back, her expression pinched with worry. I force a smile and turn to leave. Weaving through the tables and out the reception doors, I half-run down the hallway that leads to the main entrance. As I push through the door and look both ways into the parking lot, a feathering of smoke permeates my senses.

I glance farther to my left. Cal is seated with his back flush against the side of the building, his knees drawn up. There's a cigarette pressed between his fingertips. "Cal."

He takes a drag, tipping his head back to the brick. His eyes are closed as he mutters, "What." It's not even a question—just a clipped acknowledgement of my presence.

"You're smoking," I say, my words as cautious as my approach toward him.

"Observant of you." He takes another drag, longer this time, blowing the smoke out through his nostrils. The tendrils curl around him before a draft carries them away. "I don't want to talk if that's why you're out here. I have an Uber on the way."

My gut twists. "Cal, please. Let me explain."

His head whips toward me, the embers of his cigarette glowing bright against the backdrop of nightfall. Almost like a firefly. "Explain?" he echoes drily, flicking ashes to the cement. "You had nearly four months to explain. But you waited until now to rip the rug out from under me."

My breath catches. I slow to a stop a few feet away from him, shaking my head. "You say it like it was intentional. Like I was trying to hurt you, but I wasn't. All I was trying to do was *protect* you."

"Protect me?" A humorless laugh falls out of him as he inhales another drag, then rises from the pavement. When he faces me, his eyes ignite to match the smoldering ash at the end of his cigarette. "Inserting yourself into my life after all these years when you're only temporary is not protecting me."

"I missed my friend."

"We were always more than friends," he counters. "You had to know what would happen when you walked through the door to my shop."

My head is shaking back and forth, wildly, defiantly. "No."

"Yes. And the first thing out of your mouth when you sat down for an interview should have been that you were *fucking dying*."

I've never seen Cal this angry before. I've seen him irritated, cold, distant, and sullen, but I've never seen him seething mad. Waves of volatile emotion ripple off of him, and I know I did this.

I'm responsible.

Tears well and fall, so I swipe them away as I resume my trek forward. He's right, in a way, but he's also not. Cal has no clue what it's like to be me. It's like walking through a minefield day after day—or, maybe I am the minefield. I'm one wrong move, one misstep away from detonating. My heart is a powder keg. "I shouldn't have said it like that," I say gently, closing in on him. "I used to have a good friend...her name was Jessica." He looks away as a thin column of smoke billows skyward from his right hand. "I met her at the hospital when I was just a kid, and we kept in touch as pen pals. She had the same heart condition as me. TOF."

Cal's jaw tics as he glances down at the ground, flicking his cigarette again.

"As we grew up, we started to spend time together in person. Sleepovers, lunch dates, movie marathons. When she was fourteen, she fell in love," I croak. "With Greg—the man you saw at the show last month. They were high school sweethearts. They had their whole life planned." I wipe away more tears and push my hair out of my face. I'm standing right in front of him now, my ankles shaking in my heels. "They were so, so happy, Cal. So in love. And then, just like that...she was gone."

His eyes lift, dark and bleak.

"She was grocery shopping, and she dropped dead in the produce aisle. No warning, nothing. She was just...gone." My voice cracks. The tears fall harder. "Her heart gave out while she was *grocery shopping*. Something so mundane and innocent. Greg came to my mom's house to deliver the news, and he collapsed on the doorstep. He was completely devastated. Broken. The love of his life was taken from him at only eighteen years old, before they could even start their life together," I sob, choking on my words. "I swore to myself that would never be me. I would never put a man through that. I saw what it did to him—I saw what it stole. Love can be a fulfilling, enchanting thing, but it can be a thief, too. It can drain you, suck you dry, strip you bare. I decided that I would never give it a taste. It wasn't worth it." My confession prickles like the ice cold gale that blows through. I watch as Cal stares back at me, only two feet away, the cigarette paper charring to his skin.

He flinches when it scalds him, tossing the burned-out stub to the ground and stomping it out with the toe of his dress shoe. The wind howls as he glances up at me again. "Is that supposed to make me feel better?"

I shake my head through a frown. "No, I just...I'm trying to explain. I'm trying to help you understand my motives."

"None of that explains why you lied to me."

My eyes round. "I didn't—"

"You told me you had fucking *asthma*," he blares, a finger lashing out and pointing at my face. "I questioned it. The mysterious scar on your chest, the fact that I never saw you with an inhaler. But you're Lucy fucking Hope, and I never in a million years thought you'd lie to me."

I'm a shaken soda can about to implode, waiting for that cap to be pulled off so I can erupt like a geyser. Guilt stabs at my chest. "I didn't tell anyone. I couldn't," I cry. "I didn't want people grieving for me like I was already gone. I didn't want to be sad all the time. I couldn't bear the looks, or the whispers."

"Sounds like a selfish reason to me."

Selfish?

Have I been *selfish*?

From my point of view, it feels like I've been anything but.

I've sacrificed love, sex, relationships, all to protect the man susceptible to the loss of me.

I swing my head back and forth, the guilt mixing with outrage. "You're acting like you understand what it's like to be me; like *you're* the one who's dying," I tell him, my voice rising over the shrill pitch of the wind. "You could never understand."

His face twists into a deadly scowl as he takes a deliberate stride toward me. "I died the day I lost her, and I've died over and over again, every day since," he spits out, teeth bared. "And then you come along and bring me back to life, only to put me right back in the fucking ground."

My lips part to speak, but nothing comes out, so I close my mouth and pull his jacket tighter around me. Silence permeates. It festers. Cal breaks our stare-off first, looking off toward the parking lot of idle cars, and my shoulders fall as I release a breath. "When I was just a little kid, right before I moved next door to you, I overheard my kindergarten teacher talking about me to another faculty member. She said I wouldn't live past high school," I say, the memory like poison. "She said it so flippantly, like the topic of my life expectancy was nothing more than lunch-room chatter. I was only five years old, but it traumatized me. I went home in tears and begged my parents to keep my secret. We moved two months later, and they kept it. They never told anyone the truth about my medical condition—they would always just say that I had asthma."

Cal's eyes pan back to me, and I swear they soften briefly.

He swallows, taking a small step forward. "Did Emma know?"

"No," I admit.

"You should have told me."

I close my eyes with a nod. "I thought it was a well-intentioned omission. I didn't think you would react like this."

"What, like I give a shit? Surprise. I fucking give a shit."

"You said..." I trail off, chewing my lip and glancing away. "You said you wouldn't love me. I didn't think it would change anything. I just wanted to be your friend again."

He doesn't say anything. A white sedan pulls up to the curb

in the midst of our tangible silence, a driver stepping out and observing from afar.

"That's my Uber," Cal murmurs, letting out a sigh.

My throat stings. "Okay." Our night of intimacy is snuffed out like the smoking remnants of his cigarette butt smoldering on the cement. Cal is leaving in an Uber instead of in my Volkswagen, and I'm returning home to my bed instead of his, the memory of his kiss still buzzing on my tongue.

I ruined everything.

He moves around me, side-stepping me, without a goodbye. Desperation has my hand reaching out and latching onto his bicep, stopping him in his tracks. "Cal, wait. Don't leave like this."

Canting his head toward me, his eyes find mine, reluctantly lingering. His muscle twitches beneath my touch. "I'll see you at work."

I can't stomach his brush-off and squeeze him tighter. "Please. I'm sorry." I step closer, right up to him, flush against him, then tentatively nuzzle my cheek to his chest, dampening his shirt with my tears. "I'm so sorry. I never meant to hurt you."

"Lucy, I have to go."

My chin pops up, my eyes wide and emotion-glazed. I drag my hand up the length of his arm, cupping the side of his cheek. His stance relaxes, just a little, by the way he leans ever so slightly into my touch. I drink in a shaky breath, grazing my thumb up and down his jawline. "I'm sorry," I repeat softly.

"I know."

"I still want you."

His eyes close, then reopen slowly, as if he were savoring my confession in the privacy of his own mind. I didn't mean to purge those words. I hadn't intended to speak so brazenly, but it's the truth. And I'm done hiding away the truth.

Cal swallows, lifting his hand and placing it along my waist. His fingers curl into me like he's still holding on, like he doesn't want to walk away just as much as I don't want him to. "I know," he echoes.

But, he does walk away.

He lets me go, his expression a mask of pain, and turns

around to leave. Cal hops into the backseat of the Uber and slams the door without another glance in my direction. I watch the car pull away, the taillights curving around the corner and out of sight. My insides pitch.

I wipe more tears off my cheek with the sleeve of Cal's jacket, then glance down at the pavement, spotting the dying cigarette. Bending over, I pick it up between my thumb and finger, noting the tiny trace of smoke rolling off the end.

Maybe Cal was right. I went about this all wrong, thinking I could keep him at arm's length, thinking I could draw that line between friendship and something more, and neither of us would be tempted to cross it.

I was foolish and naïve.

I was playing with fire.

And I realize now...

The hotter the flame, the faster it burns out.

CHAPTER 20

I wouldn't say it's strange to see Dante manning the front desk when I plod through the front door on Monday morning, but the sight of him, and only him, does raise an eyebrow or two. "Good morning," I greet, hoping the forced cheer in my inflection matches the jingle of the holly berry bells above me. Glancing up at them, my heart sinks at the memory of Cal telling me of their true purpose.

"Morning, sweetheart," Dante says, quirking a smile when his eyes lift to mine. "Do you always come in this early?"

"Usually, yes. I'm a morning person."

"What's that like?"

I flip my hair over my shoulder with a shrug. "Less preferable when sleep never came the night before." I'm not a huge makeup wearer, but I'll admit I used more than a few dabs of concealer when I woke up in order to camouflage the dark circles under my eyes. "Where's Cal?"

"Sick," he sniffs, leaning over the computer desk. "The flu or something."

My insides swirl with dread. I'm more inclined to go with *or something*. "Is he okay?"

"I'm sure he's fine. He texted me to come in early and take care of some things." He waggles his eyebrows at me, in that flirty-but-still-professional way I'm all too familiar with.

"Oh." The tone of my voice falters and dips, and I'm helpless to it. "I see."

Dante's eyes narrow studiously. "Lovers' quarrel?"

"What?" The question takes me off guard, and my purse strap slips off my shoulder, making a clumsy trek to the lobby floor. I lean over to sweep my lip gloss and bobby pins back inside, then straighten with far less gumption. "What do you mean by that?"

"Pretty straightforward question."

"We're not...*lovers*. I'm hesitant to even call us friends," I fluster as Cal's tormented, betrayed expression flashes through my mind, just like it has over and over again for the past thirty-six hours. He hasn't texted me, hasn't called. I word-vomited a grand apology speech into his voicemail Sunday morning, but his only response was my loathsome foe: radio silence. I had to shut my phone off to avoid acting like an unhinged, jilted lover, and leaving him a thousand more messages. "Anyway, tell him I hope he feels better."

"You can tell him, yourself," Dante breezes, panning back to the computer screen. "I bet he'd love to hear from you."

"I doubt that."

He looks back up, knowingly. "I knew it. You're fighting." Straightening, Dante sucks on one of Ike's lollipops that are strewn around the shop like we're always journeying across a Candyland game board. "You sleep with him?" he inquires. "Wait, let me guess, he boned you, then didn't call you, and now he's too much of a pussy to face you. Fucker."

My face flames. I start chewing on my thumbnail as I make every attempt to avoid eye contact on my way to the break room. "No. He wouldn't do that."

"He'd definitely do that."

I force back the sting of implication, sparing him a quick glance. Dante is leaning forward on his palms, his Cal's Corner t-shirt chopped off at the sleeves, turning it into a tank. "Regardless, that's not what happened. I'm sure he's just sick."

"Maybe. Weird that he's never once called in sick to work, though. I figured it either had something to do with you, or the fact that Allanson is on the schedule today."

I shrug. "Roy is just misunderstood." As I move around the desk, I reach for the remote control and flip on the mini television I had Kenny install the month prior. *Growing Pains* shines back at me once I land on the channel I'm looking for, the laugh track posing as a jarring contrast to my mood. "I brought banana bread if you want some. It's in the car."

He claps his hands, swiping them together. "You're a saint."

After I clock in and put my purse away, I bring in the platter of banana bread and set it on the break room table. Chewing on my cheek, I whip out my cell phone and snap a picture.

ME:

> Good morning. I brought you banana bread if you're feeling better later. Get well soon :)

He reads it, and the three little dots bob to life.

Then, they vanish.

Cal never responds.

I text him every morning that week in the wake of his five-day absence.

Good morning!

I hope you're feeling better.

I miss you.

He never responds to any of them.

It's the following Monday when Cal finally makes it into work. An entire week dragged by, my heart shrinking more each day, while the bags under my eyes grew twice their original size. I set a fresh vase of green orchids on his desk to symbolize good health. I'm not confident he was ever sick in the physical sense, but I'm beginning to realize that emotional sickness doesn't feel any better. In fact, I'm willing to bet it's the very worst kind.

"Can I get you anything?" I ask as Cal storms past me toward his office. It's already four p.m. and he hasn't even gifted me a glance. Not a single one. "Are you feeling okay?"

My own neediness grates me. I'm yearning for something from him, anything, even the driest, smallest crumb. I'd prefer he unleash his anger on me than act like I'm not standing right in front of him, my every heartbeat acting as a plea to make this right.

He must see right through me because he continues to avoid me.

No response, no wayward glance in my direction, not even a grumble or a scowl.

He's blank.

I don't exist to him.

I told him I'm dying, and he's acting like I'm already dead.

Cal disappears into his office and slams the door, just as Ike saunters out of the service area, swiping a big bear paw over his bald head.

I wilt like a droopy orchid. "Hey," I acknowledge bleakly, collapsing forward on my arms.

"You okay, doll? You haven't been yourself lately," he notes. A patched denim vest is draped over a familiar yellow t-shirt, both articles straining against his broad shoulders. "Is it the boss? Ya'll have us walkin' on eggshells around here."

"Sorry," I tell him, and I mean it. The last thing I ever want to do is contribute to a less-than-sunny working environment. "Everything is fine. What can I get for you?"

"Nothin'. Bishop wants to see you in his office," he shrugs, scratching the blondish stubble along his jaw. "I'll watch the desk."

"What?" My spine goes ramrod straight as my eyes flare. I'm instantly sluiced with anxiety. "Cal?"

"That's the one."

I swallow, but it's more of a painful, brittle gulp. "Okay. Sure." Instinctively, I swipe away the wrinkles from my wrinkle-less jeans, tinker with the long sleeves of my blouse, and fix my hair in an invisible mirror before heaving in a breath of courage.

"You're pretty as a picture, don't you worry." Ike gives me an affectionate wink as he shoos me away from the desk. "I got it covered."

"Thank you." I move around him, pacing languidly toward

Cal's closed door. I'm not sure what he wants, or what to expect. I'm uncertain if I should have another apology lined up, or if I should pretend like nothing ever soured between us.

I'm the poster girl for good health. My heart is strong and eternal. We never left each other in shambles the prior weekend, and we've spoken every day since.

Everything is wonderful.

The fantasy is enough to pick up my pace as I knock softly on his office door.

"Come in," he clips, his tone brimming with venom.

The fantasy promptly crumbles at my ankle boots. My hand shakes as I lift it to the knob and twist. The creaky door is the only thing louder than my thundering heartbeats—I think. Truthfully, I'm not even sure of that. "Hi," I choke out, stepping inside.

Cal sits behind his desk in a faded gray sleeveless shirt that's practically painted onto him and a dark navy beanie. He's leaning back in his rolling chair, pivoting side to side. The green-petaled orchid has been pushed to the far corner of his work surface, and the plate of banana bread I brought him is still wrapped in plastic, untouched. "Shut the door and have a seat."

I feel like I'm in trouble.

At the very least, my heart is in trouble, on the verge of fracturing irreparably.

I shut the door behind me. "Everything okay?"

"Sit." He points to the seat across from him, his eyes fixed straight ahead, away from me.

"Cal."

"Lucy, sit."

Even though he's giving me orders like an ill-trained puppy, I still obey, gliding quickly over to the unoccupied chair. I swallow a few times to moisten the desert in my throat, then sit down. My eyes lock on his face, while his eyes pan downward, fixating on the desk. On nothingness. Nothingness is preferable to the sight of me. "Hey. Are you feeling better?"

He sighs, and it's a long, drawn-out sigh. "I wasn't sick. I was avoiding you."

I wring my hands together in my lap as my skin flushes at his admission. "At least you're honest."

I regret the comment the moment it leaves my mouth.

"That makes one of us," he replies easily.

Swallowing for the gazillionth time, all I can manage is a nod. I suppose I deserved that.

"We should talk."

Nodding again, I know I deserve that, too. I deserve a conversation. An explanation as to why he's shut me out in the wake of my hard truth. "We should."

Cal leans back farther, fishing through his blue jeans for something, then pulling out a nearly full pack of cigarettes. He plucks one from the box and searches for a lighter in his drawer.

My chest pangs at the image. I hated that he'd smoked that cigarette outside the wedding venue, but I figured it was a one-time thing. A moment of weakness amid a moment of something far worse. "You're smoking again?"

"Sometimes," he mumbles through the rolled paper and nicotine. He lights up, blowing the smoke to his left. "Needed something stronger than the gum."

Because of me.

I deflate in my seat, trying to keep the tears at bay. Guilt and culpability filter through me. "I hate that," I whisper. "I really do."

When I cough on a cloud of smoke that floats over to me, Cal stills for a moment, his attention finally pinning on me. He blinks through the smoke, then waves it away and pulls to a stand. "Sorry," he murmurs, stalking to the lone window and tugging it open. He stubs out the cigarette and tosses it outside. "Wasn't thinking."

"It's okay."

He starts to pace around the room, hands planting on his hips. "I'm just on edge. Pissed off, resentful," he says, moving toward me, then spinning around to walk the other way. When his back is to me, he finishes, "Wishing I could just hate you."

I rise from my chair. "I don't wish that. I don't wish that at all."

"It would make this a hell of a lot easier."

"It would make what easier?" I step over to him, directly behind him, and extend my hand until it's brushing his shoulder. "Cal..."

He whips around. "I'd seen you play before."

I stare at him for a moment, slowly processing.

What?

Shaking my head, I wet my lips. "What do you mean?"

"Before you applied for a job here. I found you on Instagram and saw you made a post from the wine bar. It was a blurry picture of your guitar neck, with a crowd of people in focus behind it. The caption said something like, '*My favorite place to be.*' I watched you play through the window a few times after work, just to hear your voice. See your smile." He swallows. "Just to know you were doing okay."

My brows bend with bewilderment, eyes misting. That can't be right. I was certain Cal had swept our friendship under the rug, and I'd never once considered the notion that he'd been keeping tabs on me; that he'd *found* me.

His words from that first day at the auto shop echo around me: "*I know who you are.*"

He recognized me. Of course he did.

"You...you never came inside," I croak, blindsided. "I never knew."

"I didn't want you to know," he says, glancing away. "I didn't want to *know* you, Lucy. I just wanted to make sure you were doing well. That you were happy."

I'm not understanding. It doesn't make sense. "But...*why?* Why wouldn't you want to reach out? I missed you so much, Cal. I—"

"Because I've lost everything I've ever loved," he shouts, temper flaring, voice rising. His arms extend at his sides, gaze aflame. "*Everything.* So, no, I don't make a fucking habit out of harnessing relationships or searching out new ones. It's easier to be alone. I *have* to be alone."

A tear escapes. My heart aches for him.

Cal and I are different in so many ways, but nothing compares to this.

My losses have shown me the fragile beauty of life. I appreciate what I have, I treasure everything that's still here. I view each day as a celebration, as a precious gift, while Cal sees life from an entirely different perspective.

To him, every day is a reminder of what he's lost.

A warning that he's still capable of losing.

I reach out my hand, as trembling as it is, wanting to comfort him in some way.

But he snatches me by the wrist before I can make contact. "I don't need your pity or sympathy. It was a mistake to get close to you."

"Nothing about us is a mistake."

"No?"

"No." I'm firm in my delivery.

Cal hangs onto my wrist, his grip loosening but not letting go. There's a wavering in his touch. A pause. His eyes hold on mine until they dip to my mouth, holding there instead. And then they track even lower, to the scar between my breasts, to the trace of cleavage peeking out from my blouse. His grasp tightens ever so slightly, his breathing unsteadying. He looks back up, and there's the smallest shift in his expression.

"What?" I breathe out, suddenly desperate to know what he's thinking. It's not the same thing he was thinking just moments ago, that much I know.

His throat bobs, jaw clenching, as he still holds onto my wrist, his thumb grazing my pulse point. "Nothing."

"Tell me."

"You don't want to know what I was thinking about, Lucy."

"Yes, I do."

"I promise you don't." He drops my arm, then moves around me, heading in the opposite direction.

My pulse revs, heating my blood. "I do." I boldly reach for his elbow as he stalks away from me, and the gesture does something.

Cal comes to a grinding halt.

Then he spins around, snatching me by the waist with both hands, practically lifting me off the ground. My feet struggle not to trip over themselves as he moves us both backward until I'm being hoisted up and deposited onto his work desk in one fell swoop. Loose papers scatter along with my breath. A stapler topples, the orchid tips.

My cheeks feel hot with the telltale flush of desire. Cal steps right between my knees, pressing our groins together as I lean back on my palms and stare up at him with parted lips that still tingle with the memory of his kiss in the gardens.

Swallowing, his chest heaves in time with mine, two hooded eyes fixed on my mouth before he slides them back up. "I was wondering what you would look like when I make you come."

Humiliatingly, a moan falls out of me.

The sound escapes unplanned, unprecedented, and it takes all of my effort to keep my arms from shaking as they hold my weight.

"I was trying to picture your eyes. If they'd be closed, lost to the moment, or wide and glazed, staring right at me while I brought you to ecstasy," he says, voice low and husky. "I was thinking about the color in your cheeks. Pink, red, something in between." He grazes a rough finger along my cheekbone. "And your mouth," he rasps. "Would you scream my name? Pant it? Beg me for more?"

My head falls back, as if the titillating words swimming through my mind are far too heavy to keep it upright. "Cal..." I part my legs wider on instinct, and he grinds against me, his erection evident. "Wh-what are you doing?"

"What do you want me to do?" Cal leans over me, his lips near my ear, arms caging me in. "Tell me what you want, sunshine."

Every part of me feels sensitized, tender, weightless, buzzing. I say it before I think it: "Touch me."

And then it's *all* I can think about.

Cal touching me.

Everywhere.

Without pause, he tears apart the button on my jeans, tugs at the zipper, then thrusts his hand down the front of my pants. I cry out and fall back against the desk as Cal's free hand lifts to cover my mouth. "Shh." He hovers over me, the tips of our noses touching, his fingers inching their way inside my underwear.

When he finds me wet and needy, his eyes practically roll up as he hisses through his teeth, "Fuck, Lucy."

"Oh my God." I writhe underneath him, my words muffled by his palm. One of my legs raises to curl around his hip while the other lifts until the heel of my boot is planted on the desk. "Oh God."

He drags his fingers down my mouth, tugging my jaw open, then replaces his hand with his mouth. His tongue plunges inside, our moans mingling. My underwear is yanked to the side as we kiss, and Cal inserts a long finger inside of me. A second one joins, sending a surge of blinding heat through me. My spine arcs off the desk, my elbows digging into the wood grains and likely gathering splinters. I don't care. All I care about is the tingle that's already climbing, sparking, enveloping my womb.

Two fingers pump in and out, hot and fast. This isn't sweet or gentle. It's rough, angry, aggressive, desperate. His erection grinds into my inner thigh, hard like steel, as our kiss turns messy—teeth clanking, tongues in a rhythmless frenzy, breaths sharp and uneven. The wet sounds of him roughly fingering me vibrate through the quiet office, mixing with Cal's groans and my whimpers. I lift a hand to slide the beanie off his head, revealing his mop of hair. It falls over his forehead, into his eyes, and I fist it as I unravel. He does the same to mine, tugging at my own tresses partially draped over the side of his desk, until he's craning my neck back.

"You're so sweet. An angel."

"Cal..."

"What do angels look like when they break apart?" he pants against the curve of my throat, laving his tongue up to the sensitive patch of skin behind my ear. "Break for me, Lucy."

I'm semi-aware of the door being unlocked, of co-workers and possible customers only a few feet away, but I can't bring myself to stop. I can't pull away; I can only pull him closer. I grip the nape of his neck, holding him to me as his hand works me. The underside of his palm rubs against my clit as his fingers curl inside of me, not too far to hurt, but far enough that my hips jolt up off the desk. "Cal, Cal, Cal," I chant his name, my eyes closing.

He takes his unoccupied hand and shoves my blouse up my chest, palming me through my shell pink bra. His tongue drags down from my neck, right between my breasts, teasing my scar before sucking my nipple through the layer of lace. "You're fucking killing me," he groans.

I hear a zipper unfasten. Forcing my eyes open, I glance down to see him pulling himself free of his jeans and boxers, then stroking his cock as he continues to touch me in a way I've never been touched before him. Tattooed fingers are fisted around his thick erection, pumping furiously, the tip leaking with precum, and the sight is enough to send me over the edge.

Mindlessly, I slap my own hand across my mouth to stifle my cry of pleasure. I wonder if I'm too loud, if the door is about to plow open, if our indiscretion will be witnessed by unpermitted eyes.

Still, I don't care.

I *can't* care.

I break apart, viciously, wholly, my body tensing and imploding as wave after wave of ecstasy ripples through me. I feel it in my core, in the deepest parts of me, and I've never experienced anything like it before. I'm flying high on the rapture of it when I feel warm spurts of liquid pool along my bare stomach. My shirt is still rolled up over my breasts as Cal releases onto me. I look up at him through drunken eyes, watching his face morph with bliss.

"Fuck, *fuck*," he grunts, jerking himself, hovering over me as he depletes.

He finishes, and we both go still, breathing heavily.

And then it's over.

I tip my head backward, half of it hanging over the edge of the desk as I drape the back of my arm over my eyes. Mixed emotions spiral through me, rendering me immobile. I don't know what to say, think, do.

What happens next, what happens next...

His weight pulls off of me, and the evidence of his orgasm turns cold against my skin. I lift up slightly, noting the way his release glistens underneath the tungsten light above us. I need him to talk to me, to tell me what to do, how to react to what just happened.

Cal breathes out deeply, tucking himself back into his jeans and yanking up the zipper. He adjusts his belt and plucks a few tissues from the box of Kleenex beside me on the desk. My eyes squeeze shut, my chest heaving, as I feel the tissue flutter and swipe across my belly and chest, absorbing the aftermath of our encounter.

I can't absorb it, though. I can't process it.

What happens next, what happens next...

"Cal." His name is a plea, a pardon. I've never felt more inexperienced than I feel in this moment, sprawled half naked on his desk as he wipes his cum off my body.

Finally, he pulls me to a sitting position. Our foreheads knock together when he leans over, and I just sit there, mutely, as my shirt falls back down. Cal tucks my hair behind my ear, then presses a light kiss to my hairline. "Lucy..." he murmurs gently.

I wait for his next words.

I need them.

I need them more than I need air.

But I nearly trip over my own heart as it bottoms out of me when he says the absolute last thing I expect him to say...

"You're fired."

CHAPTER 21

12/25/12

"Last Christmas"

You want to know the worst song ever made?
Last Christmas by Wham!
It's a song about heartbreak, betrayal, and loss,
and I can't think of a worse thing to sing about
during such a magical time of year. I think I'm
going to write my own Christmas song, and I'll
call it Every Christmas. It'll be about eternal love
and hearts that don't know how to break. They can
only celebrate, only love, only sing with joy and
wonder.

Every Christmas, I give you my heart
And every night, you hold it so tight
Each year, I have no more tears
Because our love is something special

There, I fixed it.

Merry Christmas!

Toodles,

Emma

The Christmas tree twinkles beneath the skylight, glittering with silvery tinsel and golden garland. *Forever Young*'s lobby is decked out to the max as potential adopters line up outside the door to snap a picture of their pet with Santa Claus, in exchange for a modest fifteen-dollar donation. We're hoping to raise funds for the sanctuary going into the new year, while getting traffic and fresh faces in the door to meet our adoptable pets.

I'm dressed like an elf, because of course I am.

Gemma, too.

Vera is adorned head to toe in a Mrs. Claus suit while her husband, Terrance, sits in the big man's chair. The costume is perfect for her, given her permanent rosy cheeks and nurturing disposition. Moses, an elderly bloodhound, drags her down the hallway on his leather lead, his nose overly curious as his reindeer ears tip charmingly off the top of his head. "Slow down, boy. These knees aren't what they used to be."

"I got him," I jump in, taking the leash from her hand. "Moses smells those holiday dog treats I whipped up, don't you, old boy?" The platter of mutt-friendly biscuits, shaped into candy canes and jolly snowmen, sit beside an array of human treats I've marked accordingly.

"You're so good to these pets, Lucy," Vera says kindly, adjusting her Mrs. Claus hat. "I can't wait until you're here more often."

I smile, and it's partially genuine, somewhat sad. After I told Vera about my recent unemployment status, she immediately offered me a paid position at the sanctuary. Only a small handful of workers are here in more than a volunteering capacity, and I didn't feel great about the idea of taking money from an establishment that survives off of donations. I never wanted to get paid for something I value doing for free.

But I was in a bind, and I can't think of a better position than to work for a cause I feel passionate about. To work at a place that appreciates me, and *wants* me there.

Cal wanted me once. So, he took what he wanted, and then he tossed me aside.

I'm still processing the shock of it all.

While I'm making less per hour, and working fewer hours in general, it'll do for now. Besides, Nash offered me a bartending gig two nights a week at the wine bar to help supplement the missing income. I'm not certified by any means, so he's going to pay me under the table until I get an actual license—if that's, ultimately, what I want to do.

I just don't know.

I'm in a current state of waffling, which never pairs well with grief.

Gemma sidles up to me in her bright green elf suit, her arms full of our favorite tuxedo cat, Mr. Perkins. "Did you see that anonymous donation that came in yesterday?" she wonders, the red streaks in her hair matching the ornaments sprinkled onto the tree behind her. "Another two thousand dollars. It might be enough to cover Mr. Perkins' dental surgery."

I give the cat a rub between the ears. "A little Christmas miracle. And here I'd been thinking we were low on those this year."

"A good Samaritan, indeed," Vera chimes in.

We spend the afternoon taking pictures, switching out holiday-inspired headbands and elf outfits for the pets, and taking part in two successful adoptions. One of our longtime cat residents, Annabel, found a home for Christmas, as did the bloodhound, Moses. Overall, it was a good day.

Before the doors close, my best friend shuffles inside with my two hooligans who are dead set on knocking her off her brand new Simon Miller boots. I may or may not have dug deep into the pits of my savings account to gift her the boots she'd been dying to have since springtime. We always partake in a holiday martini night and gift exchange sometime before the big day. Alyssa bought me the newest KitchenAid mixer in rose pink, along with her great grandmother's handwritten recipe card for key lime cookies. It was such a thoughtful gift.

"Lucy!" Alyssa calls out, just as my own furry Key Lime breaks free and dives at the leftover people treats like the dirty rascal she is.

She always knows exactly what's *not* meant for her and takes supreme interest in it anyway.

Kind of like me.

"Sorry you're always getting stuck with my heathens, Lys," I chuckle, pulling off my elf ears and racing to grab the leashes. Alyssa brought the dogs by for a picture because I'm helpless against photographic evidence of my fur babies in impossibly cute reindeer outfits.

And she's helpless against my shameless begging.

"The things we do for love," she winks, shrugging out of her coat. "I'm also here for selfish reasons. I think I want a dog or something. Maybe a cat. What do you think?"

My eyebrows arc with intrigue. "Really? I'd go with a cat due to your busy work schedule. Less maintenance."

"Valid point. Show me the kitties, please."

Elation trickles through me as Gemma and I lead Alyssa back to the cat room while Vera and her husband de-Santa Claus the front lobby. There's nothing that gives me more joy than finding the perfect forever home for an animal in need. As we spend quality time with each of the seven available cats, Alyssa brings up a topic that has my elation plummeting into a black hole of dread.

"Have you heard from Cal at all since The Incident?" she asks cautiously, not making eye contact, instead focusing on the little jingle bell collar secured around Sully's neck.

I try not to go pale, but I'm certain the remnants of my red lipstick are the only source of color visible on my face. "Nothing aside from that one text." I clear the tickle from my throat, the pain still raw. "It hurts too much."

Gemma rubs my back with affection. "It's a shitty situation. I don't blame you for cutting off contact."

Nodding, I look away before they can see the moisture springing to my eyes. It's not like me to dodge or deflect in times of crisis. Normally, I'm the first person to pry into the whys and what ifs, press for answers, and attempt to fix.

Fix, fix, fix.

But words couldn't fix this. Nothing Cal could say would lessen the sting of the wound he'd carved into me after I gave him something precious, something I never intended to share with anyone, and he threw me out like a piece of trash.

He fired me while I was still coming down from the most potent bliss I'd ever felt, my jeans unbuttoned, my heart in his hands, his release slow-drying on my skin.

The timing of it was unbearable.

Unfixable.

And this was after he'd spent the whole week ignoring me, *avoiding* me, after I'd confessed to him that my heart was on borrowed time.

I screenshotted the text message he sent me later that night to Alyssa, after I stumbled out of his office amid a fit of gut-wrenching sobs, trying to avoid Ike's concerned questions as I clocked out of the auto shop for the very last time.

CAL:

> I'm sorry. I didn't mean for it to go like that. I called you into my office to let you go because it's no longer a comfortable working environment for either of us. We're in too deep. The timing was shit, and I'm sorry for that, but it only reinforced my reasoning. Please try to understand where I'm coming from. It was business, it wasn't personal. Call me when you get this.

Business.

What a terrible phrase.

All business, nothing personal.

It *was* personal because there was a person on the other end of that cold, ruthless business decision. A person who thought

Cal Bishop truly cared about her. A person who trusted him to protect her heart.

He put me in an unfair place, leaving me stranded, forcing me to pick up the pieces of our shared mistake.

And I realize I told him we weren't a mistake, but I don't think I believe that anymore.

After all, he flat-out told me that he wouldn't love me, and I should have taken his words at face value and run the other way. A man unwilling to love when love makes a worthy case for itself, is a man who will only ensure a future of disappointment. Life's too short to pursue disappointment.

Especially my life.

My overtly sunny thought process has been tested since that day in Cal's office, infected with lightning and rain clouds, and I don't like it.

But I can't prevent the unstable air: I can't stop the storm.

All I said back to him was, *"I'm okay."*

Not that he'd even asked how I was, but it was all I could muster at the time. Alyssa made the forty minute drive to my house that night to hold me as I rocked and cried and told her everything—from our kiss in the gardens, to the truth about my medical diagnosis, to what transpired in Cal's office. She insisted he didn't deserve me, and it was a small solace...but it didn't ring true.

Cal deserved me. He just failed to believe that he did.

And somehow, that feels even worse.

I'm overcome with shortness of breath, my chest achy. I rub a hand over my heart to subdue the sharp pang, knowing I need to keep my anxiety low, but the notion feels next to impossible.

When the topic quickly shifts from Cal, to Gemma and Knox's wedded bliss, I notice the song from the speaker change from Mariah Carey to Taylor Swift's version of *Last Christmas*. My insides hum with unease as I internalize the lyrics and think about Emma and her journal entry. It was titled "Last Christmas" —little did she know, it would end up *being* her last Christmas.

Emotion catches in my throat, heating my skin.

It's a terrible song, worse than *Blue Christmas*.

It's sad. Everything feels sad.

Sad songs everywhere; it's all I can hear.

Standing from the floor of the cat room, I pace around for a few moments, then lean back against the wall and place my hands over my ears to block it all out.

My chest hurts.

My heart hurts.

Tears trickle down my cheeks as my friends watch helplessly.

Cal told me to break for him, and that's what I'm doing.

Optimists fall, too.

This is how we break.

Pinky the panda bear sits across from me in the rocking chair on Christmas Eve, while my mother and I sip eggnog by the tree after an evening of making porcupines and dozens of homemade cookies. My feet are pulled up beside me, encased in fuzzy twinkle light socks, and my eyes are pinned on the stuffed toy with a defective ear.

Cal told me the panda looked sick, and that I shouldn't choose that one.

I wonder if he thought the same thing about me.

"My baby girl is turning twenty-three tomorrow," Mom coos beside me, playing with my hair, while her own hair reflects with silver streaks against the luminous tree. "I wish I could freeze time."

I force a smile, still staring at the little toy. I've slept with it every night since Cal won it for me, crying into its worn fur, wishing he was the one I was holding onto. "Wishes are silly and unproductive," I murmur. "They hold no weight. No value."

Mom straightens from the couch, her features pinched with alarm. Two dangling Rudolph earrings flutter as she tilts her head toward me. "Are you okay, sweetheart? That doesn't sound like something my eternal ball of sunshine would say."

She laughs a little, but it's strained, just like my heart.

"Sorry. I'm in a mood, I guess," I swallow, picking at a loose string on one of my socks. "I miss Dad. And Emma. And Jessica."

And Cal.

"Oh, Lucy," she sighs sadly, wrapping a loving arm around me. "You know they're never far."

"They're too far. Too far to hold, too far to touch."

"They live inside here, which is as close as they can get." She places a tender palm against my chest, reveling in my heartbeats. "Dad lives in the strings of your guitar. Emma in the fireflies on a warm summer night. Jessica in your laughter and every inside joke. That's not far, honey. That's not far at all."

A tear slips.

God, I'm being so depressing.

It's my favorite holiday. My birthday is officially in three hours. I'm here, I'm breathing, I'm alive and loved, and all I'm doing is being ungrateful.

I'm mourning when I should be relishing in my blessings.

"You're right," I sigh, intaking a full breath. "Sorry I'm being emotional. It's been a rough month." My chest starts to ache again, just like it did at the sanctuary. I squeeze the front of my shirt, trying to intake a full breath as my mother spares me a worried glance.

"Are you all right, honey?"

I nod quickly, rubbing the space between my breasts as the feeling climbs, then fades out. "I'm fine."

"Lucy, you need to make that cardiologist appointment. I'm serious."

I know I do.

I just can't fathom spoken confirmation that I'm dying right now—that my time is running out.

It's too much.

"It's not that, Mom," I assure her. "It's just stress."

"I know," she nods, sighing sadly. "The situation with Callahan was...unprecedented. But I'm sure he had your best interest in mind."

I gave my mother the cliff note version of my termination from Cal's Corner, omitting the part about me getting fingered to oblivion on his work desk.

My cheeks burn at the memory.

"I'm sure he did," I mutter.

"Romantic entanglements in the workplace never end well. It's for the best that you keep your personal lives separate from your professional lives. It'll all work out...you'll see."

I wish I could see it from that perspective, but my heart was entangled in that job. That job brought me back to him. I looked forward to those jingle bells chiming every morning, signaling a new day. A new chance to turn our messy past into a brighter future.

I fill my cheeks with air and blow out a breath. "Thank you for coming over tonight. What time is my birthday dinner tomorrow?"

"Six o'clock," she smiles, unraveling her arm from my shoulders. "Your aunt and uncle will be joining us. Your cousins, too."

Warmth tickles me, filtering out the rotten thoughts. "That sounds great. I can't wait."

"I'll let you get to sleep," she says, moving to stand. "It's getting late."

"Okay, Mom. Merry Christmas."

My mother wraps me in a big hug, kissing my temple, humming the tune to *Jingle Bell Rock* as she floats out the door. A smile lingers on my lips as her headlights illuminate my front window, and her car pulls out, disappearing down the neighborhood street.

Rising from the couch, I snatch up my cell phone, along with Pinky, and make my way down the short hallway to my bedroom.

I hover in the doorway of Emma's old room for a moment, chewing on my lip.

Maybe it's the splash of liquor Mom snuck into my eggnog, or maybe I'm searching for a Christmas miracle—whatever it is, I find myself dialing Cal's phone number with shaky fingers, bringing the cell to my ear as I wait.

Ring, ring, ri—

"Lucy?"

The sound of his voice is a miracle all in itself. "Merry Christmas," I squeak out, tears imminent.

"Christ, I've been worried about you."

"Why did you do it?" I blurt. It's not what I meant to say, but I can't stop the dam from breaking now. "Why did you use me and discard me like that?"

A beat passes, like he's having trouble processing my questions. "What?"

"I gave myself to you, Cal. I trusted you, and you threw me away. You broke my heart."

"Jesus, Lucy, it wasn't like that. Letting you go from the job was a practical, healthy move for both of us. You have to see that."

"All I see is you taking what you wanted from me, then leaving all the rest."

"No. That's absolutely not what happened, and this is why I wanted to have a conversation with you," he says wearily, his trademark sigh evident. "Can I come over? I want to make this right. I hate hearing you like this."

I sniffle, clutching Pinky to my chest like a child who's lost her best friend.

I would know—I *was* her, once upon a time.

Shaking my head, I muster a reply. "No. I'm not ready to see you yet," I confess, wanting nothing more than to see him. "I just wanted to know why."

"I told you why."

"But why...like *that*? Why in that moment, after I gave you something so valuable to me?"

"Because I'm fucking *helpless* against you," he shouts, anger flaring. Emotion escalating. "Every day I'm around you, I become more and more goddamn defenseless. I can't think straight. Rational thought goes out the window. I'm no fucking good for you, but somehow, you're the best thing about me—it's a recipe for disaster."

My breath hitches. I squeeze the phone tighter as I make my way to the bed and plop down.

"Do you want your job back? Would that fix this? Fine, I'll rehire you. But you'll see exactly why I think it's a huge mistake."

I shake my head again, knowing it's too little too late. "No, I'm working at the animal shelter now. And I start working with Nash after the new year."

Silence crackles for a few charged seconds before his terse reply meets my ears. "The bartender? Why?"

"You didn't leave me with a ton of options, Cal. He offered, and it makes sense."

He sighs again, longer this time, his tone laced with more frustration than ever. "Lucy. Let me come over so we can talk this through. Just because I let you go doesn't mean I...let *you* go."

"It's not a good idea. It's too soon."

I know exactly what will happen if he comes over right now.

I'll give in, fall into his arms like he didn't shred my heart to smithereens, probably sleep with him because I'm helpless, too, and then I'll hate myself tenfold come sunrise.

He clears his throat and says, "But it's your birthday."

My eyes close as I lean back against the headboard of my bed. "I've managed a whole lot of birthdays without you. I'll survive one more."

Cal goes silent again.

I don't know what to say, either.

Honestly, I'm not sure why I even called him in the first place. I didn't want to end the night like this, with falling tears, with whisperings of things that'll never come to be. "I'm sorry I called you," I tell him, strengthening my voice. "I just wanted to say Merry Christmas. I hope you have a good day with Cricket. I hope..." I heave in a rickety breath, finishing, "I hope you have all the good days."

"Lucy..."

"Goodnight, Cal."

"Luc—"

I hang up.

I hang up and shut off my phone, swiping away the tears with the sleeve of my pajama shirt. Swatting my hair out of my face, I drink in another breath and climb off the bed, falling to my knees beside the loose floorboard.

It's partially open, Emma's long lost treasures staring up at me. I move the plank aside and stare into the dark cubby, savoring the memories.

Cal's old clarinet, patched up and glued back together with love.

Emma's diary filled with all of her precious pieces.

Notes, stickers, wishes that never came true.

I smile down at everything she was, at everything she was meant to become, and I add a final trinket to the pile.

Pinky the panda bear.

I stuff the toy inside the hole and cover it back up, securing the floorboard into place, hiding it all away where it belongs.

Then I climb into the guest bed and fall asleep, dreaming of Emma, dreaming of Cal, dreaming of my adventure people.

But, there's a fine line between adventure and disaster.

And little did I know, as I chased fireflies and wishes, lost in a beautiful dream, that disaster would strike in the worst possible way on the day I turned twenty-three.

CHAPTER 22

CAL

Age 15

THE NIGHT SHE LEFT

She's still in her recital dress when I hand her the orchid. I swiped it from Lucy's mom's living room, which doubles as a greenhouse, because it was more convenient than riding my bike to the local Woodman's.

They say it's the thought that counts, so I'm going to go with that.

Emma's eyes light up like pennies under the sun. "You got me flowers?"

My sister gives her dress a twirl before she grabs the pot of violet petals from my hands, popping her eyebrows up and down. I quirk a grin, pleased with my pilfering. "Of course. It was your first piano recital. Isn't that customary or something?"

"Not from stinky big brothers."

"I don't stink," I say, sparing my sweat-stained jersey a glance. After being cooped up in that auditorium for three mindless hours, I had to let off some steam when I got home and shoot hoops in the driveway. Not that I regret going to the recital—Emma was flawless in her performance. A natural-born. And the smile she wore the whole time, braided with joy and confidence?

The absolute best.

It was the remaining two hours and fifty minutes that had me bored numb.

In true stinky big brother fashion, I pull Emma into a hug, infecting her with the stench of my one-man game. She squeals and squirms, pushing against me with one hand, the other holding the orchid high above her head. "Gross, Cal! Let me go."

"Say I don't stink."

"Fine, you reek."

I shove her head in the direction of my armpit, pulling a diabolical shriek out of her. Laughing until my stomach hurts, I finally release her, relishing in the murderous glare in her eyes. "You totally deserved that," I wheeze through my laughter.

"You're the worst." Her words are eclipsed by the upturn of her lips and the way her freckles scatter when her cheeks stretch. "But you got me flowers, so bonus points for that."

"Points, huh? Are you keeping score of my awesomeness?"

"Yes. Lucy's winning by a thousand points."

"Not possible. I did the dishes for you last night so you two could write songs in your room, pretending you were the future Spice Girls."

Her nose scrunches up. "Which Spice Girl would I be?"

I don't miss a beat. "Scary Spice."

"Ugh." She swats at my shoulder. "You lost fifty points. Go back to your corner."

Shrugging, I saunter backward until I collapse into the giant bean bag chair in my designated "corner." Emma surprised me last Christmas after I fell asleep on the couch by sneaking into my bedroom with Mom and decorating the far corner of my room with basketball posters, a navy beanbag chair, stacks of sports magazines, and a homemade clarinet she made with Dad. She cut out letters from newspapers and magazines, taping them to my wall, spelling "Cal's Corner."

It's my safe haven, a little sanctuary, where I write music, play the clarinet, listen to my headphones, and do homework. I'm still trying to think of a gift worthy of topping it, but everything comes up short. She's pretty much the best sibling ever.

She has all the points.

"Are you and Lucy having a sleepover tonight?" I wonder, clasping my hands behind my head.

Say yes, my mind adds.

A pout steals her expression. "No, I'm having a sleepover with Marjorie. Her mom is having all the recital girls over to celebrate."

"No fair. I was hoping to torment you both until sunrise."

"Of course you were. I have no idea what Lucy sees in you."

Her red dress tickles her ankles as she bobs her hips back and forth. Emma told me that red makes girls look older—according to Lucy, anyway—but I disagree. Her bony frame, gummy smile, and crooked ponytail tell me she's all innocent kid. When her words register, I narrow my eyes with mock disdain. "She sees utter perfection, clearly."

"You're such a doof."

"A perfect doof."

A smile lingers as she sets the orchid on my dresser. "I really do appreciate the flowers. Orchids are my favorite," she says softly.

"I know." I do know—if it wasn't totally dweeby for a teenage boy to like flowers, I'd say they were my favorite, too. They remind me of my sister...and of the girl next door. "Do you need a ride to Marjorie's?"

"You only have your learner's permit, Cal. I'd rather not die tonight when you inevitably crash into an unsuspecting lamppost."

"I resent that," I frown. "I'm a great driver. Ask Dad."

"Dad said you ran over a squirrel last week."

I thin my lips. "It bolted right out in front of me. It had a death wish."

"Well, I don't. I'll walk," she breezes, turning to leave the room.

I'm on my feet in an instant, searching for my shoes. "I'll walk you there. It's already dark outside. Better to be safe."

Emma spins back around, shaking her head. "I'll be fine. She only lives one street over, and I've walked there a million times." When her eyes pan over to my sheet of half-written music, she adds, "Besides, you were excited to work on that song you were writing. I don't want to interrupt."

"What about Mom or Dad? You shouldn't go alone."

"Dad's working in his office, and Mom passed out with a migraine. I promise I'll be fine."

I do want to work on my song. I'm writing it for Lucy as a birthday present. I realize I'm jumping the gun a bit since her birthday isn't until Christmas, but it's my very first song, and I want it to be right. I want it to be perfect. "Yeah, okay. If you're sure."

"I'm sure. I'll go change and pack, then head out," she smiles. "Maybe tomorrow we can practice what you've written on the piano together."

I chew on my fingernail, debating the offer. I'm pretty bad at the piano, but Emma has been a good teacher, and I could use the added lessons before I play for Lucy. "Sounds good. Text me when you get there so I know you made it okay."

"I will." She holds up her phone and gives it a shake as confirmation.

"I'm serious, Emma. Don't forget."

"Cal, I'll be fine. I promise I'll text you."

I know she will. She's good about it. "All right, have fun. See you tomorrow."

Emma leans over to give the purple flowers a final whiff before spinning on her heels. "Toodles!" she chirps, skipping out of my bedroom.

It's the last thing she says before I hear the front door click shut twenty minutes later.

Twenty more minutes tick by as I lose myself to chords and notes, unworthy and imperfect melodies, tapping the pencil to my chin as I attempt to piece together the greatest piano song ever written for the greatest girl I've ever met.

Then another twenty minutes pass.

And another.

A whole hour rolls by when I realize her text never came.

PRESENT DAY

I stomp through the bays while Alice in Chains blares from the overhead speaker, telling me I made a big mistake.

"I knew I'd find you here on Christmas day, you lonely bastard."

A cigarette is pressed between my fingers as I glance across the garage at Dante hunched over an engine. His smirk is obscured by the cloud of smoke I blow out through my nose. "Yeah, so? I've got work to do. What are you doing here?"

"Same as you. Takes one lonely bastard to know one."

"I'm not lonely. I like being alone."

"The difference?" he quips, turning his back to me.

"Choice."

An unconvinced grumble is his reply as he reaches for a hex-key wrench. "What's your woman up to today?" he wonders as an early morning sunbeam peeks through the garage window and lights him up. "Probably hoping Santa gifted you with syphilis."

"Go fuck yourself." My words fall flat because his aren't wrong. "She's not my woman."

"Not anymore," he says. "You're an idiot."

Also not wrong, but I'll never admit it to him. "We've already had this discussion. Wasn't your business then, and it's not now."

Dante swings around on his stool to shoot me well-earned glare, his tan coveralls stained with a smudge of black grease to match his hair. "She was part of the crew, man. We all liked her, and you sent that poor girl away crying her heart out. I'm not even sure how you sleep at night."

"I don't."

Folding my arms across my chest, a muscle in my cheek twitches. Guilt stabs at places long since sealed as I force my eyes away from the forthright look on his face.

He's right.

He's absolutely fucking right, and I can't muster the lie to deny it. I was an asshole, one hundred percent. While I don't regret firing her because it was the only scenario that made sense for us, and I sure as hell don't regret a single second of making her come apart on my desk with my fingers inside of her, watching her head fall back in ecstasy, reveling in the flush of desire stained on her cheeks—I *do* regret doing those things at the same time.

The timing was shit.

The timing was a poorly aimed arrow to her heart.

And mine.

On instinct, I sift through my pockets for my cell phone and glance at the screen, itching to see a missed call or text from her.

Nothing.

It's eight a.m., and I know she's up by now, but she's clearly not thinking about me or the tentative plans we'd made for the day consisting of monkey bread, gift opening, and reminiscing by tinsel and tree light.

Dante can see me sweating, so he adds to my self-inflicted torment. "She's too busy crying to text you, bro."

"You're an asshole."

"Like I said, takes one to know one." A half-smile shines back at me, lightening the tension. "Go comfort her. Stop being a cowardly shit and admit you fucked up."

I swallow, shoving the phone into the deepest recesses of my pocket so I'm not tempted to keep checking it. "She doesn't want to see me," I confess, my voice cracking enough to erase Dante's grin. I clear my throat. "It's fine. She's better off."

Based on last night's emotion-charged conversation, I don't think it's a lie. The heartbreak in Lucy's voice haunted me all night. I couldn't sleep, couldn't rest. I even kicked my poor kitten out of the bed when she tried to bring me a semblance of solace, purring and nuzzling the crook of my neck, because I didn't feel like I deserved the relief.

I take an extra long drag on my cigarette until it chokes me.

"That's exactly what a coward would say," Dante replies, leaning forward on his elbows. "She's not better off being sad as shit on Christmas. It's her birthday, too, right? Goddamn,

Bishop, go make it right. And give that girl her job back while you're at it."

My muscles tense as I flick some ashes to the garage floor. "She's already got another job."

With that bartender—*Nash.*

What the actual fuck?

It's obvious he's trying to get into her pants, and now she'll probably let him. The thought makes me want to vomit.

And yet, I still can't bring myself to pretend Dante's assessment is lacking any truth, so I dig for my cell phone again and type out a quick message, one-handed, hoping Lucy isn't actively wishing syphilis upon me.

ME:

> Merry Christmas. I'm coming over whether you want me to or not. I have something for you.

It's true, I do.

It's not much, but I didn't know what to get her that showcased value in all the right ways. Lucy isn't the materialistic type, so shoes, or a new purse, or a pretty sweater wouldn't do. It had to be special, so I had something custom-made for her shortly before her wedding night bombshell detonated, causing a catastrophic eruption we never fully recovered from.

I still can't process that truth bomb.

Maybe it's denial, maybe it's the bone-deep fear of losing Emma all over again, but the thought of Lucy's heart being anything less than fully intact and unimpaired, isn't something I can fathom.

And the fact that she kept it from me, all while whittling away my walls and steamrolling my jagged edges, was just another well-hidden landmine I stepped right onto.

I never saw it coming.

I never saw her coming back into my life, and now she's all I can see through the smoke.

The phone is heavy in my hand as I wait for my text message to show "read," but it never does. It only shows delivered, acting as a glaring parallel to my own misery.

"I'm dying."

Delivered, but not read.

Spoken, but not registered.

Given, but not accepted.

Fuck it—I'm just going to show up on her doorstep, and she'll have no choice but to let me in. With a long sigh, I throw my cigarette butt to the floor, stomp it out, then toss it in a nearby trash can. Before I turn to leave, Dante calls out to me.

"Hey, Bishop," he hollers, pulling my attention back to him. "Good luck. And Merry Christmas."

I falter, my throat tight. "Yeah. You, too." Nodding a curt farewell, I head out of the shop.

It's an easy ride to Lucy's house on my bike, but what comes next is anything but easy. I've been over here a few times now, but never inside. Never too close. I can't linger for long, or look too closely at the attached one-car garage, or focus on how nothing about the damn house has changed in almost a decade, the bricks still honey-yellow, the shutters only slightly weathered.

Even the basketball hoop still stands, rusted and unused, the net only slightly more tattered than it used to be. The rose bushes are still lined up, three in a row, and the leafless maple tree towers over the roof from its familiar perch in the backyard.

The only difference is the special touches she's brought to it.

The string lights strewn around the bushes and porch pillar because she couldn't reach the roof. A light-up snowman inflatable in the center of the lawn, teetering when a draft rolls through. A gold and green wreath, possibly handmade, hanging from the front door.

Oh, and the color of that front door.

It's red now.

Like mine, like Emma's last recital dress, like Lucy's reception attire with such a steep V-neck, all I wanted to do was dip my tongue between her breasts and make her mine.

Like her lips when they parted for me, succumbing to our inevitable kiss.

Like the color in her cheeks when I made her come.

My skin heats at the memory, distracting me just enough so I can pull off my bike and trudge through her frost-tipped front lawn. The grass blades crunch beneath my boots. My heartbeats thunder with a swell of anxiety, uncertain of what the fuck I'm even going to say when I see her.

I'm sorry for avoiding you for a week because I couldn't process the thought of a life without you.

I'm sorry for firing you.

I'm sorry for finger-fucking you until you chanted my name, and then breaking your perfect heart.

I'm sorry for not being able to love you, because everything I love dies.

And if I lose you, it'll finally be the goddamn end of me.

I'm not a groveling man, and no speech is prepared, but I hope I'm enough.

Me, and the little gift tucked inside the pocket of my jeans.

I blow out a breath, watching it plume against the chilly air like the cigarette smoke I'm desperate to suck into my lungs. The curtains covering the bay window are cracked, giving me a partial view of her illuminated Christmas tree sitting behind the pane of glass—in the same place we used to put it. I refuse to think about that last Christmas ten years ago, that last worthy, laughter-lit Christmas, and pool all my energy into salvaging all I can of this one.

My knuckles tap against the screen door. I wait, shuffling from foot to foot on her stoop, fidgeting with the box of cigarettes calling to me from my back pocket. I close my eyes and blow out another breath, waiting, still waiting. It takes a solid minute for me to register the fact that her dogs aren't barking, so I lean over to the window and try to peer inside.

The tree is too big, and I can't see shit.

I twist around and double-check the driveway, confirming that her black Passat is, indeed, still sitting there dormant. I didn't imagine it.

A pang of anxiety settles in.

Familiar twinges of worry churn in my gut.

Nausea swirls, my mind reeling with worst case scenarios and memories of my little sister walking out the front door and never coming back.

No, this isn't like Emma.

She isn't Emma.

Swallowing back an acrid lump, I turn toward the quiet street, taking in the stillness of the air and noting how it was blowing angrily only moments ago, and now it's lifeless.

The snow-dusted streets are empty, everyone tucked inside their warm homes, sipping cocoa and opening gifts.

I move off the step, eyes scanning left to right, then I pull out my cell phone.

It's still blank. My text was never opened, never read.

My heartbeats kick up. My lungs feel tight and smothered.

Inhaling a worried breath, I begin to stalk back toward my bike, deciding on my next move.

That's when something catches my eye. At first it doesn't register, doesn't compute, and even though my eyes are witness to two familiar dogs running straight at me, their leashes dragging behind them, it doesn't make any sense.

Lucy's dogs, loose and racing down the sidewalk.

Lucy's dogs, but no Lucy.

No Lucy.

Where's Lucy?

I'm frozen to the cement, my blood turning ice cold. The cell phone falls from my hand, cracking when it hits the pavement.

Kiki and Lemon storm at me, Kiki barking her head off, Lemon frantically circling my ankles, both of them pawing at me, stressed and whining.

I start to sweat, start to wither, start to die a little inside.

When the dogs decide they have my full attention, they take off running back in the direction from which they came, and a rush of adrenaline triggers my legs to move.

I chase after them.

I bolt, run, flee, follow the animals until I'm being led around the corner to where I make a discovery that knocks the air right out of my lungs.

Lucy.

She's lying in front of me, collapsed on the sidewalk.

Sprawled out on her stomach, her long hair billowing from underneath a winter cap.

Lifeless, colorless, motionless.

The dogs sniff her, paw at her, cry and mourn as they run around in anxious circles.

"Lucy..." Breaking into a sprint, I skid to a stop beside her. I reach down and scoop her up into my arms, knowing that maybe I shouldn't move her but unable to stop myself. "Lucy, Lucy, Lucy." My voice breaks on every syllable, my heart cracking in two.

I hoist her in the air as I stand, and then I book it. I'm racing down the sidewalk, shouting for help at the top of my lungs.

I don't know where my phone is. Maybe I dropped it, lost it, never had it.

I can't think.

Can't breathe.

"Somebody help me!" I bellow into the too-quiet morning, desperate for help, desperate for this to not be happening.

Lucy is a ragdoll in my arms, unmoving. I'm not sure if she's breathing.

Is she breathing? Is she fucking breathing?

"Help!"

A neighbor pokes his head out of one of the houses; I think he does, but everything's a blur and maybe he didn't. I'm still running, half slipping on patches of ice, Kiki and Lemon frantic beside me as I beg for someone to turn back time and make this not true.

"Breathe, Lucy," I whisper into her hair as I cradle her to me.

Someone is running at me. A stranger, two strangers. Talking in tongues with blacked-out faces.

"Sh-she fainted. Collapsed, I don't fucking know. Call 9-1-1," I ramble to everyone, to no one, nothing making sense. "Help her. Please fucking help her."

A man assists in lying her down in the grass near the side of the road and starts doing chest compressions as a woman puts a phone to her ear.

Why didn't I think of that?

CPR. She needs CPR.

"Breathe, Lucy," I repeat, falling to my knees beside her and breathing life back into her lungs. "Breathe."

Sirens blare in the distance at some point. Two minutes, five minutes, maybe more. Maybe a lifetime passes, maybe no time at all. I fall across her chest, burying my face into her puffy coat.

This can't be happening.

This isn't real.

"Breathe, Lucy," I croak, squeezing her, holding her, loving her in all the ways I swore I'd never love her.

My greatest fear has come true.

Lucy, Lucy, my sweet Lucy.

Her fucking heart broke.

To Be Continued...

The story continues in book two:
A Pessimist's Guide To Love

CONNECT

Feel free to join my reader's group:
Queen of Harts: Jennifer Hartmann's Reader Group
Follow me here:
Linktree: @jenniferhartmannauthor
Instagram: @author.jenniferhartmann
Facebook: @jenhartmannauthor
Twitter: @authorjhartmann
TikTok: @jenniferhartmannauthor

Leave your thoughts on Amazon, Goodreads, and Bookbub!

♡
www.jenniferhartmannauthor.com

MORE FROM JENNIFER

THE DUET SERIES — ARIA & CODA
When the lead singer of his rock band starts falling for a pretty
waitress, Noah will do whatever it takes to make sure she doesn't
get in the way of their dreams.
But it would be easier if that waitress didn't accidentally spill her
darkest secrets to him one night, triggering a profound
connection neither of them saw coming.

CLAWS AND FEATHERS
Small town cop, Cooper, is intrigued by the mysterious new girl
who walks into his father's bar, but the last thing he expects is for
her to go missing that same night.
Finding Abby is just the beginning. The only way to truly save
her is to unravel her secrets—a task that proves to be more
challenging than he could ever anticipate.

STILL BEATING
#1 Amazon Bestseller in three categories!
When Cora leaves her sister's birthday party, she doesn't expect to wake up in shackles in a madman's basement.
To make matters worse, her arch nemesis and ultimate thorn in her side, Dean, shares the space in his own set of chains. The two people who always thought they'd end up killing each other must now work together if they want to survive.

LOTUS
To the rest of the world, he was the little boy who went missing on the Fourth of July.
To Sydney, he was everything.
Twenty-two years later, he's back.
This is Oliver Lynch's story...
This is their story.

THE WRONG HEART
Audie Awards Romance Finalist 2021!
When my husband died, he left my broken heart behind.
He left another heart behind, too—his.
I know it's wrong. I shouldn't be contacting the recipient of my husband's heart. I don't even expect him to reply...
But there's a desperate, twisted part of me that hopes he will.
No names.
No personal details.
Just a conversation.
The only thing I have left of my husband is inside him.

THE THORNS REMAIN
Vengeance.
Hiding deep within the shadows of human nature, it smolders...
simmers...
Waits.
The day I discovered the wrongs committed against me,
vengeance clawed its way right through me.
In the end, I never expected things to be worse than when it all
began.
I never expected the wreckage left in my wake.
I never expected *her*.

ENTROPY
*Surviving Monday might be the biggest accomplishment of their
lives.*
By 9:03 A.M. Monday, bank manager Indie Chase thinks her day
can't get worse.
She's wrong.
In a matter of moments, that day becomes the stuff of nightmares
when she's caught in a robbery with retired hockey player, Dax
Reed.
It's going to take trust.
It's going to take strength.
It might even take ... *each other*.

JUNE FIRST

Want to know what happens to a man who barely claws his way
out of a tragedy, only to fall right into the arms of the one girl in
the world he can never have?

Another tragedy, that's what.

ABOUT THE AUTHOR

Jennifer Hartmann resides in northern Illinois with her devoted husband and three children. When she is not writing angsty love stories, she is likely thinking about writing them. She enjoys sunsets (because mornings are hard), bike riding, traveling to eternally warm places, bingeing Buffy the Vampire Slayer reruns, and that time of day when coffee gets replaced by wine. She is excellent at making puns and finding inappropriate humor in mundane situations. She loves tacos. She also really, really wants to pet your dog. *Xoxo.*

Made in the USA
Middletown, DE
29 August 2024

59999404R00177